Running to Daylight

by

Kim Janine Ligon

The Wild Rose Press, Inc.
PO Box 708
Adams Basin, NY 14410-0708
Visit us at www.thewildrosepress.com

Publishing History
First Edition, 2025
Trade Paperback ISBN 978-1-5092-6138-3
Digital ISBN 978-1-5092-6139-0

Published in the United States of America

Dedication

As always, this book is dedicated to my husband, Jim, for his unfailing loving support and for the book's title.

Thanks to Millie and Beverly for being beta readers and chief encouragers. Special thanks to Bev for her social media skills.

I never intended to write a fourth Lansdale story, but my characters insisted on it and you, my readers and blog followers, had other ideas. I hope you enjoy meeting Elsie and Mark and seeing some familiar faces on these pages. Thanks for reading and reviewing my books and for following my author journey on my blog.

Thank you Kaycee John for taking on editing my book.

And thank you to the good Lord who continues to guide me on me on this adventure. I am truly blessed.

Chapter One

Beads of perspiration seeped under the sweatband, ran between my eyebrows, and off the end of my nose. The odometer on my wrist pinged and flashed—seven miles—a new personal high. No wonder the strip of terrycloth couldn't keep my forehead dry. I pulled the hem of my T-shirt out of my shorts, found the driest section, and wiped off my face.

Almost home.

My favorite part of my daily run has always been when I turned the corner and started up the driveway. After ten yards, I saw the house I love come into view—its newly-tuck pointed bricks and green shutters shining brightly. At this time of day, the sun creates a halo around my home making the gleaming white double front doors look so welcoming, so eager to open in hello.

The car in the driveway didn't look at all familiar—and Mom didn't tell me we were expecting guests.

The door was ajar. Mom *never* left the door open, she's too worried about the neighbor's cat getting in. One litter of mewing black and white kittens in the middle of a partially completed sweater in her knitting basket made her hyper-vigilant about closing the door tightly. The unexpected company must have distracted her.

Where did the odd aroma—cherries, vanilla, and tobacco—come from? It doesn't smell anything like her menthol cigarettes.

What was Mom doing in the kitchen? The dark roasted coffee aroma wafted through the air saying she just brewed a new pot. I could use a cup before my shower. When I'm fresh from a run, Mom makes me sit on the deck to drink it so I don't sweat all over the faux leather-covered kitchen chairs that are relics from Dad's college days.

Wait.

Unfamiliar angry voices.

Two men.

Maybe more.

They have gotten louder.

Was Mom crying?

I took a deep breath, then carefully pushed the swinging door between the dining room and kitchen open very slowly. Everyone stopped talking. I continued forward acting like everything was normal.

Mom was in her usual chair seated at the end of the table nearest the stove. I couldn't see anyone else without going all the way into the kitchen. She looked more pale than I'd ever seen her. Her eyes blinked rapidly and kept blinking. SOS in Morse code—something she taught me for a long ago scouting badge.

I nodded toward behind the door. Her eyes darted and she tilted her head slightly in that direction.

Wham!

I slammed the door open and hit something. Correction. I hit someone. Curses flew. Something metal clattered to the floor.

Mom hollered, "Run, Morgan! Run!"

I hesitated. Too. Long. A hand reached out, grabbed my arm, and jerked hard. A strange face appeared inches from my own. "So this is the infamous Morgan Tucker we've been waiting for. Doesn't quite live up to all the hype."

I choked back a gag. His breath was beyond foul—a putrid ragout of tobacco, garlic, and alcohol. A fire-red scar ran from eyebrow to chin down one side of the ruddy, pockmarked face. It looked recent and poorly stitched together. Thinning brown hair barely covered part of his gourd-shaped head.

He was larger than Dad or Uncle Paul or me—very tall and broad. His crooked teeth were yellow, almost green. But it was the eyes that made me shiver. They were steely gray orbs shooting lasers of pure evil. Those eyes will haunt me for the rest of my life.

"Get out of our house. I'll tell the cops you were here. You'll be arrested." Where was that bravado coming from? I channeled someone much stronger and surer than I was. Could they tell it was more bluster than probability?

After my threat, maniacal—no more precisely—demonic laughter echoed through the room. The nicotine-yellowed fingernails dug into me in a painful iron grip. I expected to see blood pooling on my arm.

A smaller, older man who looked familiar sat at the table almost caressing my mother's hand. He was well-dressed. In different circumstances, I might have said he looked distinguished. His full head of salt and pepper hair did not have a strand out of place. He stared at me with inky black eyes that seemed to know my every thought. His pipe rested in the ashtray next to Mom's ever-present cigarette. A wisp of cherry vanilla smoke slithered from the bowl.

I knew him. He'd been in the shop on the day my father died in the fire that this man had ordered set. But he'd been arrested, hadn't he? What was he doing at our kitchen table with my mother?

"Delores, explain the facts to your kid," the elegant man said. "As much as you mean to me personally, I can't allow testimony from one of my own."

"Sal, you can't hurt my only child," Mom pleaded.

"You have my solemn promise, you won't lose your child—unless I'm left with no other option."

His smile was pure evil. "Don't back me into a corner, dear. It's enough for the kid to just disappear. You, I'm not worried about, but this one is too much Tucker."

"Tell the goon to let go of my child. Now." Mom's voice was strong, unwavering. I had only seen that look of barely controlled anger in her dark eyes once before today.

The older man nodded. Red finger marks encircled my freed arm as aching pain shot up and down it. Cold metal pressed hard against my back. Not much of an improvement.

"Mom, is this about the fire at our shop?"

"Yes. They want you to go with them to ensure no one can identify the arsonists in court on Monday." How could she sound so calm?

"But, Mom, Dad died in the fire. I know who did it. I picked the guy who lit the torch out of a lineup. I have to testify. Dad would want me to do the right thing. He can't have died for nothing. Why are you here with that cretin?" I pointed at the man whom I'd thought was safely in jail. "He ordered Dad's murder. He was

4

there."

The older man shook his head. "I told you, Delores, too much Tucker." He turned to me. "If you insist on being unreasonable about this issue, Morgan, I'll have no choice, but to break your sainted mother's heart and put you permanently out of reach of the court."

I swallowed the bile rising in my throat. "You mean kill me?"

"Yah, that's what he means," old yellow teeth chuckled. "And I'll get to be the one to do it."

Mom took another drag off her cigarette and slowly pushed up out of her chair. "Sal, let me talk to my child for a moment, privately, please."

The old man nodded. Cold metal no longer pressed against my spine. Mom pulled me by the arm into the corner of the kitchen farthest from the table and nearest the back door. She hugged me close and whispered, "When I say the word *choice,* run as fast as you can out the back door into the woods. Don't stop. You have to testify on Monday, no matter what. They won't dare to hurt me. Go directly to the State's Attorney's office. Get police protection."

Sal said, "Speak louder, Delores. I can't hear you."

Mom stood straighter, released me from her embrace, and stepped toward the table, leaving me close to the back door. "Morgan, honey, I love you very much. I know walking away isn't what your father taught you. The men who killed him must be punished. We need to do all we can to get justice for him."

"A little faster, Delores. This isn't being filmed for posterity." The old man paced on the other side of the kitchen. Old Yellow Teeth slumped in a chair at the table with the gun on the scarred tabletop within hand's reach.

Mom stepped closer to the table. Her voice got stronger and louder. "I have a young adult who understands sometimes we have to do things that disgust us because we simply have no other choice."

I turned and shot out the door as soon as *choice* left her lips. I raced across the deck and down the steps into the muddy backyard. The sucking sound my shoes made in the mire was muffled by my mother's scream. I couldn't stop. Mom knew what she was doing. She told me to keep going. No matter what, I have to testify.

"You stupid kid. Get back here."

A bullet whizzed past my left ear, missed me, but clipped leaves off the back hedge. I ran harder, aiming for the gap in the greenery. I tried to catch my breath, but the pain in my chest made it hard to breathe. I could do this. I knew I could.

I hit a huge puddle and left my right sneaker in the murky brown water. Cold, slimy mud oozed through my sock and squished between my toes. Branches whipped at my face, burning my cheeks. Briars stung my bare calves.

Behind me, someone hollered my name, but I couldn't stop. Finally, I saw daylight ahead and the street on the other side of the woods.

Almost there.

Something hit my left shoulder with a hard, burning blow. I reached back and touched it. My hand came back, covered with red, slimy liquid. Blood. The sickening coppery smell gagged me. *This was not the time to get queasy, Morgan, power through. Run to the daylight.*

Finally, I was there. I leaped off the curb and saw a car moving toward me down the street. Waving wildly, I jumped into its path.

The driver slammed on the brakes, slowing enough for me to climb in the passenger side. "What is wrong with you? I could have killed you! Get out of my car!"

"I've been shot."

That was all he needed. He hit the gas, and we burned rubber. "Where to first? The ER or the police?"

"No, not the hospital," I panted. "Not yet. I have to get to the State's Attorney's office in the courthouse. Please, it's a matter of life and death."

And justice.

****

The sheets were soaking wet, reeking with the foul odor of fear sweat. A smell I have known far too well. A damp, mangled, wad of foam that used to be my pillow covered the bed. I reached back and touched the spot on my left shoulder, expecting it to be gaping and bloody. Instead it was a bloodless, marble-sized, rock-hard knot of flesh. A parting gift from old yellow teeth.

It was an all too vivid dream. No—it was a remembered event masquerading as a nightmare and relived under the cover of darkness.

Evil thrives in darkness.

Why had my mind gone to that day now? The anniversary of the escape was months ago. It was not my birthday or Mom's. The nightmares had completely stopped—until this morning at four a.m..

The letter came yesterday from an unreadable postmark. The address was typed. A clipping from some unknown newspaper without a date, a note, or a signature drifted out of the envelope and onto my table.

Mobster Salvatore Scachhi Dies in Federal Prison was the headline. Scachhi had been serving multiple life sentences for arson and murder.

Mom's second cousin, Sal, the distinguished looking pipe smoker, whom I last saw from the witness box in federal court on the day I testified. The one who ordered a fire to conceal my father's murder.

It was too late for celebrating. It wasn't even a relief that Scachhi can no longer hurt me. I couldn't visit Mom since she's been gone five years. Cancer was the physician's diagnostic guess. I knew better. It was loneliness and a broken heart. I couldn't contact her without The Family finding out. That was against the rules I have had to live by all these years.

I have always been a 'follow the rules, do the right thing' person. Always. At all costs. Ten years has been a long time to stay this hazardous course. I have had to watch every step to stay on the straight and narrow never-ending path toward daylight.

I was finally free, but I have nowhere to go. No one was waiting to welcome me back into the bosom of my family. They were all gone. No one knew Morgan Tucker any longer. I sacrificed my life so that my father would get the justice he deserved. I would do it again. It was the right thing—the only choice. Mom understood the truth as well as I did. Perhaps even better.

I testified. The bad guys went to prison. I have been reborn into a new life under the protection of the U.S. Marshals Service. I'm living proof that when you do the right thing everything will work out in the end.

Wait.

Who knew to send me a letter to an address in Lansdale, Wisconsin?

To the *new* me?

If the sender was only trying to scare me, they have succeeded in spades. Who would still be alive to care where I am? Who I am?

Lord, please don't leave me. I need your protection now more than ever. Shield me from the darkness. Lead me to the daylight.

Chapter Two

Mark Trask tugged the brim of his baseball cap down farther on his forehead to block the sun as it drifted lower on the western horizon. The week had been perfect—just him, his thoughts, and a fishing pole. He was finally free to make plans. To do what?

He'd eaten well even if it was his own cooking. The fish had been biting—so much so that he was tired of eating fresh pan-fried trout. By the fourth day, he'd broken out the bratwurst. They had been his failsafe food so he wouldn't starve if he didn't catch anything. The rest of the week, he cleaned and filleted his daily catch and packaged the fish in freezer bags to save and enjoy this winter—after he'd forgotten how wonderful trout you caught with your own two hands could taste. He might even drop some off at Mrs. Ritterskamp's house. She had told him more than once how much fresh fish reminded her of her late husband, Karl, who'd been an avid angler.

A genuine old-school country and western song came on the radio. One he remembered his mom had liked. Mark cranked the volume a couple of notches higher. The truck was old, but the radio still worked. He threw back his head and sang every word about his friends in low places. Something about singing the old song made him feel unfettered for the first time in over a decade. No more waiting for the other shoe to drop.

At thirty-one, maybe it was time to think about finding someone to share his life. He could even picture himself as someone's dad one day. Of course, he'd need to find the perfect mom first. No time like the present to set those wheels in motion.

It was kind of Chief Davis to offer the use of his riverside cabin for Mark's vacation even though it might have been a consolation prize. Chief Davis's retirement after decades in the position marked the end of an era. For many people Mark's age who had lived in Lansdale all their lives, Chief Davis was the only police chief they'd ever known.

In his heart of hearts, Mark had never really expected to be named Lansdale's new Chief of Police when Davis retired, but he was qualified for the position. He'd been on the force since he moved to town ten years ago. He'd received great annual reviews and was well-liked in the small town. He had fit right in from the very beginning—as if he'd always been a small-town boy.

At least he'd served as some competition for Randy Miller. He didn't coast into the Chief of Police job because he was the only candidate. Randy started on the force one week before Mark had, but he was a local boy born and bred, third generation in the rural Wisconsin hamlet. In the end, Mark believed Randy's being a native was the tipping factor in his favor. The choice was between hometown boy makes good or a "new guy originally from the east" takes the reins. You're always the new guy in a situation like this, even when your *new* is over a decade old.

The decision hadn't upset him as much as he had expected. He liked Randy and they'd always gotten along. He liked his job and his adopted hometown. He hoped he wouldn't have a reason to consider going anywhere else. Ever.

High beam headlights topped the hill, temporarily blinding him. A black monster truck barreled down the middle of the road, increasing speed as he got closer—and aimed straight at Mark. "What the heck?"

Hoping to get the driver's attention, Mark laid on the horn and flashed his lights. A solid limestone cliff loomed on the opposite side of the road. If he leaped the metal guard rail beside him, it was straight down into a wooded ravine. The black truck bearing down on him didn't move.

At the last possible moment, the renegade vehicle veered into its own lane, clipping Mark's driver's side headlight and sending him careening toward the guard rail. Mark pumped his brakes and hung on. By some miracle, he didn't go over or through the guardrail. His truck stopped, suspended atop the sturdy metal rail with three of the four tires completely off the ground. Only the left front tire, on the damaged driver's side, still had contact with the pavement.

Bottom line, he was still alive and not laying at the bottom of the ravine encased in the steel tomb of a mangled truck.

Mark saw no one else around. The driver who'd forced the accident apparently didn't feel responsible enough to stop and check on the havoc he'd left in his wake. He'd seen a lot of wild things in the last ten years of patrolling the highway, but this was the first time he'd been a victim.

First order of business was to get off this guard rail. Fortunately, his phone had stayed safe in his shirt pocket during the daredevil driving exhibition. He turned off the radio and immediately hit speed dial for Pop Skelton's Garage. Pop himself answered even though it was Sunday evening. "Hiya. What's up?"

"You're not going to believe where I am," Mark began.

He gave Pop his exact location and his predicament. After Pop stopped laughing, he told Mark he'd be there in about thirty minutes with the tow truck and his son. Mark turned the radio on again and sat back.

Nothing to do but wait.

As promised, Pop and his son, Mike, arrived thirty minutes later. After Mike took pictures of the accident, they got the tow hooked to Mark's vehicle, then gently pulled the old truck off the guard rail it straddled. When all four tires were touching the ground on the roadside, Mark crawled out the driver's door.

"My insurance guy is never going to believe this," Mark said as he viewed the pictures taken by Mike. "I don't believe it and I was there. Thanks for providing the video proof."

"You were certainly working your angels overtime tonight," Pop said. "I won't know the damage until I get her on the rack in the morning. C'mon, Kris is waiting supper. You want to come and eat with us before you go home?"

"I appreciate the offer, but I should get home," Mark said. "I need to get the cooler out of the passenger side. Don't want to lose the fruits of my labor from this past week."

He got the cooler out of the truck and transferred it over to the wrecker. Pop dropped him at his house before they towed the truck to their shop and went home for their waiting supper.

Mark waved goodbye, hefted the cooler in front of him, and slogged to the front door. He sat his burden down on the stoop and dug in his pant's pocket for the house key. Dang it. He hadn't gotten it off the ring when he gave Pop the truck keys. The house looked dark but maybe his housemate Phil was home.

He pressed the doorbell button three short rings. It was the housemates' signal it was them, not a salesperson or lost soul at their front door. No response. Maybe Phil was asleep. He was an amazingly heavy sleeper. Mark tried the doorbell signal again. No luck.

"Now what?" He leaned his back against the door. Half a moment later he was flat on his butt sitting on the gray tiled entryway floor. The door hadn't been completely closed. How long had it been left open?

And more importantly, where in the heck was Phil?

Mark carefully got off the floor. Various odors of rotting food assaulted his nose as soon as he brought the cooler in off the stoop and closed the door. He followed the putrid smell to the kitchen.

Both sides of the double farmhouse sink overflowed with used dishes and glassware. The round oak kitchen table held at least two meals worth of silverware and condiments to feed a small army. Phil must have been entertaining while Mark was away. He never had visitors in the past. He must have morphed into a real party animal to leave this big a mess.

Phil was a pig. No doubt about it. He only cleaned up after himself when Mark nagged him into it. Some days it took less energy to do the work than to prod Phil into doing it. Phil expected him to be home tonight.

Why would he leave the whole week of kitchen mess rotting in the sink? It was a good thing his boarder wasn't home. Mark would pop his top if he laid eyes on his housemate right now.

Hindsight was twenty-twenty. Phil wasn't his first choice of housemates, but he was the one he had been with for a decade. Mark owned the house and Phil was his tenant. Phil lived in the upstairs where he worked from home. Mark hadn't been in the apartment in years. No telling how filthy it was. Except for the aversion to cleaning, Phil was the perfect tenant. Quiet. And he was willing to look after things when Mark was out of town. That was a big plus.

Mark unloaded the cooler into the freezer. He didn't have the energy to deal with the kitchen tonight. Maybe he'd get lucky, and Phil would feel guilty when he got home and clean up his own mess.

Sure. That's what would happen. Dream on.

He turned off the kitchen light and checked the lock on the back door. Wait. Something was scratching at the screen door and whining. Domino. In all the trauma of the wreck and the horror of the kitchen, he'd forgotten about the dog. He flipped the light on again. He opened the back door and barely avoided being bowled over by a wiggling mass of black fur.

Domino licked his hands and, when he bent down, his face. Mark was never certain exactly what breeds made up his rescue dog's pedigree. He was the size of a standard poodle with silky, longish, black hair everywhere except for three perfectly round white spots down his back. They were so perfectly circular they looked like decals had been applied to the dog's back. He was stocky with muscular legs and the square jaw line of a boxer, canine not pugilist. He didn't bark unless there was a good reason and had never gone through a chewing stage since Mark had owned him. He was perfectly content to stay in the fenced in backyard while his master was at work. The mutt usually slept across the foot of the king size bed in the master bedroom.

Domino went to his bowls and took a long drink of water. Then he came over and blocked Mark from leaving the kitchen. He kept trying to herd his master toward the pantry.

"Haven't you eaten today, big guy?" Mark patted the dog's side. Was he thinner than usual? "Maybe not." He got the kibble from the pantry and put two large scoops in Domino's bowl. The animal didn't waste a second digging in. "I'm sorry. It's not like Phil to forget to feed you. What's been going on here?" The hungry dog didn't acknowledge his question.

After Domino had eaten his fill, they headed to the bedroom. Mark had to have a shower. The fish smell was everywhere. He couldn't stand himself. Even Domino seemed to be keeping his distance after the initial euphoria of his master's return had passed. When he came out of the bathroom, Domino was stretched across the bed sound asleep. Mark wasn't too far behind him.

Chapter Three

Mark didn't stir until almost nine o'clock the next morning. Usually he was awake and around no later than seven. Working the evening shift meant he had to be organized to get his errands done before he went to work. Nothing was open when he got off work, except Murphy's Bar. He'd learned early on that stopping for a beer on the way home usually meant staying until closing time and it didn't bode well for getting anything done the next day before time for work. It was much better for his to-do list and his liver to go home straight from work.

He wandered into the kitchen in his pajamas. Domino followed close at his heels. Apparently, no domestic fairies had arrived in the night to spirit away Phil's mess. He put the coffee pot on, refilled Domino's water bowl, and scooped out his morning kibble.

The sun streamed in the kitchen window over the sink. Not a cloud in the sky. Mark poured a large mug of black coffee and took it out on the deck. No reason to sit in the middle of all the filth when it was a beautiful day and very comfortable outside.

The air smelled almost spring-like. Faint hints of floral mixed with...bleach? Yep, bleach. Mikal Reynolds was hanging white sheets out on the clothesline. He didn't think anyone still had plain old white sheets. They must be some of Polly's. Mikal usually did her grandmother-in-law's laundry.

She waved and hollered, "Good morning."

Mark returned the neighborly greeting. He walked to the edge of the deck while downing the last of his coffee. Phil's car was in the driveway. Had he come home late last night? Mark hadn't checked to see if the car was there before he went to bed. Maybe Phil left with someone. Or if the car was there when he came home, maybe Phil was upstairs but injured or worse so he couldn't respond to Mark's calls.

The kitchen had to be cleaned before he left for work. He didn't want to face this mess when he got home after his shift. But first, he needed to know if Phil was home.

He hurried to the top of the stairs and rapped on the door. There was no answer, and he couldn't hear anyone stirring. He cautiously unlocked and opened the door and hollered to his housemate. No response. He walked down the hall. The upstairs apartment was remarkably neat and clean. The bed was made and didn't appear to have been slept in last night. Nothing seemed unusual except there was no Phil. Mark was thankful he hadn't stumbled on a corpse.

The housemates had exchanged vehicle keys early in their relationship so they could back one another up in an emergency. Mark left Phil a note explaining he was borrowing the tiny car Phil drove, then taped it to the apartment door.

All the household chores took longer than he expected. By the time he finished, it was past ten-thirty. He sat down at the desk in the hallway and looked through the pile of accumulated mail. Phil had it all sorted between bills, junk mail, and magazines.

He opened the bills. Nothing needed his immediate attention. If he got ready now, he would have time to drop the fish at Emma's and stop at Whistler's Diner downtown for a late lunch before going to work. He called Emma Ritterskamp to make sure she'd be home in about forty-five minutes.

During his week in the woods he hadn't bothered to shave. His beard was filling in nicely. He sort of liked the look of a hairy face. He had morphed into someone else. Kind of funny the whiskers were more reddish than dark brown like the thinning hair on top of his head. He knew it was a cliché that balding men grew beards but there was a reason for the adage. He turned on his electric razor and shaved. His head, not his jaw.

Not bad. A totally new look for the next phase of his life. Would Poppy Caldwell like it? They'd only dated a few times. He had no idea about her facial hair preference or how she felt about bald guys. Guess he'd find out when he stopped at the diner for lunch.

He put on his uniform. He got an envelope from the desk drawer and put the cabin key in it with a note saying 'Thanks'. Chief Davis lived between Emma's and Whistler's. He'd drop the key off as he went past.

"C'mon, boy. You know the drill. It's back to work for me today." Mark carried the dog's water and kibble out onto the deck and coaxed the animal outside. "I'll let you in late tonight, unless Phil arrives first and lets you back in."

The dog strolled down the steps into the backyard and flopped down in the shade in front of his doghouse. Mark grabbed a couple of bags of trout fillets out of the freezer and put them in a mini cooler to transport.

Fortunately, Phil's little car started after a minimum amount of spitting and sputtering. Mark couldn't remember the last time he'd seen Phil drive it—and the gauge hovering barely above E told him the car needed gas. He stopped at the first station he came to and filled the tank, then headed to Emma's.

As Mark knocked on Emma's door, he saw her peek out the window and frown. "Hello, may I help you?"

He smiled. "Emma, I called and told you I was coming."

"Mark? Mark Trask? With the beard and bald head I had no idea who was at the door. You do have on your uniform, but where's your truck?" Emma opened the door wide. "Please come in."

"I was in an accident last night on the way home and my truck is at Pop Skelton's. I've got Phil's car. I stopped to share the fruits of my labor. I know you're partial to rainbow trout."

She clapped her hands together. "You, sweet boy. Claire and I both love it. I know what we're having for dinner tonight." She stood on tiptoe and kissed his cheek. "Thank you for thinking of me."

"Glad you can use it. I'd better get going. Still some other stops to make before work."

"I can't get over how different you look with the beard. It's a very masculine look. Quite interesting. If I'd run into you on the street out of uniform, I'm not certain I would have known who you were. Thank you again." She waved and closed the door.

It was a short drive to his next stop. Chief Davis wasn't at home. Mrs. Davis said he had a whole list of *retirement* projects to work on—starting with a new fence for the backyard—so he'd made a trip to the hardware store. Mark left the key with her. He was getting hungry. It was a short drive downtown.

The lunch rush was definitely over by the time Mark settled into one of the red Naugahyde booths in Poppy Caldwell's section at Whistler's Diner. He glanced at the menu. Monday Specials were the same as always—meatloaf or chicken and dumplings. He liked this smidgen of consistency in his life. Eating a bigger lunch before he went on shift meant he could get by with a sandwich at supper time. He was positive it was better for his waistline to eat his biggest meal earlier in the day.

A tall, well-built, brunette came to the table with her pen ready to write his order on the pad in her hand. "What can I get you, sir?"

"What do I usually have on Monday afternoon, Poppy?"

"How would I know?" She looked confused, then burst into a smile. "Mark Trask. Boy, what a difference a week makes. Why'd you shave your head?"

He winked at her. "The more important question is do you like it?"

"Too soon to tell. I've never kissed someone with a beard before. Does it tickle?"

"I don't know, I haven't lip-locked with a beard-wearer either. My great Aunt Martha only had a mustache." He laughed. "Want to give it a try now?"

Poppy blushed. "Are you crazy? I am not kissing you in the middle of Whistler's. I'm going to put your order in." She whirled around and headed toward the kitchen.

"What are you putting in?"

"Same as always. Meatloaf, mashed potatoes, green beans, and start with a small salad with French dressing but no tomato."

Mark chuckled. He leafed through the newspaper someone had left in the booth. In no time, Poppy delivered his meal. She slid into the booth across from him to visit since he was the only patron in the place. "Was it a relaxing vacation?"

"The best. Fishing, thinking, sleeping in."

She batted her emerald-colored eyes flirtatiously. "Did you miss me?"

"Yep."

She looked out the window. "I don't see your truck out front."

Mark explained about the careless driver and Pop Skelton's rescue operation.

"You're lucky you're not at the bottom of the ravine."

"Don't I know it. Say, have you got any apple pie left?"

Poppy smiled. "I do. I put one piece back hoping you'd be in today."

"How can I thank you for taking such good care of me?"

She blushed. "I'm certain we can think of a way if we put our heads together."

"Maybe Saturday night?"

"I'll plan on it." Poppy added the pie to his bill, put the check on the table, cleared away the dirty dishes, and went to get his pie.

****

He had just enough time to stop by Pop Skelton's before clocking in. He parked in front of the garage. His truck was up on the rack. Judging by the overall-covered legs, Pop was underneath it.

"Am I going to have to sell my first-born child to get this fixed?"

Pop laughed. "Not sure I can wait that long to be paid. Considering where you were when we found you, there isn't too much damage. The rail scraped the under carriage a little but none of her vital organs, like the brake or fuel lines, were hit. I want to run a few more tests, but I think I can give her back to you by Thursday."

"Hallelujah! What great news. I'll check back a little later in the week. Gotta get to work now."

Chapter Four

Mark took a lot of razzing from his fellow officers as soon as they spotted his new 'look'. One asked if he'd discovered a genie in a lamp on vacation.

The dispatcher gave him a lollipop out of the jar they keep for little kids who visit. "Who loves ya, baby?"

The desk sergeant handed him a mop. "Look who's here to cleanup."

Everyone's a comedian.

He got the news on what had happened during his week off and especially how the first week of Randy Miller's tenure as chief had gone. Chief Miller was off to a good start in the opinion of his evening shift. He was approaching the job with the "if it's not broke, don't change it" attitude. It was a major relief to everyone, especially some of the old timers. A lot of them had been on the force more than twice as long as the new chief. They'd already broken in one boss, Chief Davis.

All in all, it seemed to have been seamless transition to the new administration. Mark couldn't help but wonder if he would have been as well received if he had been named chief instead of Randy Miller. No use wasting time on 'what ifs'.

It was a normal Monday night in Lansdale. A domestic disturbance rose to the level of police involvement when the man of the house got home from a long weekend to find all his belongings strewn around the front yard. He'd neglected to tell his wife that his very attractive, much younger secretary would be accompanying him, purely for business reasons, of course, on this important weekend trip. The official police assessment was she didn't believe him.

Then there was the teenaged female driver who pulled out of The Purple Cow parking lot with two of her male friends clinging to the hood of her bright red sports car. She protested getting a ticket. The young gentlemen were harassing her—she claimed—and she couldn't think of another way to get them off the car so she could get home before curfew. Her dad was very strict. Officer Trask wondered what her father would think of his darling little girl getting a ticket.

A complaint about a howling beagle next door came in from Mrs. Martha Hall who was trying to sleep. The same beagle made his displeasure known every time his owner stopped at Murphy's on the way home from work instead of rushing home to feed the dog. Mark was well acquainted with Marlon, the beagle, and the sleep-deprived Mrs. Hall.

At eleven-thirty p.m. Officer Trask turned the patrol car keys over to the night shift officer replacing him and clocked out. He hesitated for a moment in the parking lot when he didn't see his truck. Right. He drove Phil's car. He'd be glad when Pop Skelton had the repairs done. It was difficult to fold his six-foot four-inch frame into his housemate's tiny clown car. But he was thankful it was available, so he didn't have the expense of a rental on top of the repairs.

Mark circled the courthouse square and turned

down Lincoln street. *Knitting Pretty* was lit brightly—
like it was open for insomniac customers. Elsie Dennis
never opened the store on Mondays and did not
normally stay open after nine o'clock at night on any
day. He parked in a space in front of the shop and got
out of the car.

A colorful banner draped across the front of the
building announced, "*Join Our Ten Year Anniversary
Celebration*". The second line said: "*Daily Specials*".

Mark peered through the glass front door and saw
no one. He pulled the handle and found it was
unlocked. He stepped inside. "Elsie?" he hollered.
"Anyone here?"

Cocoa, the store's resident Seal Point Siamese cat,
leaped down from her perch and rubbed against Mark's
legs meowing loudly. He reached down and scratched
behind her ears. "Where's Elsie?"

He heard a thud and rattling like a jar of beads
falling on the floor. "Oh sassafras!" It came from the
adjoining storefront where the shop held classes.

Mark followed the sound with the cat close at his
heels. Elsie Dennis sat on the floor amid large
cardboard boxes with her head in hands sobbing. Her
mop of black hair falling in her eyes.

Mark had never seen Elsie cry in all the years he'd
known her. She was one of those positive people who
was usually upbeat. He'd rarely seen her without a
smile which told him it must be bad.

He cleared his throat and moved forward. "You
should lock your door when it's after hours and you're
by yourself."

Elsie looked up and jumped to her feet, hammer in
hand. "Stop. This store is protected by an attack animal,

and I'm armed."

Mark chuckled and backed away from her. Cocoa chose that moment to rub against his legs. He bent down and gathered the large feline in his arms. She immediately began purring. "Cocoa isn't much of a threat. Can I help you with some of this?"

The hammer stayed at the ready. "Who are you?" She stared at him. "How do you know my cat? What are you doing in my store in the middle of the night?"

"You don't recognize me? Think a minute. I do have on a policeman's uniform. Cocoa knew me right away."

She took a step closer yet kept the hammer between them. "Mark? Mark Trask? I'm so embarrassed and way past exhausted." She reached out and rubbed his bald head. "I can't believe I didn't recognize you."

He smiled. "Was that for luck?"

"Would it work? I could use some of the immediate magical kind."

He pointed to the floor littered with screws, bolts, and wooden pieces. "What are you doing?"

"The store's tenth anniversary celebration starts tomorrow. I had this notion of having six spinning wheels set up for people to have hands-on lessons. Polly Rogers volunteered to be the teacher. Unfortunately, the shipment was delayed and only arrived this afternoon. The class is tomorrow afternoon at two and I only have two wheels put together. I can't change the class time now. People have pre-registered for it and paid a fee." She stopped and took a deep breath. "Just before you came in I dropped a sleeve of parts and they flew everywhere. I may have to go to

Plan B, except I don't have one. I barely had an adequate Plan A." A tear ran down her cheek.

"I never thought I'd see Elsie Dennis ready to quit. You're usually the roll-up-your-sleeves-and-plunge-back-in type." He held out his hand. "Give me a screwdriver and point me to the directions. I can read instructions with the best of them. I was on my way home, but I'm happy to stay and help. Can't have your celebration start off on the wrong foot tomorrow."

Elsie threw her arms around Mark. "Have I told you lately how much I absolutely adore you? With your help, I may actually get this done in time to sleep before I open at ten in the morning."

He chuckled. "If I'd known wielding a screwdriver would evoke such an affectionate response, I would have done it a lot sooner. Let's get to it."

Elsie blushed. "Timing is everything. It might not have worked years ago."

Mark plopped down cross-legged on the floor and Elsie slid an unopened box to him. "You start with a new one. I'll gather the parts from the floor and finish this one. You'll need the screwdriver, little hammer, and the Allen wrenches. I'll put the tools here between us."

They worked well together, sharing tools but speaking little. Mark took the opportunity to study Elsie's face while he was working. It was a kind face but there were a few worry lines beginning to settle on her forehead and at the corners of her kissable lips.

Kissable lips? Where did that thought come from?

He needed to pay more attention to the task at hand and less to his coworker before he hammered his thumb.

By two in the morning, they had all six spinning wheels ready for use and Elsie had briefly tested each one. She pedaled and Mark tightened screws and placed drops of oil strategically until each wheel spun noiselessly without any wobble. Elsie placed them in a semicircle facing a small, raised platform where the teacher would work. Seeing the completed project gave him a sense of satisfaction. He was particularly happy to see a smile return to her face.

She had a spinning bench to go with each wheel. They got to work and finished putting those together in short order. They had a lot fewer pieces. Then they put them in place behind each wheel.

Elsie stepped back to get the full effect of the view and tripped into Mark. Fortunately, he caught her before she hit the floor. "Sorry to be such a klutz. Thanks for saving me…again." She whirled around and kissed his cheek. "Mark, you're blushing all the way across your bald head." She patted his shoulder. "Thanks for saving my celebration. I couldn't have finished all this without you."

"My pleasure. I didn't expect such an exuberant thank you. Please, lock your door when you're working after hours in the future. Cocoa's not much protection if someone intent on evil came in."

"Yes sir, Officer Trask. I am past ready to go home. I have a busy week planned. Stick your head in tomorrow before you go on shift and see the fruits of your labor in action. Your neighbor, Polly Rogers, has been spinning for over seventy years. She'll have the whole class going like pros in no time."

"I'll be certain to do so. C'mon, let's go. Is the back door locked?"

"Yes. I'll go out the front door." She waved him away. "You don't have to wait on me. I only live four blocks away."

"It's late and you're alone. I'll drop you at your house on my way home."

"Don't be ridiculous," she protested. "I walk to and from the shop all the time."

He raised one eyebrow. "After two-thirty in the morning?"

"Well, no."

He stood with his hands on his hips. "Humor me. It's my responsibility to protect and serve. Let me do my job."

"Good to know you've only been doing your job tonight."

"I was helping a friend in distress." Mark winked at her. "Fortunately, I can do both at the same time."

Elsie reached overhead and petted Cocoa stretched out on her perch just inside the front door. "Keep everything under control. I'll see you in the morning." With a loud purr, the cat nuzzled her hand.

Chapter Five

After Elsie got into Phil's car, she said, "Mark, I'm four blocks straight down the street."

"I know. Remember, I've been there several times and it hasn't been that long ago."

"I hadn't forgotten your visits. I wasn't sure if you had." She sat quietly staring at his profile as he drove to her place.

The light on the front porch was on. The rest of the white two-story house on the corner of Lincoln and Pine was completely dark. Mark parked at the curb, then got out of the car and was at the passenger door before Elsie unfastened her seat belt.

She got out of the car. "My goodness, this is service. I even get walked to the door."

"Yes, ma'am. Your shrubs are pretty high around the perimeter of the yard. Anything could be behind them, and you would not see it until your assailant was on top of you."

"Do all police officers see danger lurking in every shadow?"

"Professional hazard, I guess. I'm glad Hubert left the light on for you."

Elsie walked up the steps and unlocked the door. "He's thoughtful. He's a good older brother. He would have come to help me tonight, but I hated to ask. He always has so many projects of his own going on and I foolishly thought I had it all under control. Plus, he hasn't been feeling his best of late. I'm not sure he would have had the energy to work half the night. Thanks again. Have sweet dreams." She stood on tiptoe and kissed his cheek before opening the door and disappearing inside.

The deadbolt sounded as Elsie locked the door. Mark strolled to the car humming softly. It felt good to help a friend. He enjoyed being with her. Once he'd thought he and Elsie might be more than friends but they both shied away from entanglements then. No. More accurately, they flew like bats out of the netherworld away from anything meaningful or long lasting. Maybe things had changed now. He knew from town gossips that she wasn't seeing anyone regularly. And those same people would probably say he and Poppy Caldwell were an item but that was a very recent development. Who knew how long it would last? Poppy wasn't as mature and settled as Elsie. She was fun, but for the long-term, shouldn't your life's mate be more than a good time? He touched the spot Elsie kissed. It still felt warm. A smile spread across his lips as he slid into the car.

No lights were on at his house. He parked Phil's car in the usual spot and walked through the open garage and through the door to the backyard. Domino flew across the yard making happy yips. Mark shushed him. No need to wake the neighbors at this hour.

He reached down and rubbed the dog's head. "Sorry to be so late. I was rescuing a damsel in distress. C'mon in. I'll get your food out. I'm beat. Guess Phil didn't come home." They climbed the steps to the deck together.

Mark filled Domino's food and water bowls, then sat at the kitchen table watching the dog gulp it down. Phil had never left the house without saying where he was going. And never for multiple nights in a row. Not in the ten years he'd rented from Mark. He'd rarely left home at all.

After he let Domino back outside, Mark checked the answering machine on his landline. A flashing red light showed three missed calls from unknown numbers and one message. He hit play.

"Mr. Trask, this is Selena Hughes, Phil's mother. I hate to bother you, but Phil missed calling me Sunday night. He always phones me right at six o'clock without fail. Every Sunday night since he went away to college. I thought he'd call Monday, but no call tonight either. Would you please tell him to call me, or would you phone me yourself? Thanks."

The machine indicated Mrs. Hughes had called at ten o'clock. He'd have to remember to call her in the morning, later this morning. He left a bright yellow sticky note on the phone as a reminder.

He let Domino back in the house. "I'm going to bed now. You may do as you like." Too tired for a shower, he peeled off his clothes and snuggled under the covers. He set the alarm as the clock rolled over to three forty-five. The fluffy mutt curled up beside him.

The next thing he knew, it was noon and the alarm was blaring him wake. Mark was lying in the exact position he'd fallen asleep in. *Clang, clang.* Domino nudged his bowls across the kitchen floor. If the alarm hadn't woken him, the dog would have. He went into the kitchen and fed the dog. He flipped the coffeemaker on.

Back in the bathroom, he ran the electric razor around his head. He definitely needed one of the specialty head razors, if he was going to maintain this new look.

He stood under the stream of hot pulsating water for a long time. The water got cooler—either because he'd gotten acclimated to it—or because the old water heater probably needed to be replaced. It was here when he moved in. When you own a house, it's always something. Somewhere to spend your hard-earned money. Whether you wanted to or not.

He wrapped a towel around his middle and padded on bare feet into the kitchen. The coffee pot worked perfectly and steaming hot nectar of the gods was waiting for him. He poured a cup, took his cell phone off the charger, and opened the "paper" online. It was nice not to have to retrieve the printed newspaper from whatever corner of the yard it had been deposited in. Not a lot of news. There was Elsie's quarter page ad announcing her weeklong tenth anniversary celebration. He made a mental note to stop in after lunch and before work.

He got dressed. The neon yellow sticky note got his attention when he walked back through the living room. No time like the present. He hit the callback button.

"Hello, Hughes residence."

"Mrs. Hughes, this is Mark Trask. I'm returning your call from yesterday. I work the evening shift, so I didn't see it until almost four o'clock this morning. I'm sorry you didn't hear from Phil, but I can't really help you. I got home from a week's vacation on Sunday, and he wasn't here. No note. Nothing. I'm not certain when he left. He didn't take his car."

"Do you think he's all right? It's not like him to disappear without a word." Was Mrs. Hughes crying?

"You're right. He's never done this since he has lived with me. I can put out some inquiries today. I'll check around with the neighbors. Maybe someone saw him leave or talked with him before he did. If you hear from him let me know and if I learn anything, I will do the same. Don't worry. I'm sure there's a logical explanation." He hoped he sounded comforting.

"Okay. Thanks for calling me back, Mr. Trask. I know I shouldn't worry about a grown man, but he'll always be my little boy. Thanks for understanding. Goodbye."

"Goodbye, Mrs. Hughes."

He was starting to worry. It's one thing to leave without telling your landlord what you're doing. It's another to disappear without letting your mom know. Maybe the next-door neighbor, Mrs. Hollis, saw him. She's in her yard all the time and more than a little bit interested in all the neighborhood comings and goings. He pulled the living room drapes open. There she was, in her broad straw sunhat trimming her rose bushes. He unlocked the front door and stepped into the sunshine.

She waved when she saw him on the front porch. "Good morning." Mrs. Hollis stopped pruning her rosebushes and put her hand up to shield her eyes. "You're coming out of Mark's house, but you don't look like my neighbor. Mark, is that you? How was your fishing trip? Catch a lot?" She smiled. Despite the sunhat her skin was bright pink, a sign of the hazards of being a redhead.

The scent of blooming roses wafted to him as he

neared the white picket fence between the houses. "It's me. My post-holiday look. I needed to change things around a bit. I did have a good vacation. It was a nice relaxing trip until I was almost home." He told her about the reckless driver and the damage to his truck.

She frowned. "I'm not surprised. Drivers glued to their cell phones seem as dangerous as drunk drivers and there's so many more of them. You're lucky you weren't hurt."

"Yes, ma'am. Did you see my housemate, Phil Hughes, last week?"

She walked closer to the fence separating them and lowered her voice as if revealing a secret. "Oh, yes. At least, I think it was him—I've only seen him a handful of times." She put her hand to her mouth and hesitated. "I hope I'm not telling tales out of school, but it was party city at your house last week. Overnight visitors with out of state plates. Lights on until all hours of the night. A constant stream of food delivery drivers—you know even The Purple Cow delivers now. It was all most unusual. Then Saturday afternoon they packed their trunks and left all at the same time." She shook her head. "It looked like a caravan heading out for the next oasis."

How could his housemate's personality have changed so dramatically? "That's not the Phil I know. Was he with them when they left?"

She nodded. "He was."

Maybe someone forced Phil to leave. "Did he seem to be going willingly?"

Mrs. Hollis hesitated a moment. "Well. He carried out his suitcases and sat them by the limousine. I was having dinner guests Saturday evening and was out here cutting some roses for the dining room table. The yellow bush has been especially prolific this year."

"And he saw you and came over alone to talk with you?" Mark asked trying to get her story back on track.

"Yes, that's what happened. He walked over to the fence while the luggage was being loaded in the car," she continued. "He told me he was sorry if they'd been too loud or disturbed me with all their activity. Of course, I didn't tell him what a ruckus they'd made. I didn't want him to feel bad after he'd apologized."

"Of course. Did he say when he'd be home?"

"Yes, kind of. He wasn't sure when he'd be coming home. He hadn't expected any company or to be leaving. Then a woman came over to his side and he stopped talking."

A woman was involved? With Phil Hughes? "Do you think he was trying to tell you he was being taken against his will?"

She cocked her head. "No, I didn't pick up any reluctance to leave from him." She stopped and put her hand on her forehead. "Oh, dear. I haven't got a brain in my head. I forgot to tell you he came over specifically to tell me to give you a message immediately when you got home. I'm so sorry."

"If he left a message for me, he probably was going willingly," he said. "What was the message?"

"Right. The message was 'don't worry about me.' I should have told you at the beginning."

"Thanks for telling me now. Something isn't right with the whole situation even if he said not to worry about him. Maybe he just decided to take a little holiday, too. He knew I'd be home on Sunday to take care of Domino. Thanks for providing some clues in the mystery of the missing housemate. I'll let you go back to your roses. They look beautiful."

"Thank you," she said leaning over to smell a bloom. "We've had perfect weather for them. Their scent is stronger than it has been in years. Let me know if you hear from Phil. Have a good day." She picked up her pruning shears. He started toward the house.

She called out, "Oh, Mark, I don't know why I remember this but the limousine he left in had a Pennsylvania license plate with only three letters, SAS and the number zero. I thought it was odd. I mean we don't see limos in this neighborhood every week and out of state plates made it stick out more."

"Thanks. Hopefully, I won't have to track it down, but this will help if I do."

Mark went in the house and called Mrs. Hughes back to report what Mrs. Hollis had told him. She was still worried and couldn't imagine who her son would go off with from Pennsylvania.

When he hung up, he stepped out the front door again. Mrs. Hollis was still there trimming the lush bushes. He walked over to the fence. "One more question, Mrs. Hollis. Can you describe the limo Phil got in?"

"It was dark colored with tinted windows. Probably black. It seemed kind of long—maybe one of those stretch limousines. The interior was black, too. I saw it when they opened the doors. It was chauffeur driven. Does that help?"

Mark grinned. "Talk about observant. You get the Miss Marple award. Thanks. It helps a lot."

"There were two other cars," she said. "They were dark sedans with tinted windows, but smaller than the limo. The people who came out of the house drove them. They both had Pennsylvania plates, too." She smiled broadly. "I've always loved detective novels."

Chapter Six

Mark walked up to Whistler's Diner just as Chief Davis was coming out with his wife. "Good to see you, sir."

"Good to see you," Davis said. "Sounds like you had a successful fishing trip. Lucky you weren't hurt on the way home."

There are no secrets in a small town.

"You're right. Very lucky. I'm glad Mike Skelton took a picture of my truck stuck on the guard rail, or my insurance agent never would have believed it."

"Emma said the rainbow trout was out of this world," Mrs. Davis said.

"If that's a hint," Mark said, "I'd be glad to drop some by your place later this week. I have plenty to share. It's the least I could do after you let me stay at your cabin."

"I should be embarrassed about begging for some, but I'll cook it if you'll bring it. Might as well plan to come for Sunday dinner and I'll feed you—something other than fish. Bring a certain someone with you, if you want." She winked and nodded toward the diner's interior. "Just let me know how many to expect."

"Thanks. I'll be there. I'll let you know about any others later this week."

Mark pushed the door open, walked into the diner and took a seat in his usual area. There were only a few other patrons still dining. A few minutes later, a friendly voice asked, "Having today's special or branching out?" Susie Powell stood at his table with her pen in hand and pad ready.

"I'm sorry," he said. "Isn't this Poppy's section?"

"It is but she didn't think you'd want to risk getting a plate dumped in your lap," she said and gave him a broad grin.

"Why on earth would Poppy want to drop something on me?"

Susie leaned so close he could smell her lemon scented perfume. "I heard someone tell her earlier that Elsie Dennis had help late last night and she was very appreciative. Let's just say our Poppy didn't take the news very well."

Mark threw up his hands. "So she's not even going to ask to hear my side of the story?"

Susie shrugged. "I'm here to take your order, not straighten out your love life. What'll it be?"

He glanced at the menu. "The special is fine. Would you ask her to stop at my table when she has a moment?"

"I can ask. Don't hold your breath. She's pretty upset." Susie went to the back to submit Mark's order.

Yep. There are no secrets in this small town.

The daily special consisted of chicken livers, squash casserole, mashed potatoes, and brown gravy over the potatoes and livers. Mark was almost finished when Poppy flopped down in the seat across from him. "Susie said you wanted to see me."

"I did. I do." He stared at her across the table. "How can I get in trouble for doing a good deed for a friend? Elsie was in a panic last night. There was no way she could get everything done on her own by today. All I did was help her put together some spinning wheels and benches."

Poppy glared at him with flashing green eyes. "I heard there was more to it than simply using a screwdriver."

"When we'd finished the work, I gave her a ride home because it was after two-thirty in the morning, and I walked her to the door for safety reasons." Mark felt a rise of heat move across his face. He wasn't sure if he was embarrassed about being told on—or angry at being distrusted.

"Hah. Since when is kissing someone goodnight a *safety precaution*?" she asked shrilly

"I did not kiss Elsie goodnight…she kissed me…on the cheek…to thank me for my help."

She cocked her head. "Are you telling me the truth?"

Mark reached across the table and laid his hand atop hers, gently caressing it with his thumb. "Poppy Ann Caldwell, what reason would I have to lie about something so perfectly innocent?"

"I'm sorry. I don't mean to be jealous. You are *usually* a good person. You help when you can." She patted his hand and smiled. "It doesn't matter who needs assistance. You're forgiven."

He pulled his hand back to his side of the table. "Hah. I have nothing to be forgiven for. Sometimes I think life would be simpler if I just resigned myself to being a lifelong bachelor."

Poppy got out of the booth, leaned down and kissed the top of his bald head. "But it wouldn't be nearly as much fun. I'll see you tomorrow."

Mark debated about stopping at *Knitting Pretty* since it would undoubtedly be reported to Poppy, but he wanted to be supportive of Elsie's celebration. He had told her he would stop. And part of him wanted to see her in the light of day. Plus, Polly Rogers was his neighbor. He'd like to see the ninety-year-old in action behind her spinning wheel. When a parking spot opened up directly across the street from the shop, the decision was made. He pulled to the curb.

The shop was standing room only. Polly Rogers sat behind a spinning wheel on the little rise at the front of the horseshoe-shaped class area. Every wheel they'd built last night was in use. Often with two women taking turns using the device.

Elsie waved at Mark from across the room and made her way to his side. "Thank you again for last night. As you see, I needed every wheel we put together."

"Glad I could help make your celebration a success. Hope your week goes well."

"It's off to a good start, thanks to you. If you don't feel like going to bed after work, stop by. Tonight, I'm assembling table-top looms and stands."

"I'll keep it in mind if I have a sudden attack of insomnia. Have a good day."

Mark left the shop humming. He was certain Elsie Dennis was flirting with him. Poppy wouldn't like it, but he was a little surprised that he did.

****

The shift went quickly. It was mostly paperwork and preparing for the annual Kid's Bike Rodeo the police department sponsored each year. It included safe bike riding classes, issuing new licenses, and carnival games with prizes and lots of food and drink. It was a good way for the kids to meet the police before they got into any trouble. Plus, the event encouraged them to look on the officers as friends instead of adversaries.

The lights were all on at *Knitting Pretty* when Mark turned down Lincoln street on the way home. What the heck. He had an invitation to stop, and Elsie was going to need more help. He was handy with a screwdriver.

He frowned when the front door was unlocked. Again. Cocoa greeted him with a loud meow but didn't bother to jump off her perch. He walked into the classroom to see Elsie in almost the same position as she had been last night—on the floor with pieces and parts spread out all around her—but tonight she wasn't crying. It was an improvement. "C'mon you stubborn screw. Go in."

Mark laughed. "I didn't know they made voice activated screws these days. What will they think of next?"

Elsie looked up and a smile lit her face. "Come in. If these can hear, they aren't responding to voice commands. I must have gotten duds, or they don't listen in English."

"How many other 'some assembly required' projects have you got planned for this week?"

"This is the last screwdriver project. I promise. The rest of the classes are things people buy here and learn how to use." She pointed to the boxes beside her. "As you can see, I'm only halfway done. I had customers until ten o'clock. I just got started."

"Point me to what you need done." She pushed a box his direction. He sat down on the floor next to her.

"While I'm thinking about it, the front door wasn't locked again. I'm serious, Elsie. It's not safe for you to be here alone at night with the doors unlocked."

"Sorry." She shrugged. "The back door is locked. I figured I'd see anyone coming in the front door."

"Somehow it doesn't give me a lot of comfort to know you would see your assailant before he acted. I guess if they leave you alive, you'd be able to identify them," he said without a smile.

She handed him the box cutter to open the carton in front of him. "I hadn't thought of it like that. Message received, Officer Trask."

By one in the morning, the looms were mounted on their stands and ready for tomorrow morning's ten o'clock class.

"Thanks again for the help," she said as she gathered up the tools. "I definitely bit off more than I could accomplish working alone this week. I probably should have asked Hubert to help. I think I told you he hasn't been feeling well."

He nodded. "You did. What's wrong?"

Elsie shrugged. "Who knows? He's tired to the point of exhaustion. His hair is falling out. He said his skin feels crawly and he can't keep enough lotion on it to prevent it from drying out."

"What did the doctor say?"

"Doctor?" Elsie rolled her eyes. "This is my stubborn brother we're talking about. You don't really know him, but he refuses to go to the clinic. He said he's too old to start seeing doctors. No point."

"You're right. I haven't been around him except briefly a couple of times when I picked you up for a date years ago." Mark hesitated. "It may be my police brain at work, but those symptoms sound like arsenic poisoning."

Elsie frowned. "Really? Where would Hubert run into arsenic?"

"Do you use any pesticides on your garden or flowers?" he asked.

"I don't think so, but the landscaping and gardening is Hubert's arena. He is concerned about pesticides leaking into the water table. I think he uses natural, non-toxic stuff. He does outside and I do inside. I do all the cooking. I'll guarantee every piece of produce is well washed before I cook it."

"You do know how to cook, right?" Mark grinned and winked.

"You are darned right I know how." She punched Mark's arm. "I'm a very good cook if I do say so myself."

"Couldn't prove it by me...I'm just going by the evidence at my disposal."

"Wait until I get past this week. You're coming to dinner—one I cooked—and I won't take no for an answer."

"It's a date." He started toward the front door. "Come on, it's past my bedtime. I need to get you home."

"I have to check a couple more things." Elsie waved him on. "You go ahead."

"Nope." Mark crossed his arms across his chest and scowled at her. "You know the drill. I go when you do."

"Fine. I'll do those things in the morning." Elsie retrieved her purse from behind the counter and turned out the lights in each room as she walked to the front door. She reached above her shoulders and stroked the cat's sleek coat. "Keep a good watch, Cocoa."

Mark opened the passenger door while Elsie locked up. "Madam, your chariot awaits."

Elsie winked. "A girl could get spoiled by this kind of attention."

A few minutes later, Mark pulled to the curb in front of Elsie's house. The house was totally dark. Not even the porch light to illuminate the steps and door lock.

"That's funny. Hubert didn't leave the light on," she commented as she stepped out of the car.

Mark got out of the car and pulled the high beam flashlight out of his belt. He hurried to Elsie's side. "Stay behind me."

They walked to the door. Elsie took her keys out of her purse. Mark held out his hand for them. He turned and started to put them in the lock. The door was ajar. No lights were visible inside the house. He pulled his service revolver out of the holster, slowly pushed the door open with the flashlight, and kept her behind him as they walked into the entryway.

Mark shone the flashlight straight ahead while Elsie peered into the darkness off to her right. "Mark, look over there."

He shone the light into the living room. Hubert Dennis slumped in the recliner, his head listing off to one side. Elsie turned on the overhead light and hurried to her brother's side. "Hubert." She gently shook him and patted his face. "Mark, he feels clammy. Hubert, are you awake?"

Mark scanned the room, then holstered his revolver, and checked Hubert's wrist. "He has a pulse but it's very weak. His breathing is too shallow. Call 911. He needs to get to the hospital."

"He'll be furious with me if I send him to the hospital."

"Would you rather call the funeral home? Do it. Now!"

Elsie made the call.

****

In less than ten minutes, the EMT's arrived. After checking Hubert's vital signs, they loaded the unconscious man onto their stretcher, flipped on their beacon light, and silently raced toward the hospital, claiming there was no sense in waking everyone in town with the siren when there was no traffic to battle.

"I have to go to the hospital," Elsie insisted. "I can drive myself. You need to sleep."

"I'll drive you over. Once he's admitted, there's nothing more for you to do and I'll bring you home. You shouldn't be alone." Mark gently led her to the front door. Elsie closed and locked the door.

Dr. Lovelady, the ER physician on duty, ordered multiple lab tests, including having Hubert's blood tested for toxins. This came after Elsie explained Hubert's recent physical complaints. The final results wouldn't be available for several days. Hubert did not regain consciousness in the emergency room to shed any light on his symptoms.

The doctor said it did sound like he had been poisoned or had been exposed to excessive amounts of carbon monoxide. The furnace in the old house hadn't run at all in the past month so that couldn't be the culprit. Dr. Lovelady admitted Hubert to the ICU and sent Elsie home with samples of a mild sedative to help her sleep. By the time they drove home, it was three o'clock in the morning according to the bank clock on the town square flashing the time.

Mark slowly walked Elsie to the door. She fumbled with the keys and finally, with tears running down her cheeks, handed them to Mark. He opened the door and gave the keys back to her. He steered her through the door with his hand on the small of her back. She put her purse down on the hall table and fell against his chest. "Can I do anything else for you?" he asked gently embracing her. "Help you get upstairs to bed?"

She lifted her head from his chest. "No, my room is back by the kitchen here on the first floor. The second floor is pretty much all Hubert's." She looked up still crying. "Thank you for insisting on bringing me home and for staying with me at the hospital. I don't know what I'd have done if I'd been alone when I found him."

He held her hand. "Should you be alone now?"

"I think I'll be okay. I just need some sleep." She got on her tiptoes and kissed his cheek.

Mark tipped his hat and smiled. "Your obedient servant, ma'am. I'll check on you tomorrow. Get some sleep. Morning is already here." He leaned down and kissed the top of her head. He gave her a quick squeeze around her shoulders and left, pulling the front door closed behind him.

****

Domino was curled in a ball just outside the kitchen door on the deck. He began softly whimpering when Mark turned on the garage light and started up the stairs. The dog raced into the kitchen as soon as the door cracked open.

Mark bent down to the animal and ruffled his fur. "Sorry, boy. I stopped to help Elsie and then we had to get her brother to the hospital. It couldn't be helped. I'm beat. Let's go to bed."

Domino licked his master's hand and made a beeline for his side of the bed. Mark wasn't far behind.

Chapter Seven

Mark turned off the alarm and wandered into the living room still in his pajamas. The message light on the answering machine flashed insistently. From a one a.m. call. Mark hadn't seen it when he came home.

"Hey, Mark. I was certain you'd be home by now. If you're there, please answer. It's kinda an emergency..." There was a delay and then Phil spoke again, clearly to someone with him, not to Mark. *"He isn't answering. He's not home. Or asleep. I'm sorry but I can't get him on the phone right now. We'll have to try again later."* Click.

The phone number wasn't one Mark recognized. He punched the call back button. The phone rang once, followed by a high-pitched squeal. *"The number you have called is not in service."* Great. He tried Phil's cell phone, but the voice mail function answered, *"The party you have called has a full mailbox."*

Unfortunately, Mark couldn't spend more time trying to track down his missing boarder. He had other things to worry about. Like how Hubert Dennis had gotten into arsenic...or some other equally lethal substance.

Domino danced around Mark until he finally made it into the kitchen and refilled the animal's water and food bowls. The dog dove into his dishes as soon as they hit the floor. Mark stood at the kitchen sink, eating a toasted bagel with cream cheese and drinking a glass of milk while he looked out at the backyard.

"What the heck?" Mark yelped.

Domino stopped munching long enough to look at his master and cocked his head as if he was wondering if he was supposed to answer.

Mark leaned closer to look through the window. An entire section of fence from the backyard was down and now propped up crossways against the opening where it had been. He hadn't noticed it last night when he let the dog in and wondered if it had happened this morning. He walked out on the deck to get a closer look.

His neighbor, Mikal Reynolds, waved from her yard where she was hanging out wash. "What are you doing with your fence, Mark?"

"Nothing intentional. Do you know when this happened?"

"Yesterday about two o'clock in the afternoon. A work truck pulled in the alley and two guys got out. They had chain saws, so I asked what they were doing. They glared at me and said they had been hired to put a gate on the fence where it opened to the alley. I asked if they had the right place since you weren't home, and Domino was outside."

"Thanks. What did they say to that?"

"Mark Trask hired them, and it had to be done today. I take it from your response you didn't hire them."

Mark shook his head in disbelief. "No. I didn't. I'm lucky Domino didn't get lost. Why would someone cut a hole in my fence?"

"They said they'd be back today to install the gate.

If I see them, do you want me to call you? My son, Will, went over when they left and laid the piece they'd cut crossways hoping it would keep the dog in the yard. Do you want to leave Domino with me today? He gets along well with our trio of fur babies."

"Thanks. I would worry a lot less if I knew he was being supervised. You still have my house key, right?"

"I do."

"When you get ready to go to bed you can let him in the house so you don't have to wait on me to get home. I really appreciate the offer. I'll drop him off on my way to work. If you see anyone out here, please do call me. Thanks, Mikal." He looked at the gap in the fence once more before going inside.

Back in the kitchen, he stroked the top of Domino's head. "You're going on a play date today over at the Reynolds house, buddy. I'm sure you'll have lots of fun with Rhett, Sheba, and Blackie, not to mention Will and his little sister, Abbie. You'll be tired enough to be trusted in the house alone when they bring you back tonight. At least until I get home."

After Mark got dressed for work, he gathered up supplies for Domino. He put the dog on the leash and delivered him to Mikal Reynolds. Domino was so excited he couldn't stop wiggling. The Reynolds's pets surrounded him and they all sniffed one another.

"Thanks for doing this. I appreciate having one less thing to worry about." Mark bent down and hugged Domino and left.

He went to Whistler's for his usual before work meal. Once again Susie took his order. He didn't even ask about Poppy. He wasn't in the mood to mess with her childish snit. Susie brought him the special and he ate in silence. He left her a larger than normal tip, paid his bill, and drove over to *Knitting Pretty*.

The store was packed again and the class using last night's building project was in full swing. All the looms they'd built were strung with colorful yarn with students at them listening intently to the instructor. Elsie saw Mark from across the room. She smiled and waved toward the rear of the store. He walked back and met her there.

"Thanks again. I talked to the doctor about twenty minutes ago. Hubert is still unconscious, and they don't have the results from the toxicology screen or other lab work yet. So basically, no change from when we admitted him this morning." She smiled, but it didn't reach her bloodshot eyes.

"I guess you didn't have time to look for poisons around the house."

"Not yet. I barely got my head down before the alarm went off. I plan to get out of here by nine fifteen tonight since I don't have to put anything together for tomorrow's classes."

"Glad to hear that," Mark said with a grin. "Look for pesticides, rat poison, weed spray, those kinds of solutions. They're the most likely candidates, if he's been accidentally poisoned. We probably need to have the space heater I saw by his recliner checked for leaks. I think they can run a diagnostic on it at the hardware store."

"Good idea. Hopefully, Hubert will come around soon. I should have insisted he go to the doctor earlier when his complaints started. But the only way I could make it happen was for him to be unconscious so he couldn't stop me. He is not going to be happy with his little sister when he comes to."

"Blame me. Tell him Officer Trask insisted. I have broad shoulders."

"Thanks. Have a good night. You've been my hero this week."

He gave her shoulders a squeeze. "I know you don't have an assembly project tonight, but if you need me for any reason, call me. Do you still have my number?"

"I do. Home and cell. Thank you."

Mark headed down to the station.

It was a very quiet shift. One barking dog call. One jilted boyfriend drunk at Murphy's and insisting on driving himself home. Luckily, the bartender was a lot bigger and held on to the keys until the patrol car got there. Mark drove the guy home and told him to stop by the station tomorrow to retrieve his vehicle.

Mark was glad to see *Knitting Pretty* was dark when he drove by. So was Elsie's house. Hopefully, she'd be able to catch up on her rest tonight. So would he.

As promised, Mikal Reynolds had let Domino in the house. The dog raced into the kitchen as his master came through the back door. Mikal left a note, offering to keep Domino the rest of the week, even overnight, until Mark could get the fence fixed on Saturday. She had been watching, but no one even passed through the alley behind his house, much less installed a gate in the gap in the fence.

"Well, boy, you must have been a model guest today since Mikal's willing to have you stay a couple of days. And you didn't mess with anything here in the house. You're a very good dog."

He petted his wiggly animal, laid a stack of mail on the hall table, let Domino outside briefly, and went to bed. The last two late nights were catching up with him.

What woke him?

The LED display on the alarm clock flashed one twelve a.m. in bright white numbers.

The dog was snoring, but not any louder than normal.

Ring.

His landline.

He got up and walked into the living room. He grabbed the phone as the machine started it's message. "You have reached…"

"I'm on the line. Let it finish," Mark hollered over the recorded voice.

When the beep sounded for a message, a voice said, "Glad I caught you tonight."

"You woke me up. Who is this?"

"It's me. Phil. Sorry, but I really need your help."

"I'm not fully awake. You don't sound normal, not that I talk to you on the phone frequently. I'm glad you called. You need to call your mom. I wanted to let you know I have been driving your car because I was in an accident with the truck…"

Phil didn't wait for Mark to finish. "Did you get a package in the mail for me?"

"A package? No. How big is it?"

"It's a padded mailer. You know, an eight and a half inches by eleven."

Mark heard whispers in the background. "It should have been there by now," Phil insisted. "It's really important. I need to know as soon as you get it."

"Where is it from?"

"That's not important. Just let me know when you get it."

"Your cell phone mailbox is full. What number should I call?"

"I'll call you again to check."

Click.

What on earth has Phil gotten himself into?

Chapter Eight

The next morning as Mark crossed the living room, he saw the message light flashing on the answering machine. Of course, it recorded the phone call from Phil since he didn't catch it before the machine kicked in. Mark listened to the message.

He hadn't dreamed the call. But Phil's voice sounded reedy and more shaky than usual—worse than it had sounded last night when the two of them spoke. Mark saved the message. He hoped it wouldn't be important later, but it seemed to be at this moment.

He got yesterday's mail off the hall table and leafed through it. A couple bills; a card from his insurance agent; a hunting magazine; and the bill for the cable service to Phil's apartment.

And there it was.

On the bottom of the stack lay the package Phil called about last night. The postmark was smudged, but there was a Priority Mail tracking number on it. Mark jotted it down and stuck the paper in the pocket of his uniform shirt. He wanted to know more about this package before Phil called to check on it tonight.

Ding. Dong. Ding.

Mrs. Hollis, all decked out in her Sunday best, stood on the front steps holding a plate covered in plastic wrap. Mark smelled her gardenia-scented perfume before he got the door all the way open. "Good

morning, Mark. I don't know if I'll ever get used to your new look. I came to let you know I'll be out of town this weekend. My two sisters, Beverly and Sue, and I are escaping to Chicago for a sisters weekend of shopping and fine dining. You remember them, right?"

"I do. You look especially lovely this morning. I've never seen you with your hair like that—very fancy."

She covered her mouth to hold in a titter. "You're going to make me blush. I don't know the last time a handsome young man told me I looked lovely."

"We're even." He grinned. "I don't know the last time anyone referred to me as a handsome young man. I'll be happy to keep an eye on your place. I'm sure you'll have a good time."

"Here." She thrust the plate into his hands. "White chocolate macadamia nut—your favorite—right?"

"You spoil me rotten. Thank you." He made a mental note to take the cookies with him to the station. Those guys would eat anything, and his waistline didn't need a whole plateful of the cookies, favorite or not.

"I'll be home by dark on Sunday. Take care."

She stood on tiptoe to kiss his cheek. He kissed her forehead and watched her carefully navigate down the porch steps, down the walk and over to her yard. He waited until she was inside before he went back in.

It was time to get Domino situated before he went to work. He gathered all the dog's paraphernalia and loaded it in Phil's car. Domino wiggled in and out of his legs with excitement. He could barely get him into the car for the very short trip. The Reynolds kids were almost as excited as the dog was to say nothing of Sheba, Rhett, and Blackie, their fur babies.

"Mikal, you have a special spot in heaven for taking in Domino. Thanks. I'll come back for him Saturday morning."

She laughed. "Go to work. We'll get along fine. Don't waste a minute worry about Domino…or me. I have lots of help."

On his way to the station Mark pulled into the Skelton Motors parking lot and walked inside. There he found his truck, up on the rack with a pair of overall-covered legs sticking out from underneath the vehicle.

He leaned down and asked, "Did you run into a snag?"

Wiping his hands on the oily rag tucked into his belt, Pop slid from under the truck. "Everything is going according to plan. I said Thursday and you will have it before the end of the day."

"Terrific. I wasn't doubting you. Can you bring it to the station and take Phil Hughes's car in? It needs a good general tune up." Mark asked.

"You bet. I'll call you when we're on the way to make the swap. I'll probably send Mike over with it between four and five if that will work for you."

"I'll leave the keys with the dispatcher if I have to go out at any time. Thanks, Pop. Sure is nice to know a mechanic who does great work and follows through on his promises."

"You might want to wait to thank me until you see my bill," Pop said with a chuckle.

"I'm sure I'll still be happy with your work even if my bank account suffers some."

****

Mark pulled into a parking space in front of *Knitting Pretty* and saw Elsie going in the front door as he approached.

"Good morning, Officer Trask," Elsie called as she walked to the back of the store.

"Good morning. Thought I'd stop to check on Hubert."

"He woke long enough to ask where he was, but drifted off again before I could respond. The doctor said it was an encouraging sign." She wiped a tear off her cheek with the back of her hand. "It's so hard to see him lying there and I'm helpless to do anything about it."

Feeling her pain, Mark pulled her into a brief hug. "You did the necessary thing to make certain he was still with us."

"Thanks. I hope he thinks it was a good thing once he's fully awake. We're still waiting for the report on the toxins. I looked at the portable heater last night. There is nothing *portable* about it. I can't lift it very easily and I'm not certain it will fit in my trunk. I wonder if the store would come and get it."

"I'm getting my truck back tonight. I could pick the heater up and take it to them."

"Thanks for the offer. I'll call the store first. Maybe they can check it at the house. If they need it brought in, I'll let you know."

Mark tipped his hat. "Happy to be of service, ma'am. What are the good ladies of Lansdale learning about today at the *Knitting Pretty* anniversary celebration?"

"Brioche knitting. Want to stay? I can scrounge up some needles and yarn for you." Elsie grinned. "It's an advanced class."

"I guess I'll have to wait until I complete my

'Knitting for Clumsy Police Officers' class before I jump into an advanced class." He gave her a little salute and left.

He enjoyed the give and take of the banter with Elsie. No tension. No hurt feelings. Must be what flirting with the right person feels like. She could tease him even though things were going wrong. Next stop, was Whistler's for his late lunch. He wasn't going to let Poppy's carping keep him from enjoying Walt Whistler's delicious Thursday special.

Poppy met Mark at the door of the diner and led him to a seat in the back of her section. "Having the fried chicken?"

"Is it Thursday?"

"Let me get your drink and put in the order."

Maybe she's forgiven me for helping Elsie.

She brought Mark's beverage and plopped down in the seat across from him.

"Nice to have you wait on me." he said with a smile.

"Well, there's no reason not to be professional despite our personal relationship issues," she sniped.

Nope. Doesn't sound like the beginning of the you're forgiven speech.

"You should know I am canceling our Saturday night date. I don't think it's a good idea for us to see one another," Poppy said rapidly, barely taking a breath.

"Okay," he said slowly. "Is this a one-time cancellation or the beginning of a trend?"

"It depends entirely on you. Are you going to continue seeing Elsie Dennis?" Her eyes—deeper green than usual—glared jealously.

Mark took a deep breath. "First, Elsie and I are long-time friends. I do have friends other than you. And some of them are female."

"You know that is not what I'm talking about." Poppy's voice got shriller.

Another deep breath. "I have been helping Elsie at the store and with some issues related to her brother. I don't think we are *seeing* one another in a dating sense. You can ask her about me yourself."

"I have no desire to speak with your *friend.*"

"If I were *seeing* Elsie or anyone else, why would you care? We've only been on a few dates. We haven't discussed being in an exclusive relationship. Or did I miss something?"

She pressed her lush pink lips into a perfect pout. "Apparently those few dates meant a lot more to me than they did to you."

"Do you realize how high school you sound?"

"I have my answer. We will not be dating in the foreseeable future. I will serve you in a professional manner at Whistler's and I expect appropriate behavior from you should I need your professional services." As the kitchen bell sounded, Poppy said, "Your order is ready, sir." She quickly got out of the booth and went back to the kitchen.

She put the food in front of Mark without a word and did not return until she delivered his check. Again without saying anything.

Mark wasn't going to get sucked into a silly spat. The cancelled date was fine with him. One less thing to fret over. Could be a good thing, he decided and headed to the station for his shift.

At the beginning of the shift Mark had a chance to

log onto the Post Office site and type in the tracking number from Phil's package. Why do they make them so long? On the second attempt he got all the numbers in the correct sequence. The site showed it was delivered yesterday. He already knew that. Where was it sent from and from whom? He clicked on the transit details. It was taking a long time to load.

"Mark, we have a domestic dispute in the front yard at 624 Frontier Street. Appears to be a man and his teenage daughter," the dispatcher radioed.

There was no time to check the package tracking details now. Frontier Street was on the far edge of town. This wasn't the first time they'd had a call out there. Likely it was a fight over the daughter's curfew again. He left Phil's car keys at the desk in case Mike delivered his truck while he was out.

Yep. It was Mr. Castlebeck, fighting with his seventeen-year-old daughter, Melissa. She wanted to have her curfew extended so she would be able to stay until the rock concert in College Park was over.

Her father shouted, "You won't need to worry about your curfew if you don't get to go at all."

She screamed, "You are the meanest father in the whole world!"

Mark stepped between them—a dangerous spot for any officer to place himself in—and herded them both into the house for a more private discussion. After twenty minutes of back-and-forth yelling, Mr. Castlebeck finally quietly agreed Melissa had earned the right for an extended curfew for this special event.

Sometimes people needed a third party to help them hash things out. Mark had never met Mrs. Castlebeck. She was out of the picture long before he moved here. He was glad he wasn't raising a teenage girl alone. Mr. Castlebeck was lucky Melissa was usually a well-behaved young woman.

During Mark's absence, Mike Skelton delivered the truck and took Phil's car into the shop. In a show of great customer service, they'd washed and waxed the old beauty. The bill was in an envelope on the front seat. He quickly checked it before going back inside the station. Not bad for emergency service on a Sunday night.

Chief Miller stayed late to work with Mark on the last-minute details for the Kid's Bike Rodeo a week from Saturday. The chief wanted to make sure his first community extravaganza was successful to set the tone for his administration.

Elsie called after eight. The hardware store couldn't pick up the heater or come to her house to run diagnostics. "If the offer still stands, I'll wait for you to pick it up tonight if you got your truck back."

"Sure thing. I'll be by a little after eleven-thirty. Won't take but a few minutes to put it in the back of the truck. See you then."

Mark responded to a call a few minutes later regarding a report of gunshots being fired, but it was a false alarm. The Welenz boys and their dad had gotten some firecrackers they couldn't wait to try out. Between the three boys and their father Mark wasn't sure who was the biggest kid. He understood why Mrs. Welenz always claimed to have four children at home. It was still over a month until the Fourth of July. At this rate, they'll have no more firecrackers left to celebrate with on the holiday.

Miss Adele Clover of 6212 Partridge Lane made

her *usual* Thursday night call about possible prowlers. Each Thursday evening, she came home from playing bridge where she had imbibed in a little wine, and she was certain someone had been in her house or was there now. She parked in her driveway, called the police, and waited on the front porch for an officer to go into the house with her so she wouldn't be ravaged by an intruder. The calls hadn't started until her older sister, Annalee, passed away two months ago. The two spinster sisters had been born in and lived together their entire lives in the brick house on the corner.

The officers responding to her call never found any evidence of another person in her home. Mark didn't find anyone there tonight. He came back to the station with a dozen sugar cookies Miss Clover had baked earlier in the day apparently in anticipation of the police coming to her home. The officers looked forward to those delicious, fresh baked cookies she sent to the station each week.

By the time Mark finished all the paperwork related to his calls, it was time to clock out. He liked being busy because the shift flew by, but he never had an opportunity to go back and check on Phil's package. There was always tomorrow.

He stopped in front of Elsie's house. She opened the front door before he had a chance to ring the bell and led him into the living room. "Thanks for doing this. Do you have time for a beverage?"

"Thanks, but I'm expecting a phone call after I get home so I better get the heater loaded in my truck and be on my way."

Elsie raised her eyebrows. "A call so late at night?"

"It's my boarder. It's a long story. I'll fill you in

later." Mark crossed the room to the heater. "This is awfully big. I see why you questioned its portability. Let's roll it to the front door. I'll go out and lower the tailgate first."

When he came back in the house, they rolled it slowly across the carpeted living room and the tiled entryway. Then they schlepped it down the two stairs and rolled it out to the truck. On three they heaved it up and sat it on the tailgate. It was definitely a two-person job to get it into the truck. Mark crawled in the truck bed and pulled the heater to the very front where he wrapped bungee cords around it to hold it in place.

"I'll drop it off in the morning," he said. "No word yet on the toxins?"

"None and Hubert hasn't wakened again since this morning. I'm beginning to get worried."

Mark jumped down out of the truck bed and secured the tailgate. "Hopefully, we'll hear good news tomorrow. I'll check in with you before I go to work. Have sweet dreams."

"You, too." Elsie stood on tiptoe and kissed his cheek. "Thanks again."

The truck ran better than ever. Mark pulled the vehicle into the garage instead of leaving it in the driveway, closed the door, and locked it. After the alley fence vandalism, he didn't want to tempt someone with the heater. It started to sprinkle rain as he walked up the stairs to the deck. Lucky timing.

It was very strange to walk across the deck and into the kitchen without Domino greeting him. He opened the front door and picked up today's mail out of the box which he piled on top of yesterday's. He would look at it in the morning. He stayed awake. It was already past midnight and Phil should be calling.

At one o'clock the phone rang. Mark answered after the first ring.

"Looks like you got the package," Phil said not bothering with any pleasantries.

"Yep. Had it yesterday but I didn't know. Sorry."

Knock. Knock.

"Who would be at my door at this hour?" Mark asked.

"It's Nico," Phil said. "Give him the package."

"Who is this Nico person? Are you in trouble? You sound upset."

"Mark, there's no time for questions. Please. Give him the package. Now," Phil insisted with a tone Mark had never heard from him.

More knocking and now the doorbell chimed repeatedly. Mark laid the receiver on the table. He grabbed Phil's package and started toward the door. "Hold your shirt on, I'm coming," he hollered.

He unlocked both locks and opened the door. Standing on the porch in the now pouring rain was a man he'd never seen wearing sunglasses and a baseball cap pulled down low over his eyes with his hands held out. He didn't say a word.

"Are you Nico?"

With a nod, the man reached over and snatched the package out of Mark's hands. He ran through the rain across the yard to a black extended cab pickup truck idling at the curb and drove away. Too quickly for Mark to read the license plate or even identify what state it was from. The vehicle looked a little too familiar for comfort.

Mark closed and locked the door. He picked up the

phone. "He has it. Who is he, Phil?"
All he heard was dial tone.

Chapter Nine

Mark sat up and flipped his pillow over, then fluffed it a little. Sleeping on his stomach didn't work. Or his back. Or even his right side. He couldn't stop the many thoughts racing through his mind.

Phil's mysterious behavior was getting stranger and stranger. Mark would make time today to check on the package and the vehicles Mrs. Hollis saw.

In the morning, he left the heater at the hardware store. After two strapping young men unloaded it from the truck, they promised to look at it later in the day. Then he drove by Chief Davis's house and dropped off the fish fillets he'd promised Mrs. Davis. He told her there would only be him for Sunday dinner after church.

"Oh, I'm sorry, Mark." Mrs. Davis patted his back. "I thought you and Poppy Caldwell were becoming an item. I guess my sources were mistaken."

He didn't go into any details about Poppy's snit or about helping Elsie. It was okay if the town gossips were confused about the details of his love life or lack of one.

Planning to tell Elsie to expect a call from the hardware store later in the day, he stopped at *Knitting Pretty*. She was on the phone. Her face was ashen. She hung up.

He dreaded hearing what had happened now.

"News about Hubert?"

"I'm glad you're here, Mark. That call was from the hospital. The nurse on my brother's unit said my uncle stopped by last night, wanting to see Hubert. She explained that since his name wasn't on the list of approved visitors, she couldn't let him in Hubert's room."

"They're probably following those new privacy protocols. They're for the patient's protection."

She looked at him; worry had turned her eyes darker and her voice almost a whisper. "We don't have an uncle."

"Maybe the nurse misunderstood what he said. Maybe it was a cousin or a friend of Hubert's."

"Mark, we do not have any living relatives. None. Hubert never sees anyone socially. He barely goes out of the house. Even after the nurse explained the patient was unconscious, the man was insistent. She offered to call me and get verbal approval. He said no, just let him see Hubert. She had to have security escort him out of the hospital."

First, Hubert was poisoned. Now, a stranger insisted on seeing him even though he was unconscious. Was Elsie in danger? "Are you certain you don't know anyone who would be concerned about your brother? Did the nurse describe the insistent visitor?"

Elsie paled. "I never thought to ask. I'll call her back and find out. She said he gave the name of Tollivan. What do you think it means?"

"I'm not certain but we need a description," he said thinking out loud. "If security escorted him out, he should be on camera somewhere. Maybe it's all innocent and he was someone you'd recognize. We need to be able to talk with Hubert, get the heater checked out, and to see the toxicology report. Lots of moving parts on this one." He picked up her soft, cold hands in his warm, calloused ones. "Be cautious, but don't worry."

"Easy for you to say." She squeezed his hands, looking intently into his eyes. "I'm the queen of vivid imaginations. I'll try to tamp down my worries. I'll let you know if I hear anything. Thanks for taking the heater in and for talking me down. Hope your shift is quiet."

He moved her hands to his lips and kissed them gently, gave her a smile, and went to work.

****

Fortunately, Mark had some time to investigate the Phil mystery a bit more. It had poured down rain most of the day. The criminal element seemed especially averse to doing their mischief while getting wet.

First, the package. He logged onto the Post Office tracking website and after punching in the number was told, *Package not found.* He typed it again and was told, *This package is no longer available for tracking.*

Mrs. Hollis told him the Pennsylvania license plate on the limousine was SAS and a number zero. After digging through the internet, he discovered SAS was a large leasing company based in Philadelphia. They leased all types of vehicles. It was nine p.m., an hour later in Philadelphia, so it was too late to check with SAS today. He put it on tomorrow's To-Do list and clocked out.

Mark pulled into the garage, walked into the basement, and up the interior stairs to the first floor.

The quiet enveloped him. He hoped the rain would end tonight so he could repair the fence tomorrow and get his personal greeter back home where he belonged. The house echoed emptiness without Domino.

He walked through the kitchen into the living room. The front door was ajar several inches. He immediately closed the door and threw the deadbolt lock into a secure position and pulled his service revolver. The stack of mail had been knocked off the hall table and strewn across the floor. The answering machine was on the living room floor smashed beyond repair.

He looked in his bedroom. Nothing seemed out of place. He returned to the front hall. There were muddy shoe prints on the entryway rug. They led to the stairway and continued to the second floor.

With his revolver still drawn, he carefully climbed the stairs. The door to the second floor stood wide open. His note was still taped to the door. The wood around the lock had been smashed. He quietly crept down the hall. He stopped.

The door to Phil's bedroom was open. The mattress had been pulled off the bed and its cover slashed open in multiple places. All of the drawers from the dresser had been emptied on one side of the room. Then the drawers had been broken completely apart. The shelves in the closet had been swept clean. Everything laid in mangled piles on the floor. The linings of all the suit jackets had been shredded with a razor blade or knife.

With his weapon still drawn, he crept into Phil's office. The desktop computer and laptop were missing. His answering machine suffered the same fate Mark's had. The desk drawers had been emptied on top of the desk and left upside down. The lock on the three-drawer metal filing cabinet had been drilled out, and all the drawers were open. There were no files anywhere in the room.

In Phil's den the big screen TV and expensive stereo system were in their usual places. All of the cushions on the wingback chairs and the sofas had had the stuffing removed and been turned inside out. The backs of the chairs and sofa were slashed open. Books had been pulled off of the shelves and left upended as if they had been shaken looking for something. This was no ordinary robbery. A professional was searching for something very specific.

He walked downstairs and called 911, then opened the front door. The rain had stopped. He turned the door mat over to a drier side and sat on the damp steps waiting for the patrol car. He explained to his colleague about his missing boarder, the package that went MIA, and the phone calls. The forensic team was radioed and appeared less than twenty minutes later.

It was two o'clock in the morning by the time all the law enforcement members left, and Mark was able to call it a night.

Chapter Ten

Saturday morning Mark rose at eight and went for a run. He hadn't slept much, but he needed to get back in the habit of morning exercise. He hadn't been running since he returned from vacation. There were too many other things on his To-Do list. It felt good to get out in the light of day, to soak in the sunshine. The air smelled different, fresher and cleaner, when he was running.

At the end of his run he stopped at the Reynolds house to retrieve Domino who wiggled in happiness to see him. He carried home as much of the dog's paraphernalia as he could. Caleb and Will volunteered to bring the rest of the dog's belongings when they came over a little later to help rebuild the fence. Mikal reported she hadn't seen anyone in the area again yesterday.

Mark called the locksmith to rekey the front door, replace the deadbolt lock with one requiring a key, and to replace the lock to the second-floor apartment. He was able to come over immediately. If he was curious about what had happened, he didn't ask. He wore gloves to remove the locks and doorknobs to preserve evidence. As much as Mark wanted to start the cleanup on the mess upstairs, he knew to wait until the detectives coming over this morning cleared it.

Shortly after the locksmith left, Detective Glen

Myers came up the walk. Mark let him in and shook his hand. "Sorry about destroying your Saturday plans. I had the locks changed earlier, but we bagged the doorknobs and locking mechanisms and Earl was careful not to touch anything without wearing gloves. Where do you want to start? Upstairs or right here?"

"Here is fine," Myers said. "This bag has your mail in it. They took it back to the station and dusted it for prints. Nothing useable was found. We still have the answering machine. Do you want it back when we're finished?"

"No, it looked like it was toast. It had my housemate, Phil Hughes's, last message on it. I guess I wasn't the only one who thought it might be important. Nothing else on this floor was messed with. I think they knew exactly where Phil's apartment was."

"Doesn't look like much else except the footprints here. I want to get some measurements and more pictures of them before you remove them. Then I'll go upstairs. I'll probably be several hours given what I heard about the condition of things in the apartment. Have the neighbors been interviewed?" The detective signaled for his assistant to come in with the camera.

"Mrs. Hollis who would be most likely to have seen something is out of town. The people on the other side of me and across the street are the Barretts and the Vanoys. I didn't speak with them, and I don't think anyone else talked to them either. I was out of the house from noon Friday until two o'clock this morning. The people directly behind me, the Reynolds family, didn't see or hear anything. My dog was with them. They had been monitoring the back of the house for me after the fence was cut earlier in the week."

"Hey, anyone here need manual laborers to repair a fence?" a voice called from the kitchen as Caleb Reynolds and his fifteen-year-old-son, Will, came in the back door with arms loaded with the rest of Domino's paraphernalia.

"Unless you have more questions for me, I'll leave you to your work. I'm in the backyard if anything comes up," Mark said to the detective, then he walked into the kitchen. "This is the place. Just put Domino's stuff in the corner."

The three of them were able to make quick work of the repair, even with Domino out in the yard supervising the work. Mark never could have done it alone.

When the work was finished, Caleb and Will sat in lawn chairs on the deck sipping on their lemonades. "Do they think this vandalism is related to the break-in yesterday?" Caleb asked.

"No one has told me yet. The detective is in Phil's apartment right now processing the area."

"I'm sure this isn't the only project for your day off." Caleb stood and set the empty glass on the table. "C'mon, Will, we'd best get home and see what your mom's 'honey-do' list for today looks like."

The Reynolds men headed back home. He was lucky to have such good neighbors.

****

Knitting Pretty was open on this Saturday from nine to three. The hardware store called to say the heater was ready to pick up and Elsie asked Mark to stop after the shop closed to take her over there. He parked in front of the store at three on the dot.

About five minutes later, Elsie came out, locked

the front door and crawled in the truck. "Thanks for helping me retrieve the heater."

"Did they give you any idea what they found?"

Seeming distracted, Elsie stared straight ahead. Finally she said, "Oh, yes. They found a hole."

Mark wasn't sure what the problem was. She usually paid more attention. "Did something else happen?"

She smiled weakly. "Nothing new. Just running through all this in my brain trying to figure out why its happening now."

As he pulled into the hardware store parking lot, her phone pinged. It was Hubert's physician. She put him on speaker phone.

"I received the toxicology report," Dr. Lovelady began. "There was a potentially lethal combination of carbon monoxide, arsenic, and an anesthetic agent called Ketamine, in Hubert's blood stream. On the street, that drug is known as Special K."

"The heater by his recliner was leaking," Elsie said. "He doesn't take any prescription medications, nor has he had recent surgery, Dr. Lovelady. And I haven't found any poisons in the garage or basement."

"Your brother is lucky to be alive. If he'd been found an hour later, he probably would have already been dead when you got home. Hubert is awake and fairly alert this morning. He is insisting on knowing who was responsible for him being hospitalized."

"Thanks for the update, Dr. Lovelady." Elsie ended the call then turned to Mark. "Could we go to see Hubert first? He may be able to answer some questions about what happened."

"Good idea. The hardware store is open until

seven, so we have plenty of time to pick up the heater."

"I told you he'd be angry about me sending him to the hospital," Elsie fretted.

"Blame me. His doctor just said he's lucky to be alive. Did we ever get a description of the man claiming to be your uncle, Mr. Tollivan?"

"No, we didn't. Let's stop at the desk before we go back to see Hubert."

It took forever to find a parking space at the hospital. Finally, someone pulled out on their third pass through the lot. They went directly to the fourth floor.

Elsie stopped in front of a nurse at the desk. "Hi. I'm Hubert Dennis's sister, Elsie. Yesterday someone called to tell me a Mr. Tollivan who claimed to be our uncle stopped by asking to see my brother. Is that nurse working today?"

"Yes. I'm the one who called. I'm Mrs. Pearson. How may I help you?"

"Could you describe Mr. Tollivan?" Elsie asked.

"Sure. He was an older man with graying hair and mustache. He was probably tall when he was younger, but he was stooped over and walked with a cane. He had coal black eyes and bushy eyebrows. He was wearing a green tweed jacket with dark brown suede patches on the elbows and dark slacks. Does he sound familiar? I can pull up a picture of him from the security footage. They gave me a picture after the guard escorted him out so the staff could keep an eye out for him." She pulled up the picture and turned the computer screen toward Elsie. "Do you know who he is?"

Elsie shook her head. "No, he doesn't look familiar to me. Thank you. It should be on Hubert's record—no one should be admitted to see my brother except me and the police."

"I see the note explaining that is already on the chart. I'll let you know if we have any more inquiries. Oh, there was one more unusual thing. There was an aroma of very sweet tobacco around him. Because so few people smoke anymore, I noticed it right away. I'll be sure to call if we see him again," Mrs. Pearson said.

As Elsie and Mark walked down the hall toward Hubert's room, she said, "This Tollivan person doesn't sound nor look like anyone I know. But something is tickling the back of my brain. Probably anxiety. Let's see if Hubert can give us any information about what happened the other night."

She knocked and pushed his room door open. Hubert was sitting up in bed with a book in his hands he held only inches from his squinted eyes. "Here you are, brother dear. It might be a little easier to read with these." Elsie handed him his glasses.

He quickly put them on. "Bless you for realizing I'm blind without them. Trying to get on my good side, so I'll forget you rushed me to the hospital despite my known desires to the contrary?" He glared over the top of the glasses at his sister.

Mark extended his hand to Hubert. "Excuse me, Mr. Dennis. I don't know if you remember me, I'm Officer Mark Trask. I was with your sister when she found you unresponsive. I insisted she call 911 and the emergency crew felt your life was in danger if you were not immediately transported to the hospital."

Hubert raised an eyebrow and limply shook hands. "Yes, I remember meeting you once or twice. Thank you for your confession, Officer, although I hardly believe anyone could convince dear Elsie to do anything she did not think needed to be done. Law enforcement or not. My sister has a very wide stubborn streak and the persistence to get her way."

Elsie laughed. "Must run in the family. I could spit on someone who has the same predispositions. He helped me get your little heater to the hardware store. They found it was leaking carbon monoxide."

Hubert hesitated. "I haven't used the heater in months. Just too lazy to put it back in the closet in case it turned cooler."

Elsie leaned over the bed and straightened Hubert's pillow. "You also had arsenic, and a sedative called Ketamine in your system. Any idea where you got them?"

"As for the poisons, I haven't a glimmer of an idea. You know I never use pesticides in the yard. I've never taken Ketamine in my life."

"Could you tell me what you did yesterday evening?" Mark asked.

"I ate supper about six-thirty. I had leftover chicken and dumplings and a small green salad with dill dressing. It was as good as it had been the first time. My sister is an excellent cook," Hubert said, nodding toward Elsie. "After dinner, I began watching a documentary on a travel show about the wine trail through Richland County, Illinois. They were interviewing a vintner at the Fox Creek Winery. He was a very entertaining fellow. Next thing I know, I'm in this bed hooked to tubes and monitors with worried looking medical staff hovering about me."

"Elsie, we didn't think to collect the dishes from his supper, did we?" Mark asked.

"No. At the time we had no idea we should."

"Given the toxicology report, I'll ask for a survey of the neighborhood to see if anyone strange was seen in the area. Of course, if they slipped behind the bushes, no one would see them." He turned toward Hubert. "Mr. Dennis, those tall hedges are an invitation for mischief. Someone could enter your property and never be seen from the outside."

"That, young man, is precisely the reason they are in place. I put a high value on my privacy and have no intention of cutting the hedges—not even one inch. They have been fine for the ten years we've lived behind them." His face reddened and his breathing got faster. "There will be some explanation for all of this, and you'll see no change in my landscaping is necessary."

Elsie patted his hand. "Don't get upset, Hubert. We can wait and talk about this when you get home."

He shook off her hand. "And when will that be? I am perfectly fine to go now."

"I'll talk with your doctor. Originally, he planned on keeping you at least forty-eight hours after you awakened to make certain the toxins had fully cleared your system. Time would be up Monday." Elsie kissed his cheek. "You relax. Read. Watch TV. Get some rest and the time will pass quickly. I love you." She hurried Mark out of the room before Hubert could protest further.

Elsie stopped at the nurse's station and let them know Hubert was alone again. She seemed deep in thought as they entered the elevator. "Penny for your thoughts," Mark said.

"What does your cop radar say about all of this?"

Mark chuckled. "My cop radar? Is that like ESP or

some other supernatural thing?"

The elevator doors opened to the lobby. "You know what I mean. Do you think someone is intentionally trying to harm Hubert?"

They walked across the parking lot to the truck. Mark opened her door and went to the driver's side. He slid behind the wheel. "You would be able to answer that better than I would. Does your brother have any enemies?"

"In Lansdale? Not that I know of. He barely knows anyone except our immediate neighbors."

"Where did he live before coming here?'

She hesitated a moment. "He's been here ten years." Elsie took a deep breath. "I hardly think where he lived before would matter."

"You may be right. I'm just trying to figure out if his poisoning is accidental or something more dangerous. I thought you might have some insight."

"Sorry I sniped. I know you're trying to help me."

Mark pulled into the hardware store parking lot and met Elsie as she got out of the truck. He held out his hand. "C'mon, let's get this resolved before we begin worrying about the next thing."

According to the hardware store repair person, the heater had been leaking carbon monoxide. There was a three-inch gash on the underside of one section that they repaired. The gash didn't seem to be a defect in the appliance, but looked like someone had taken a flat edge screwdriver and repeatedly driven it into the underside of the heater. The repair person didn't think it could have been used more than once in that condition without effecting whoever was nearby. He assured Elsie it was safe to use again.

The two young men who had unloaded the heater, reloaded it into the bed of Mark's truck. He secured it with bungee cords before they left.

As he started the truck, Mark glanced over at Elsie. "I know you don't want to hear this, but I think the heater was deliberately sabotaged and used without Hubert's knowledge but in his presence."

She didn't speak for several minutes, just stared at him with a furrowed brow. "You're right. I don't want to hear it. I can't wrap my brain around all of this." Mark parked in front of Elsie's house. "It's almost six o'clock," she said. "Would you like to have dinner with me before you go home?"

"First, we need to get this heater out of the truck and back in the house."

Mark got out of the truck, then stepped up into the bed. He untied the cords holding the heater and slid it across the bed. He jumped out of the truck. It took both of them to lower it to the ground. They pushed it together down the sidewalk and lifted it onto the porch.

Elsie handed the keys to Mark at the door. She smiled. "What can I say? I kind of like having you look after me."

Mark unlocked the door and bowed. "After you, madam. But I need your muscle to get it in the house." They hefted the heater up over the threshold. Elsie told him to leave it in the hall closet.

They walked through the living room into the large eat-in kitchen. The maple dinette set was off to the left in front of a hallway. The backdoor to the porch was straight ahead. On the right-hand side there was an island covered with mosaic tile in bright turquoise, blue, and white. Tall cabinets painted pale blue were above and below the counter-top between the sink and stove. A window over the sink looked into the fenced backyard lined with rosebushes. A basic white refrigerator stood beside the sink.

"A cozy kitchen," Mark said.

"Thanks. I like it because everything is convenient when I'm cooking." Elsie put Mark to work setting the table while she put together an impromptu meal of green salads with blue cheese dressing, salmon patties, wild rice, and fresh asparagus. "The plates are in the cabinets on the left-hand side of the sink."

They chatted about the weather, living in Lansdale, Hubert and Phil. Everything except themselves.

Mark pushed away from the table. "You do know how to cook. Your brother was right. It was delicious and a whole lot better than anything I could have foraged for at home."

"I'm glad you'll concede the point," Elsie said. "Speaking of home, why didn't you tell me you had a break-in?"

"Seemed like you had enough to fret about without taking on my stuff, too. How did you find out?"

"From one of my customers. Guess you've already figured out that I'm a fixer by nature. I like to try and make everything work well for everyone."

"Yep. I remember that about you. I used to try to fix everything, too, but I learned a long time ago I'm not really the one in charge. The world, thankfully, is in much more capable hands than mine."

"Point taken, Officer Trask." She began clearing the table and putting dishes in the dishwasher. "Thanks for staying for dinner. I wasn't ready to be alone."

"My pleasure." Mark stood and looked out the

back door. "Your roses are beautiful. Do you use any insecticide to keep the aphids away?"

"I don't think so, but I don't know. I only cut them for bouquets. All Hubert's rose treatment stuff is on the potter's table on the back wall of the garage. Want to take a look?"

"Might as well since I'm here. I know Hubert thinks he only uses nonpoisonous stuff, but it could be a source of the arsenic."

Elsie flipped on the outside lights, grabbed the key off the hook by the door, and went out to the garage. She showed Mark where insecticides would be. The area was very neat. The only insecticide was supposed to be the non-toxic, people and pet friendly kind. No arsenic there.

Back in the house, Mark took some of the dill dressing Hubert had eaten the other night and dropped it at the lab for arsenic testing.

Chapter Eleven

Mark woke refreshed and ready for the day. No late to bed last night. No mysterious phone calls. At seven, he rousted Domino and they went for a jog. The sun was bright and beautiful. When they got home, the dog headed for the cooler kitchen tile floor and collapsed. Mark jumped into the shower.

He made it to the adult Sunday School class and had actually read the lesson ahead of time. When the service started, Elsie slid in the pew beside him. Mrs. Davis invited her to join them for lunch. She accepted. Elsie followed Mark home. He left his truck in the garage, and she drove them both over to the Davis house.

The chief had been busy planting flower beds that burst with red, orange, and yellow blooms. In the far corner of the yard, he'd installed a two-foot-high waterfall surrounded by a rock garden covered in moss and phlox. He had also completed half of a new redwood-stained board fence around the entire backyard.

"Looks like you had a lot of pent-up demand to exercise your landscaping talents," Mark said.

The chief laughed. "A little was my idea. Mostly it came from years of the missus making honey-do lists for me. I think she's been looking forward to my retirement almost more than I."

"Well, it is all beautiful. Maybe someday I'll have time to flex my creative muscles," Elsie said. "I get to do a little at the shop teaching others, but it's not the same as doing something new simply because you want to."

"I enjoyed your celebration classes and specials," Mrs. Davis said. "I went every day to see what new and wonderful thing you had to offer."

"Thanks for coming in. I hope you learned something new you'll love to do and won't wait another ten years to come back in the store. Lunch was delicious. Would you let Mark and me clear the dishes?"

"No. The busboy job is already taken," the chief said with a wink. "Good to see you both. Hope your brother is released from the hospital soon, Elsie. Mark, I hope Phil returns unharmed. He's certainly been a lot more problem for you being gone than when he's home."

"Amen to that," Mark agreed.

They stopped at the hospital to check on Hubert who was sound asleep. The nurse said he'd been resting comfortably. The doctor had made a note about discharging him tomorrow if his lab work and vitals continued to improve. They left without disturbing the patient.

****

Domino and Mark jogged past Elsie's house about eight o'clock Monday morning. A few minutes later, Mark heard footsteps accelerating behind him. Elsie fell into step at his side.

"I know you'd never believe it to look at me." She took a deep breath. "But I used to run track in high school. I never missed a day running no matter what the weather was."

"I believe it. You can run and talk at the same time. Only experienced runners have enough wind to do both." Mark accelerated slightly.

"Trying to lose me, Officer Trask?"

Mark ran harder until he reached the pavilion in the park. Moments later Elsie caught him. Domino collapsed panting in the shade under a picnic table. Elsie bent over resting her hands on her knees. His position mirrored hers.

He laughed. "Maybe none of us are in prime running shape yet."

"It's a good start. How long have you been running?"

He raised his head and smiled. "This morning or ever?"

"Both."

"This is the third day in a row for this round. I used to do about three days a week except in the coldest part of winter. I'm getting back in the habit since my vacation. I ran cross country in junior and senior high. I need the exercise. I enjoy the sunshine and fresh air. Sitting in the patrol car or doing paperwork at the desk isn't much cardio activity. The doctor has reminded me since I turned thirty that exercise is a key to longevity."

"I get the same mantra from my doctor. Some days I think living longer isn't an unequivocal good. I'm pretty sure you're not required to jog after you pass through the pearly gates, unless it brings you joy." She laughed. "The doctor is releasing Hubert this morning. I'm glad it's today since the store is closed on Monday and I'll have plenty of time to get him settled in. I better head back home. If I'm not there at the exact moment the doctor signs the release, my brother will be angrier at me than he already is."

"Do you need any help?" he asked.

"I've got it covered. Thanks for the offer."

****

When Elsie walked into the hospital room, Hubert was sitting in a wheelchair with his belongings in a bag at his side. "I thought you'd never get here," he said testily. "The doctor came in and released me ten minutes ago."

Elsie started to step behind the wheelchair. "Sorry. I'm here now. Looks like you're ready to roll."

A young man in a blue uniform came in the door. "Ma'am, it's my job to transport Mr. Dennis to the discharge lobby. You can go ahead and pull your car under the canopy there. Mr. Dennis will need to sign out once we get downstairs. Then I'll wheel him out to the car and he's officially all yours."

Hubert shooed her out of the room, "Go get the car."

By the time Elsie's car rolled under the awning, Hubert was exiting the hospital. It only took a couple of minutes to get him loaded in the car.

"I'm glad you're coming home," she said.

"I shouldn't have been there at all," Hubert snarled.

"I'm afraid if I hadn't called the ambulance, I'd be very lonely now."

"How's that?"

"I would be living alone and only visiting you in the cemetery."

Hubert didn't respond or even look in her direction the rest of the way home.

Elsie pulled into the driveway, popped the trunk lid, got out of the car, pulled out Hubert's bag, and went to the passenger side to help him out of the car. He had the door open and had pivoted to get out of the car on his own.

"Do you need help?"

"Does it look like I do? I'm a little weak, but perfectly capable of getting out of the car without assistance." He waved her away. "Go ahead and unlock the back door. I'll be there in a minute."

Hubert seemed to be struggling to get to his feet, but Elsie was unwilling to be scolded again, so she did as he directed. She set his bag on top of the washer as she passed it. A to-do for later today. Hubert gripped the railing with white knuckles as he navigated the three steps up to the back door and slumped into the nearest chair as soon as he reached the kitchen.

"Do you want to trade bedrooms with me until you're a little steadier on your feet?"

"No. I can't stand the mattress you have," he snapped.

"It's adjustable. We can change the setting to suit you."

"No. I am sleeping in my own bed tonight. If you'd never sent me to the hospital we wouldn't be having this discussion. I'm still angry with you for doing what you knew I would not want."

Elsie rolled her eyes. "We've had this discussion. You would be six feet under, and I'd be planning a funeral instead of being chastised."

"No, I wouldn't. You know I want to be cremated."

Elsie gasped. She looked at Hubert, he winked and broke into a grin. "I should be thankful you took such good care of me. And for the record, I do want to be buried, not burned. I'll see the fires of hell soon enough without having the mortician speed things along."

"What a thing to say," Elsie scolded.

"Sorry to be so cranky. I am a little tired. Contrary to what doctors believe, a hospital is not a good place to rest. I'd like to stretch out in my recliner for a while, if you'd help me get settled in there. I don't think I can balance a glass of ice water and stay upright to walk to my chair without some assistance."

"I thought you'd never ask."

Once Hubert was ensconced in the recliner with his ice water, Elsie said, "We do need to think about taking the hedges down. Mark is right about them blocking the visibility to the house."

"No. I won't discuss it. I'm not so weak that I'll cave on maintaining my privacy. Case closed."

As she didn't want to aggravate him further, she tabled the topic until a better time.

****

Mark bought a new answering machine and installed it before he went to work. Hopefully he'd hear from Phil again and get more details about his disappearance and learn who the mysterious Nico was.

He grabbed a cheeseburger, fries, and a creamy chocolate malt at The Purple Cow and ate in his car before his shift. He wasn't in the mood to tolerate Poppy's attitude. All the relationship angst wasn't good for his digestion. Lately, he'd been chewing antacids way too frequently.

It was a very quiet Monday at work. Everyone must have gotten their mischief out of their systems over the weekend.

He tried the post office tracking number again. Same message: *No longer in the system.* Mark called the SAS leasing company in Philadelphia. They did have a limousine with a SAS 0 license plate and confirmed it had been rented for out of state use the week Mark was on vacation. They would not release who had rented it without a court order. The woman on the phone said she had told him too much already. Mark was certain he didn't have enough information to justify getting a warrant. Even with the break-in, he wasn't sure there was any evidence to link the limousine service to any crime.

Chapter Twelve

Tuesday morning an envelope was laying on the entryway floor. Morgan picked it up. The name and address were typewritten. No return address. No stamp. No postmark. It must have been pushed through the mail slot in the door. Inside was a single page of white typing paper with a warning in all capital letters cut from a magazine or newspaper. Morgan paled clutching the anonymous note in trembling hands.

Danger is stalking me and closer than ever.
I still need protection.
Who can I trust?
Lord, please stay close. Pull me out of darkness and toward the light.

****

Elsie fixed Hubert's breakfast and left him chicken salad in the refrigerator for lunch. Mrs. Johnson from across the street was going to check in and make sure he ate something. She was a sweetheart. She and Hubert were about the same age and enjoyed playing cribbage together. One less thing for Elsie to worry about.

Hubert was in his recliner devouring the morning news shows. Elsie kissed the top of his head and made certain the TV remote control was at his side, then she walked to work. Her resolution to reinstitute a daily run in her schedule had lasted one whole day. Today she'd have to settle for getting a little exercise going to and from work. She needed a good dose of fresh air and sunshine to help clear her head. Too much was happening. Too quickly. She'd expected changes, but good ones.

The *'For Sale or Lease'* signs in the two storefronts adjacent to *Knitting Pretty* were replaced by a bold yellow and black *Sold* sign. Brown craft paper covered the windows. Something new must be coming. She hadn't heard anything in the Merchant's Association meeting last month. More shops locating downtown helped all the existing ones by giving everyone another reason to shop local. Who would the new neighbors be?

The shop had some business trickle in all day long. Not the crowds that attended last week's anniversary celebration, but a little slower customer stream would give her a chance to replenish supplies. Today she'd order more fiber to feed the spinning bug she'd bitten so many with last week. Polly Rogers was a great help. All week she kept saying if a ninety-year-old woman could spin—anyone could. Might as well order another spinning wheel or two also. She was a pro at putting them together now.

When Elsie got home from the shop, Mrs. Johnson and Hubert were involved in the rubber game of their cribbage match. She'd been in and out all day making sure Hubert was comfortable and ate his lunch and dinner.

****

Mark stopped in at Whistler's for a late lunch. He couldn't resist Walt's chicken livers, the Tuesday special. For them he'd suffer Poppy's mood du jour. He had barely slid into the booth when Poppy rushed to his table. "I heard you had a break-in. Did you lose anything valuable? How stupid does someone have to be to break into a cop's house?"

Mark explained what had happened after Poppy put in his order. Everything seemed back to normal. Guess they were going to ignore last week's kerfuffle. It was fine with him. A little less drama in his personal life was always desirable.

****

Mark put the finishing touches on the plan for the Kid's Bike Rodeo layout when he got to the station. He was looking forward to the event and appreciated all the responsibility and authority Chief Miller was giving him this year for the big event.

A call came in at eight-fifteen about a window broken out of a front door. Mark recognized the address. It was Elsie's house. He was there in less than fifteen minutes. Her front door window had two holes in it where the round red glass designs in the pane had been knocked out. They were laying on the entryway floor. The projectiles had not been found.

When the incident occurred, all the lights in the house had been out except for a small lamp next to Elsie's recliner where she was sitting alone reading. She didn't hear any noise before the glass breaking so it probably wasn't a bullet.

With the hedges around the perimeter of the yard, the objects must have come from straight down the sidewalk to the front door. They had enough force they probably weren't just thrown.

As soon as she heard the glass break, Elsie ran to the front door and flipped on the porch light. She didn't see anyone outside, but she heard footsteps running down the street toward the park. Mark carefully scanned the area. Then he saw the culprits. Two small smooth rocks—perfect ammunition for a slingshot—rested a step apart on the stairway. They had the 'what' broke the window. Now they needed the 'who' and the 'why'.

Elsie assured Mark she'd be all right. It had shaken her, but she didn't believe she was in any danger. He slapped some duct tape over both sides of the broken panes. It would keep insects out until the glass could be replaced. Mark said goodnight and waited on the front steps until he heard the deadbolt turn in the lock before he returned to the patrol car.

****

Mark stopped at Elsie's house Wednesday morning while on his run. Her eyes were bloodshot, and she was much paler than usual. She made no attempt to smile.

"Did you get any sleep last night or lay awake worrying?" he asked when she opened the front door still in her nightgown and robe.

"The latter. I don't know why. Worrying never solves anything. It was such a freaky thing. Just the two little red circles out of the flower design. After Hubert's *accident* last week, I guess I'm getting edgy. I feel like there might be a target on my back."

"You've never found the arsenic or the Ketamine, have you?"

"No. Thanks for checking on me this morning, Mark. I'm glad you were the officer to respond last night."

"The day shift officers will be here interviewing your neighbors later this morning to find out if anyone saw or heard anything last night. I kind of doubt they did since no one came out of their houses while I was here. Usually, I get greeted by a witness if they think they may have seen something important. Hope your day isn't too taxing and you can get some sleep tonight. I'll let you know if we hear anything."

He gave her a brief hug and kissed the top of her head.

Chapter Thirteen

A steady parade of vehicles were in and out of the alley behind *Knitting Pretty* to deliver supplies and workmen to the stores next door. The cacophony of hammering, drills, and saws was almost constant. Elsie's head pounded in rhythm with the noise. She ate a sandwich at her desk and drank a diet cola. A little ibuprofen for dessert and she was feeling nearly human.

Chime. The front door opened. A tall man with straight coal black hair slowly entered the shop. Cocoa hissed, arched her back, yowled loudly, and leaped onto the man's back, thrusting her rear claws into him.

"Get this beast off me. Hurry!" He spun in a circle trying to buck the cat off of him.

Elsie ran to the front and extracted Cocoa's claws carefully from the man's clearly expensive shirt, apologizing the entire time. "She's hissed at patrons before, but she has never attacked anyone. I am so very sorry." She held the now purring feline close to her chest.

"You're telling me she's harmless even though you have a warning posted about the premises being guarded by an attack cat?" the man asked sarcastically. His coal black eyes glistened with anger.

"The sign is a joke. A friend bought it to be funny. I promise Cocoa has never attacked anyone before today. I can't imagine why she chose you to be her first victim." Hoping to keep the animal calm, Elsie continued petting the feline.

"No matter. I do not care what she has or has not done in the past. Keep her away from me. I am looking for Ms. Elsie Dennis." He stayed at least three feet from her and the cat.

"Look no further. You have found her."

He stepped forward and extended his hand to her. "Sullivan Stalatti. I recently acquired the two properties adjoining yours."

Elsie let Cocoa gently to the ground and the cat quickly retreated to her perch by the front door. She clasped the offered hand. "Welcome to the neighborhood. I wondered who was coming into the new stores." He held her hand a fraction longer than Elsie was comfortable with.

"Actually, I'm not alone. My sister, Siobhan, will run the *Sips to You* coffee shop next to you and I will have *The Book Nook* bookstore at the end of the row."

"Sullivan and Siobhan—unusual first names with a clearly Italian surname."

"It's what you get when your father who is countless generations of pure Italian as far back as you can go marries your Lace Curtain Irish mother. Please call me Sully. All my friends do."

Did he wink at her? She wasn't certain. "Welcome, Sully. Glad to know we can be friends despite Cocoa's hostile greeting. You're wasting no time jumping into renovations."

"We're on a 'take-no-prisoners' timeline. We want to be operational in both shops in the next thirty days, less if possible. I needed to talk to you before we begin the upstairs work. We plan to live over the shops and have quite a bit of work to do to get everything updated to meet residential code. Do you know the building's history?"

"Not really. I can only speak to what has happened in the ten years I've been here."

"The balcony needs to be totally rebuilt and replaced."

Elsie nodded her head. "I've never gone up. It looks too rickety to sustain any weight on it."

"Probably prudent on your part. Currently, it spans the entire back of the building, both our properties. Do you want to retain a joint balcony?" he asked.

"I think one balcony is fine. I had been thinking about making one or two apartments above my shop. Are you open to your team evaluating my space for renovations? There may be some efficiencies in having things like rewiring all done at one time by the same person."

"Excellent idea, Ms. Dennis."

"Elsie, please. Even if we share a balcony could we have a stairway at each end? It would be more convenient for any tenants."

"Also a good idea. I'll talk to my contractor today and let you know. Hopefully, your security animal will be more relaxed the next time we meet."

"I will make certain of it."

Sully reached out and shook her hand, then left. His handshake was firm, but his skin was cool and soft. This wasn't a man who had done much manual labor. Something about him seemed off to her, but she couldn't figure out what.

Elsie gathered the cat into her arms and cuddled her close. "Cocoa, we didn't make a very good first impression. Why did you attack Sully? Didn't you like his cologne? I don't think I do either. I'm not sure what it is. It seems familiar. Maybe next time you'll be expecting the aroma and not feel compelled to attack him."

The cat looked at her as if she understood, yowled, then jumped out of her arms and roamed toward the back of the store where her food and water was hidden away along with her litter box. Elsie had the strange feeling the new neighbors were bringing more than business to Lansdale.

****

Elsie's landline was ringing as she walked in the back door. Mark wanted to know if he could come over now on official police business. She said yes. Hubert was snoring in his recliner. Mrs. Johnson left a note by the front door saying he'd had a good day. Elsie would have to do something special to repay the sweet neighbor for her nursing and companionship during Hubert's recovery. She hated to wake him, but she did so he could retreat upstairs.

Fifteen minutes later, Mark pulled his patrol car to the curb in front of the house. Two dark-haired boys who looked to be twelve or thirteen and a middle-aged man got out of the back. Before they rang the bell, Elsie opened the door and invited them in. The young men were introduced as Billy and Bobby Taylor. Their father, Peter Taylor, was with them. He sat down on the sofa. The boys remained standing in front of him.

Mark began, "Ms. Dennis, the mystery of who knocked out part of the pane on your front door window has been solved. Which one of you wants to explain?" He gestured toward the youngsters.

The boys looked at each other. The slightly taller one, Billy, said, "We found a really cool slingshot yesterday."

Bobby continued, "We'd gathered the right size rocks and pebbles and were going to go to the park to practice with it. When we got across from your house the streetlight was shining on your front door. We didn't see any lights on in the house. We decided to aim for the red circles in the flowers on the window—to try a target that didn't move. We each hit one of the red circles on our first try."

"Then the lights came on inside and we ran home as fast as we could," Billy finished.

"I didn't know what had happened until the police came to our door asking if we'd seen or heard anything last night," Mr. Taylor explained. "The boys confessed what they had done; they have been grounded for the entire summer."

"Ms. Dennis, if you press charges, they will be on probation and have to do some community service work," Mark said.

"We're very sorry, Ms. Dennis. It was a stupid thing to do," Billy said.

Bobby said, "We're sorry we scared you. We're glad no one was hurt."

"Do you want to press charges?" Mark asked.

The boys stood silent.

"Could they serve their community service sentence here at my house without me formally pressing charges?"

"What did you have in mind?" Mark asked.

"My brother won't be able to do the mowing and trimming this summer. It needs to be done about every other week. Would you boys serve your sentence working for us?" Elsie asked.

"Yes!" the youngsters said in unison.

"The juvenile counselor will have to agree with the deal. I'll get things in motion," Mark said. "Thank you, Ms. Dennis, we won't take any more of your time."

Mr. Taylor extended his hand to Elsie. "Thank you. The boys have learned a valuable lesson from you about the spirit of mercy. Bless you." He took his sons each in one hand and led them to the waiting patrol car.

Chapter Fourteen

Mark couldn't roust Domino out for the morning run. When he jingled the leash, the dog looked at him, whimpered, and rolled back into a ball on his side of the bed. Clearly, Domino wasn't as worried about creating healthy habits as he was.

It was a lovely morning. Bright sunshine. A gentle breeze. No lights were on when he passed Elsie's. He guessed her resolve for exercise had dissipated, too.

On the way to work, Mark made five stops to pick up donated used bicycles. Tonight, he and his shift mates would see how many could be made useable for the Bike Rodeo on Saturday. The hardware store donated a brand new ten speed he loaded in the truck, too. A black pickup truck made the same stops he did all morning long—always staying at least half a block behind him. Mark never saw the driver get out of the vehicle. He never saw a license plate and didn't have time today for further investigation.

****

Elsie finished writing out the order to place in the morning, checked to make certain the back door was locked, and turned off the lights on the classroom side of the store. When she walked into the main shop, a young woman with straight black hair down to her waist rummaged through the clearance bin. Cocoa paced around her meowing.

"Sorry, I didn't hear you come in. May I help you find something?" Elsie asked as she bent down and scooped the cat into her arms.

"I meant to get over here much earlier in the day, Ms. Dennis, but time got away from me." The woman extended her hand. "I'm Siobhan Stalatti."

"Elsie, please." She grasped the hand. "It's a pleasure to meet you. Are you a fiber arts person?" Her eyes were as coal black as her brother's.

"Yes, when I have the time. I'd like to knit a shawl for my favorite aunt's birthday. It needs to be in reds, oranges, and yellows. I have a pattern for number eight needles. Do you have anything to fill the bill?"

Elsie led her to the wall of hand spun yarns. "I think this will do nicely." She pulled out a skein of yarn in vivid colors and handed it to Siobhan.

"This is the perfect weight and color combination." She flipped over the label to check the yardage. "Dawn Arrives. What an apt name."

Cocoa jumped out of Elsie's arms and climbed onto her perch by the door keeping her eyes locked on the visitor.

They walked back to the cash register. "Oh, I'm keeping you after closing time. I apologize. Getting busy on this project will make the evenings in the hotel room pass more quickly. Thank you." She handed Elsie cash.

Elsie bagged her purchase and gave it to her. "I put one of my cards in the bag. The store number and my cell are on it. Emails, too. Please let me know if I can help you in anyway. I'm looking forward to having neighbors."

Elsie made a call before she left the shop. She

turned out the remaining lights, patted Cocoa's head and left. She stopped at the nearby sandwich shop to get her order—half a dozen foot long subs, each cut into four pieces.

At five forty-five, Elsie walked through the open garage door attached to the police station. "It's suppertime!"

Mark put down a wrench and smiled. "How did you know we hadn't eaten yet?"

"I called the dispatcher before I left the shop. There's a good selection. Hopefully, everyone can find something they will like." She put the sandwiches on the counter at the back of the garage. Plates, napkins, and forks appeared from the overhead cabinets. This wasn't the first time they'd had meals out there.

The three other officers working on bicycles thanked Elsie, grabbed something to drink, and sat down at the picnic table outside the garage door to enjoy the break in the pleasant evening. Mark walked over to Elsie.

"How kind and unexpected." He gave her a brief hug. "Have you eaten yet?"

"No. I like everything I brought so I'll take whatever is left after all of you get yours."

She stood back watching Mark make his selection. A quarter of a Black Forest ham with Swiss cheese was left. She put it on a plate and sat next to Mark at the picnic table with everyone. The others finished rather quickly and returned to their repair projects after thanking Elsie again.

"I better get busy, too. We have a lot to do to be ready with enough bikes for Saturday. The good news is the bike/trike donations have been pouring in. The bad news is most of them need work. We have sixty kids registered for the rodeo and only half of them have their own bicycles. Luckily, we've gotten some monetary donations so we can buy supplies for the repairs, and we have four brand new bicycles that just had to be put together. Thanks again for feeding us." Mark leaned down and kissed her cheek.

"Oh, you're not getting rid of me so easily. You helped me in my hour of need. More than once. I'm here to return the favor. You know I can use a screwdriver and a wrench. Where do you want me?"

"Wow. Great timing. You are exactly what we need. We have newly painted bikes on the far wall. They're dry now. They all need baskets and bells attached. Some are front handlebar baskets and some saddlebags for the back. Will you take that project on?"

"You bet. I love this." She pointed to the painted cycles. "You have tricycles and bicycles. Do we have training wheels to put on the two-wheelers?"

"We do, but we'll install them at the rodeo only if they are needed," one of the other officers said.

Music from a country and western station played overhead. Occasionally the guys would sing along. Elsie loved the camaraderie between them, and they all accepted her as one of the gang. Once again, she and Mark were sitting on the floor with screws, nuts, bolts, and tools spread around them.

The dispatcher stepped into the garage. "It's Thursday night, boys. You know what that means."

Officer Mel Caldwell said, "Miss Clover has an intruder. I think it's my turn. I'll be back shortly with our dessert." He put down the screwdriver, put on his hat, and left the garage.

Thirty minutes later, Mel came into the garage carrying a plastic bag full of sugar cookies. "Here you go. Hey, Mark. Make a note. Miss Clover wants someone to come over Saturday morning to pick up the cookies she's going to bake for the rodeo. She saw it advertised in the paper and wants to do her part."

"The event starts at one in the afternoon. How early did she say to come over?" Mark asked.

"She said they'll be ready by noon," Mel said.

"Okey dokey." Mark grabbed the clipboard on the counter and added Miss Clover's name under the refreshments category.

"Do you want me to stop by for them so you don't have to?" Elsie asked.

"Are *you* planning to come to the rodeo?"

"I wouldn't miss it. I want to do my part for the community, too. I plan to close the shop at noon instead of three o'clock. Won't you need volunteers to help?"

"Yes, Ms. Dennis, we will." Mark added a note to the clipboard. "I'll call Miss Clover and tell her you will be the delivery person. Otherwise, she doesn't open the door to strange people who aren't in a police uniform."

Elsie enjoyed looking at the just-like-new bicycles she'd helped to refurbish. The hours flew by. Mark walked Elsie to her car at eleven o'clock. "You're a great worker. Thanks for the help. Once the ten bikes we painted tonight dry, we just have to basket and bell them and we'll have forty-five bicycles ready for Saturday."

"I thought you only needed thirty."

"We always have kids come who didn't get registered ahead of time. I'd rather have a few too many ready than to have to disappoint even one of the kids," Mark explained.

"You're a good man. I had fun." She smiled at him. "We work pretty well together."

"We do indeed and we're getting a lot of practice." Mark reached into his pocket and pulled out his wallet. "Let me pay you for the sandwiches. They really hit the spot."

"I won't take anything. Chalk it up to doing my part for the boys in blue."

When they got to Elsie's car, she stood on tiptoe to kiss his cheek. He gently put his hand under her chin and tilted her face up. Then slowly, sweetly, kissed her waiting lips.

"Thanks for everything," he said.

Elsie got in the car and slowly pulled away.

Mark didn't return to the garage until her taillights disappeared around the corner.

Chapter Fifteen

The next morning, when he came out the front door for his daily run, Mark noticed a black monster truck idling at the curb. Domino emitted a low growl in the vehicle's direction. Mark locked the front door but by the time he got down the steps, the truck had raced down the street and turned the corner.

He never saw its license plate. Again. He wasn't certain it was the same truck he'd encountered before, but it could be. And it looked a little like Nico's truck. Why was it hanging out in front of his house?

****

Mark went into the station about ten a.m. to finish the rest of the bicycle repairs and refurbishments. But first, he checked to see if there were any reports of stolen or missing black pickups. He couldn't find any reports on the truck. He really needed a license plate number to do effective research.

He finished the rodeo preparations. Bikes and helmets were all ready for transport to the city park tomorrow morning. There were going to be a lot of very happy—and safe—kids after tomorrow's event.

Since Mark came in early, he got to leave at six-fifteen. He saw lights on at Elsie's, so he parked in front of *Knitting Pretty* just as she was coming out the front door. A tall, ebony-haired man followed her out of the shop. They talked for several minutes before she realized Mark was there waiting at the curb. She said goodbye to the man and he walked down the street. She came over to the truck, leaned in, and talked to him through the passenger side window.

"I got done early, so I thought I'd give you a lift home. Did I interrupt your plans?" he asked trying not to sound as jealous as he was feeling.

"No, I didn't have any plans."

He tried to coax a little more information from her. "Are you sure? I thought maybe you planned to go with the guy who walked out with you. I don't want to be a bother."

"Oh, that was just Sully."

Mark waited. "Sully...I don't believe I've ever met him."

"I guess you haven't. I told you the other half of my building recently sold. Sully and his sister, Siobhan, are the new owners. They're putting in a coffee shop and a bookstore. He stopped to give me a quote for the renovations of the apartment space over my place."

"So just a fellow merchant, not your new love interest." He winked. "You'll have to introduce me the next time he's around. Would like a ride home?"

"Yes." She opened the passenger side door and got inside. "I have had a been-on-my-feet-every-single-minute kind of day. I'm beat." Mark slowly pulled away from the curb and saw the man talking to a workman in front of the building. Sully smiled and waved. Elsie returned both. Mark waited for more information about the dark-haired stranger, but she seemed content to remain silent. At one point, he would have sworn her eyes were closed.

Mark pulled to the curb in front of her house. No

lights were visible. "Is Hubert home?"

"Yes, but he retreats upstairs earlier and earlier since the hospital stay. I'm worried he's not completely well yet but, of course, there is no discussing his health with him. I don't think he'll ever fully forgive me for the ambulance ride. Would you like to come in for dinner? It will probably be something warmed up."

"I don't think so."

"What about for an adult beverage to prepare for tomorrow's melee?"

Mark didn't answer immediately. "I thought you were exhausted."

"I am. Have one beer with me and I'll set you free. I don't want to drink alone."

"Okay." He turned off the truck. "Only one. I need to get a good night's sleep."

He hurried around the front to open the passenger door. "Hey, those hedges are a full foot shorter than they were. And it looks like the lawn has been mowed."

"Yep. Bobby and Billy arrived ready for work this morning before I left for the shop. Hubert supervised them. I think he ran the hedge trimmer, too. He was nervous about them using power tools. They were his apprentices, bagging all the trimmings at his strict instructions."

"It's a start," he said. "If a full-grown person walked by, he or she could now be seen. The bushes probably need to be shorter, but I understand Hubert has to get used to the idea."

She unlocked the door. "I was thrilled he was willing to relent and take anything off." She led him back to the kitchen. "Want to sit on the back porch? It's usually pretty pleasant this time of the evening."

"Sounds great."

Elsie grabbed a couple of long-necks out of the refrigerator. "Need a glass?"

"No, but a koozie would be nice."

She pulled two koozies out of the basket on the island and signaled for Mark to follow her. The screened-in porch held a swing and three overstuffed chairs with a low table in front of them. Elsie sat down in the swing and patted the seat next to her. Mark took the hint.

"This is one of my favorite places to sit this time of year. Sometimes in the morning I bring my first cup of coffee out here while I'm still in my nightgown. It's nice and private. My bedroom is down the hall behind the dinette. It's always pleasant to smell the roses in bloom and listen to the babble of the little fountain Hubert installed in the corner of the yard." She pointed to the bubbler. "It was my birthday surprise last year."

He looked around the private area and agreed it would offer concealment. "I can see why you like to relax here. I like my deck, but I need to be clothed to go there. It isn't anything like this for privacy. The neighbors wave and holler back and forth when they see me out."

Mark laid his arm across the top of the swing behind her. Elsie laid her head on his shoulder. The swing slowly rocked back and forth as they were each lost in their own wordless thoughts for a while.

She laughed softly. "Were you jealous of Sully?"

Mark hesitated. "I didn't know him and you were smiling the whole time you were talking with him. Not a lot of tall, good-looking men frequent yarn shops. I was curious, not jealous."

"Oh, you thought he was good-looking?" she teased. "You were only curious...about the handsome man in my shop." She sat up straight.

"Maybe I was turning a tiny bit green around the edges." He squeezed her shoulder. "Sorry."

"Nothing to apologize for. It never occurred to me you would react like that." She laid her head back on his shoulder. "It's kinda nice to have someone who cares."

"This is too pleasant. I need to get home. I have to start early in the morning to get the city park lot ready. We'll have to do this again sometime—soon."

He leaned over and kissed the top of her head. She turned and caught his lips with hers and murmured, "Real soon." They walked through the house hand-in-hand. "See you in the morning," she said.

As he thought about her comment, Mark was surprised when that shot of jealousy had torn through him outside Elsie's shop and he saw her talking with this Sully. He couldn't remember ever feeling it with anyone else. Only Elsie.

It was a little scary...and slightly wonderful.

Chapter Sixteen

When Mark opened the back door to leave the next morning, he saw a black pickup truck that looked like the one from yesterday idling behind the house. It tore off down the alley in a spray of gravel, too fast to get a full license plate number, but he saw the color of the letters and numbers. Not from Wisconsin.

Who the heck was stalking him? Or were they watching for Phil's return? There were a lot of black pickup trucks in the area. He might not be seeing the same one every time, but his gut instinct said he was.

The city park lot in the middle of the soccer and baseball fields was the perfect venue for the Bike Rodeo. Plenty of parking on the soccer fields side of the lot and on the baseball fields side room for all the rodeo stations. The weather was going to be slightly overcast, but the rain was predicted to hold off until tomorrow.

The check-in area would capture all the information about the riders. Those who had bicycles with them would have them safety checked and tuned up. Those without bikes would select one with the help of a volunteer. Every child received a bike helmet. Then they etched a registration number on each bicycle and tricycle to help identify the bikes, if they were lost or stolen.

There were a dozen stations in all. The children received a tote bag with the Lansdale Police logo and phone number on it that fit on the handlebars. As they successfully completed each station, they filled it with prizes local merchants and civic organizations provided.

As promised, Elsie stopped at Miss Clover's house shortly after she closed the shop at noon to pick up twelve dozen freshly baked sugar cookies with multicolored sprinkles. The little woman told her she'd been awake since four a.m. baking to ensure they would be as fresh as possible. She'd even bagged each one in its own plastic bag so they could be given as prizes.

Elsie took her post on the tricycle obstacle course which had a long line of riders waiting to compete.

"Here are some more prizes," a familiar voice said after Elsie had been there about fifteen minutes.

She turned around to look at the speaker. "Oh, thank you, Sully. Nice to see you...and Siobhan getting involved in the community so soon. What do we have?"

"A coupon good for a free copy of the children's book, *Adam and the Purple Bicycle* or *Charllean Learns to Ride*. They are appropriate for ages three to six. I have a large supply of both," he explained. "Plus, Siobhan has coupons offering one free grande latte for the moms and dads."

She secured the coupons on the prize table at her side. "I'm sure both will be a big hit."

"Looks like you need to issue some prizes to your finishers, Elsie," Mark said as he walked over to her station. He extended his hand. "Hi, I'm Officer Mark Trask. I don't believe I've had the pleasure."

"Certainly," Sully said shaking his hand. "Sullivan Stalatti, Officer Trask. I go by Sully. My sister, Siobhan is over by the bicycle obstacle course. We dropped off some prize coupons for our coffee shop and bookstore to show our support of our new community."

"Thank you. This event is a great place to meet people," Mark said. "Come with me, I'll introduce you to the rest of your police force." He wanted to get the guy away from Elsie. He didn't understand Stalatti's motives, but he gave off a vibe that raised Mark's cop radar in a bad way.

Mark led Sully away from Elsie's station toward Chief Miller. He continued to find people for him to meet until he had to go call a race.

****

They ended the day with only two unclaimed bicycles. Lots of people pitched in to clean up the area and load the trucks to return cones, tables, chairs, and the extras to the police garage.

Elsie made her way through the dwindling crowd. "Mark!"

He waved and walked toward her. "Thanks a million for your help. I'll have to personally let Miss Clover know we didn't have a single cookie left. She outdid herself. Looked like you had a full obstacle course most of the afternoon."

"I had a blast," she said. "I can't believe I've lived in this town for ten years and this is the first time I've volunteered for the rodeo. Since I don't have kids, I never thought about what it takes to put on an event like this. Do you want to come to the house for some brats and burgers?"

"That sounds great."

"Wonderful. We'll head over and get things started. Come after you unload your truck at the garage." She turned to leave.

"We?"

A woman waved from behind Elsie. "Hi, I'm Siobhan Stalatti. Elsie was kind enough to invite Sully and me to the cookout since we had no other plans for this evening. I hope you don't mind a couple of extras."

Sully stood next to Elsie now and nodded at Mark, wearing a smug look on his face.

Mark took Elsie by the hand, "Can I talk to you a minute?"

She went with him.

"When you asked me over, I thought you meant it was us, not we."

"Sorry for the confusion. You said you wanted to meet them."

"I already did meet him. Earlier. No matter." He leaned over and kissed her cheek. "I'll be there shortly."

****

It took a little longer than Mark expected to unload at the garage. Or maybe he wasn't moving at top speed. Then he remembered that the more time it took him to get to Elsie's, the greater her exposure to Sullivan Stalatti's charms without him there for comparison. He finished quickly and drove to her house.

He parked in front of the house and walked around to the back where he found all of them on the screened-in porch. Hubert had joined the party and was telling a complex joke accompanied by wild gestures and facial expressions. Mark had never seen him so animated. Something about the company must have inspired him. Mark laughed at the end with everyone else, although he had no idea whether it was funny or not.

Elsie handed him an icy cold long neck wrapped in

a koozie and kissed his cheek as soon as he walked in the door. Maybe she wasn't as susceptible to Sully's charms as he had feared. Everyone shook hands and resumed small talk while Hubert started the gas grill. Elsie came out of the kitchen of a platter of cheese, summer sausage, and crackers and went back in to return with a platter of cut-up veggies and dip. Something for everyone.

"You have a lovely home, Elsie. So private," Sully said.

"A house this size would cost a small fortune back at home. Especially with your secluded back porch and lovely landscaping," Siobhan said.

"It was like this when we moved in except for the fountain," Elsie said. "All we had to do was give it a new coat of paint inside and out."

"How did you two make it all the way to Wisconsin from the east coast?" Hubert asked.

Sully looked surprised. "I don't remember telling you where we were from."

"You didn't have to," Hubert said. "It's your accents."

"I've heard similar accents today," Siobhan said. "I met a doctor's wife today who was from Philly, too. A Katrina Merrick."

"You're right. She's been here eight or nine years," Elsie explained. "Her mother was originally from Lansdale. Katrina and her son moved here because she had such fond memories of visiting her grandparents here."

"Were your grandparents from here as well?" Sully asked Elsie.

She took a deep breath, then looked directly at the

questioner. "No. A cousin on my father's side, whom Hubert and I had never met, died unmarried and without children. He left this house to us a little over ten years ago. I didn't think I still had an accent."

"And what's your story, Mark?" Sully asked.

"Broadening my horizons looking for a job. Mom wasn't happy about me getting so far away, but she thought small town police work would be less dangerous than doing the same thing in the city. Sounds like we're all transplanted Midwesterners now. Why did you say you came here?" Mark asked.

"I didn't," Sully said.

Siobhan punched her brother lightly on his bicep. "Don't be so mysterious, Sully. They'll think we have something to hide. We come from a family of entrepreneurs but wanted to be somewhere new to make it on our own. Many years ago, an aunt and uncle once or twice removed lived in Lansdale and had nothing but positive things to say about it. We remembered their stories and the property downtown was available for the right price and voila. Here we are."

"Who were your relatives?" Mark asked. "Maybe I knew them."

"I'm sure you didn't. They've been gone quite some time," Sully replied quickly. "Hubert, I didn't think I was hungry, but the aroma emanating from the grill is making my mouth water."

"Still a few minutes," Hubert announced as he flipped the burgers.

Elsie and Siobhan went in the kitchen to get plates, silverware, and condiments.

"Sully, have you ever heard of a leasing company in Philadelphia called SAS?" Mark asked.

"I'll have to think about it. Possibly," Sully answered. "Did you have a problem with them?"

"Not exactly. It's a long story involving my missing roommate. He was last seen getting in a chauffeur-driven limousine from SAS Leasing several weeks ago."

"Chow time!" Hubert announced, interrupting Mark's story.

The burgers and bratwurst were tasty. Hubert definitely knew how to use his grill. Everyone swore they ate too much. The conversation centered mostly around work on the coffee shop and bookstore and the upstairs living quarters and nothing more about anyone's east coast roots.

Sully and Siobhan excused themselves after dinner when Elsie declined their offer to help with cleanup. Hubert cleaned the grill and picnic table while Elsie and Mark returned food to the refrigerator and disposed of dirty plates and silverware. Hubert said good night and retreated to his room upstairs as soon as everything was clean.

"Got time to sit a minute?" Elsie asked.

"Sure. Inside or outside?"

Elsie opened the back door. "It's still lovely out here." She sat on the swing.

He stretched out next to her. "It's been a long day, but a rewarding one. The Rodeo is better attended every year. It's always fun to make a child's face light up when they get a bicycle of their own to take home." He laughed. "I feel like a summer Santa Claus."

"I can see why the department goes to all the work to have it every year. You did a great job coordinating everything. I'm sure Chief Miller was pleased."

He clasped her hand. "Thanks. I think he was. It was good to have your help."

"It was nice of the Stalattis to jump right in and participate in their new community."

"They're good business people."

"You think it was a promotion strictly to increase business?"

"Yep," Mark said without hesitation.

She pulled her hand out of his grasp. "I never thought you were cynical. I may have to reassess my initial impressions."

"It's not cynicism. It's my law enforcement observation skills kicking in."

"I didn't know you were from the east coast," she said.

"Right back at ya. Did you live in Philly, too?"

"Too? As in the same as Sully and Siobhan? Or the same as you?"

"It's fine. You don't have to tell me. I don't have to know." He kissed her cheek. "I better get home. See you in church in the morning?"

"I plan to be there."

Mark and Elsie stood at the same time. She leaned over and kissed his cheek. "Never thought I'd fall for a Philly boy."

"You mean me or Sully?" Mark winked before he turned and exited out the screen door.

Chapter Seventeen

The sermon on Sunday was about offering the hand
of friendship to newcomers to the community
recognizing they were strangers in a strange land. Elsie
squeezed Mark's hand as the pastor made his point. He
shrugged.

Maybe he was being a little cynical about the
Stalattis. He simply did not like Sully. At all. It struck
him oddly that suddenly there was all this activity
coming out of Philadelphia. Limousines carting Phil
away. New business people moving in. Maybe even
black pickup trucks. The timing was troubling. Was it
jealousy or some gut feeling warning him? It was too
soon to tell.

Elsie invited Mark for lunch after church. They
were having last night's leftovers. Mark declined. He
needed to get home and start cleaning Phil's apartment.
The longer Phil was gone, the more Mark wondered if
he'd see his boarder again. It had been two weeks since
he left and more than a week since the ransacking. Not
a word since.

Mark made a bologna and pimento cheese spread
sandwich and wolfed it down while standing over the
kitchen sink with Domino at his feet, hoping for his
master to be sloppy enough to let some goodies fall to
the floor. The dog whimpered when Mark finished
without leaving a morsel for him. Mark grabbed a dog

treat off the top of the refrigerator and his pet immediately sat up on his hind legs to beg for it. He tossed the biscuit. Domino leaped off the floor and caught the biscuit in midair. Then he took it to a corner of the kitchen and loudly munched on it.

Mark made several trips upstairs carrying the empty plastic tubs. He decided to fill those before schlepping more of them to Phil's apartment. He started in the living room area. It was the biggest mess. One room done and two tubs used. He went downstairs and retrieved three more empties.

In Phil's study he swept everything off the desktop and into one of the plastic containers. In the bedroom he used a couple more tubs. Nothing to be done in the kitchenette.

The apartment wasn't back to normal, but it looked a lot better than it had. Hopefully, he'd made it less overwhelming for his boarder. He was left with only one spare storage tub. At least for the moment.

****

The next morning, Mark looked out the front door window before leaving for his run. There was the same black truck idling at the curb again. He'd had enough. He went out the back door and down the alley. He crept around the side of the house staying close to the shrubs. He planned to sidle up next to the vehicle and confront the driver. He crossed the street crouching. It had an Iowa license plate. Could he remember the number until he got in the house? He got close to the passenger side and moved forward.

Suddenly, the truck pulled away from the curb quickly and Mark fell. Lucky that he did. It was all that kept the vehicle from running over his feet. He skinned his elbow breaking his fall, but fortunately, didn't seem to have broken any bones or have lacerations requiring stitches.

He limped back in the house and wrote down RJP9988—while he could still remember it. A quick trip to the Iowa DMV website should help him track down his stalker.

He washed his elbow, doused it in iodine, and bandaged it after the stinging subsided. His run would have to wait until tomorrow morning. He hadn't thought through the idea of confronting the guy. What if his stalker had been armed? He'd have to form a better plan for capturing the guy. Why was he being targeted? Or was the guy looking for Phil? He was a little relieved the truck didn't have Pennsylvania plates.

****

Mark intended to check the Iowa license plate when he got to work. He'd forgotten the station's entire computer system was scheduled to go down beginning at four o'clock for a hardware installation and new system release scheduled to take until tomorrow morning at seven o'clock, so he put the paper with the license plate number under the paper weight on his desk. He'd have to wait until tomorrow for a look.

Chief Miller thanked everyone for the highly successful Kids' Rodeo and said they were all on the hook for a repeat performance next summer. He was pleased to have his first public event as chief be so well attended and come off without a hitch.

Mark drove by *Knitting Pretty* after his shift. He was glad it was completely dark. Elsie frequently went into the shop even though it was closed on Mondays. Maybe she took the whole day off and relaxed for a change. Her world had been so chaotic lately between the anniversary celebration, Hubert's hospitalization, and the hubbub of new neighbors moving in by the store. She needed a break.

He found himself driving the extra block to pass her house before turning toward home. Maybe she was still awake, and he'd stop by just to say 'hi'. Why did he feel the need to see her tonight? Or was he checking to see if she was alone? Where did that thought come from?

Mark approached the corner of her block when he saw black smoke billowing out of the second-floor windows of her house. He slammed the truck into park and ran to the front door. The handle was hot to the touch. He didn't hesitate. He pulled out his phone and dialed 911 as he ran to the back door.

"Fire." He gave the address and hung up.

The screen door to the porch was locked, but he was able to push the screen in and open the door with the handle. The kitchen door was locked, too. He raised a heavy planter from the porch and swung it against the window, shattering it on impact. He turned the deadbolt open and popped the button doorknob. No smoke in the kitchen yet.

Mark hollered as he ran through the kitchen. "Elsie! Elsie! Hubert! Wake up! Fire! Fire!" He didn't bother to knock. He threw Elsie's bedroom door open still screaming.

Elsie stirred and slowly sat up. "Mark, what are you doing here?"

Mark grabbed her robe off the foot of the bed, threw it to her, and began dragging her out of the bedroom. "The house is on fire. You have to get out.

Now!"

As he pulled her out of the house into the driveway, smoke began drifting into the kitchen. She collapsed sobbing on the ground. "Hubert! He's still upstairs."

"Stay here. Don't move. The fire department is on the way."

Mark charged back into the kitchen with a handkerchief across his nose and mouth. The smoke was blacker and thicker than it had been moments earlier. His eyes watered so badly he couldn't tell where he was going. Then a blast of heat singed his face, and he heard a loud crashing sound near the stairwell in the front hall. He turned and ran out of the house. His lungs burned. He laid on the ground next to Elsie gasping for breath.

The siren stopped as the fire truck parked in front of the house. "Is there anyone left inside?" one of the firemen asked as he raced toward them.

Mark struggled to his feet. "Upstairs. Hubert Dennis is still upstairs," he yelled as loudly as he could.

Elsie got to her feet and joined Mark standing on the sidewalk in front of the house. Flames shot out of the roof. She pointed to the window where Hubert's room was located. Flames and smoke poured out of it.

A fireman broke through the front door. Smoke billowed out. He came over to them. "We can't go up the stairs. They're gone. We're getting the ladder."

An explosion rocked everyone off their feet as debris flew over their heads. Mark instinctively covered Elsie's body with his own. The back of his right calf radiated pain. A small piece of metal was sticking out of it. An ambulance pulled in next to the firetruck. An

EMT was at Mark's side as soon as he sat up. They treated his injury and got both he and Elsie equipped with oxygen masks. She was sobbing hysterically. Mark held her in his arms as she rocked back and forth. The EMT wanted to transport them both to the hospital for further treatment for smoke inhalation immediately. Elsie refused to leave, insisting they had to find Hubert before she went anywhere.

A second firetruck had joined the fight. Both vehicles kept steady streams of water blasting the fire. It didn't seem to be going out. Another explosion injured one of the firefighters. The ambulance took him immediately to Garland Regional Medical Center.

The fire chief stood in front of Mark and Elsie. He helped them to their feet. Mark kept Elsie in his embrace. The roof to the front porch crashed to the ground tearing down part of the front wall of the house. Elsie turned her face toward Mark's chest keening and shaking. He was at a loss as to how to comfort her.

The fire chief spoke, "I'm sorry, Ms. Dennis. We couldn't get to your brother. Judging from the preliminary smoke and fire patterns, it looks like the fire may have started in his room or nearby on the second floor. Was there a kitchen up there?"

Elsie shook her head. Tears trailed down her soot-stained cheeks. "Only bedrooms and his den. He smoked a pipe on occasion, but not every day. In the winter he had an extra heater in his bedroom. Nothing to catch fire this time of year. Nothing."

"I know this is difficult. I am certain your brother is no longer alive. I am sorry."

Elsie trembled and fell further into Mark's arms. She cried hard, ripped off the oxygen mask and began coughing violently.

"You need to go to the Emergency Room, please," the fire chief pleaded. "You've been through an ordeal, and you may have lung issues from the smoke. The ambulance is back. Would you go now?"

"No," she insisted as she wiped her face with the sleeve of her robe.

"Elsie, I can drive. My truck is here. Let's go. Come on." Mark led her by the hand. "I need to be checked, too."

Debris had fallen in the bed of Mark's truck. There was a dent on the hood from something heavy thrown onto it during one of the explosions. Thankfully all the windows were intact and the tires fully inflated. He eased Elsie into the passenger seat and fastened her seatbelt. She never stopped sobbing.

A short time later, they pulled under the awning for the Emergency Room entrance at the hospital. Two aides with wheelchairs instructed them to sit in the chairs, then took them straight back to exam rooms while a valet moved Mark's truck to the ER parking lot.

Mark didn't see Elsie again for several hours. They met in the discharge area after both were treated for smoke inhalation and Mark's injured calf was further treated.

"Where am I going to go?" Elsie asked with a quivering voice. "I have no home."

"You're coming home with me." Polly Rogers stood near the ER entrance with her arms open wide. "I have lots of space and you're more than welcome. One of your neighbors called to alert us about your fire. We knew you'd need a place to stay. My grandson, Caleb, will take us both home. Mikal is gathering clothes and toiletries for you. You'll be all set soon."

Elsie seemed unsure what to do. She looked to Mark for guidance.

He gave her a squeeze. "Elsie, Polly lives right behind my house. It will be easy for me to check on you. Go with them and I'll check with you later this afternoon. Okay?"

She blinked back tears. "But I have to make funeral arrangements and everything."

"Yes, you do." He guided her toward Polly. "But not right this minute. You need a hot shower and a soft bed. I'll come over about three. You'll be fine with Polly. You know her. Go on." He gave her a peck on the cheek, and she hugged him. Polly wrapped a shawl over Elsie's shoulders since she was still in her nightgown and robe.

Mark waited for the valet to retrieve his truck. He'd need to have Pop Skelton look at the dent later. He could drop off the truck and get Phil's car. It had been ready for a while. He hadn't had time to coordinate picking it up.

He drove to Elsie's. The fire was still smoldering in the back, the last area to burn. The fire inspector had a team combing through the charred debris for two reasons: the first, to try and find Hubert Dennis's remains and the second, to determine the cause of the devastating blaze.

The inspector signaled for the waiting gurney to be brought over. Mark saw them remove what looked like a large, ash-covered log. He knew it had to be Hubert, but doubted there would be any way of positively identifying Elsie's brother.

The inspector raised his arms to stop him from

coming closer. Mark waited where he stood. "Oh, it's you, Trask. As you can imagine, we've had lots of nosy neighbors trying to see what happened here. How are you doing?"

"Some oxygen and I'm right as rain." He pointed at the gurney. "Was that Hubert Dennis?"

"It was a large body. It was found in what remained of his bed. Did you know him?"

"We've met. I'm more a friend of his sister's." Mark shook his head. "Such bad luck. He was hospitalized not long ago from carbon monoxide poisoning and now this horrific accident."

"It may not have been an accident. I won't know until all the testing comes back, but the intensity of the fire in the bedroom points to accelerants."

"Arson? With Hubert a target—again?"

"Don't discuss this with anyone yet," the investigator said. "I shouldn't have said anything. I haven't seen this type of house fire in the fifteen years I've been on the job here. We'll know the cause for sure in a couple of days. I'm trying to gather all the necessary evidence now to beat the storm that's headed our way. Gotta get back to it." The fire inspector returned to supervise the work crew.

Who wanted Hubert Dennis dead and why?

He was too tired to think about it. He was sure Chief Miller would get involved soon. Mark needed to go home, take a long shower, and hopefully, score a little sleep before time to get out of bed later today. He trudged back to his truck and pointed it for home.

Domino was on the deck huddled against the kitchen door when Mark dragged himself up the steps. "Sorry, boy, it's been a wild night."

He fed and watered the dog, called the station to request a couple of personal days—Elsie would need his support—and got into the shower. No amount of soap seemed to lessen the smoke smell. It didn't matter. He dried off and sat on the edge of the bed. He was positive he'd never sleep after all the turmoil of the night.

He was wrong.

Chapter Eighteen

Was the phone ringing? No. It was the doorbell.

What time was it? One o'clock. In the afternoon?

Mark threw a tee shirt over his head and stumbled barefooted into the front hall. He looked through the peep hole and saw Mrs. Hollis standing on the stoop with a plate of cookies.

"Did I wake you, Mark? So sorry. You're usually up and around by now. Are you sick?" She handed him the plastic-wrapped plate.

"Not sick. I didn't get to bed until after eight this morning because of the fire."

"You were at the Dennis house? Oh…were you the young man who saved Elsie Dennis's life by pulling her out of the house?"

"I guess I was. But I couldn't get to her brother in time."

"You poor dear." Mrs. Hollis patted him on the back. "Poor, poor dear. You go back to sleep. I'll not keep you any longer."

"I need to get out of bed. I have things to do today. Thanks for the cookies."

He stumbled to the kitchen and started a pot of coffee. Domino was patiently waiting by the back door to go out. His food and water bowls were empty. He got the dog situated and called Polly Rogers. Elsie had just gotten out of bed and was anxious for Mark to come over. He planned to be there in about half an hour. He downed a cup of coffee and took another shower. Maybe he smelled less smoky. He threw on jeans and a T-shirt.

He walked to Polly Rogers's house. Polly greeted him at the back door with a strong, two-arm hug. "Elsie's at the kitchen table. Would you like a cup of coffee or something cold to drink?"

"A glass of ice water would be perfect, thanks."

Mark walked over to the woman hunched over a cup of coffee at the round oak kitchen table. He bent down and gave her a hug. She craned her neck high enough to kiss his cheek. "Thanks for coming, Mark. I still can't believe what happened. It's like a nightmare. If you hadn't come when you did, I'd be dead, too. Poor Hubert. He was always such a sound sleeper." She laid her head on her arms on the table sobbing.

Mark rubbed her heaving shoulders. "I'm thankful I knew where your bedroom was. If you hadn't invited me in the other evening, I wouldn't have known where to find you. Have you heard from the fire chief or anyone about when Hubert's body will be released?"

She looked at him. "No. Not a peep." She sat up straighter. "Why would they keep it?"

He quickly said, "Oh, I don't know. I'm used to dealing with the legal side."

Polly's landline rang. "Hello, Rogers residence…Yes, she's here. So is Mark Trask…okay, I'll tell them." Polly hung up. "Chief Miller and Fire Chief Gilliland are on their way over to see both of you. They should be here in fifteen minutes. Can I get either of you anything?"

"I'd have more coffee, please." Elsie handed the

empty mug to Polly. "Why would Chief Miller come, too? Is it normal for the police chief and the fire chief to follow up on a house fire?"

"I don't know. I've never witnessed a house fire before." Mark sat down next to Elsie and held her hand until the two men arrived.

They took seats across from Elsie and Mark. Chief Gilliland began, "It appears the fire started on the second floor in Mr. Dennis's bedroom. Probably at least thirty minutes before you spotted the smoke, Mark. There is no easy way to say this, Ms. Dennis. Your brother was burned beyond recognition. Normally, we would use dental records to help confirm the identity, but no teeth were found by the medical examiner on initial review of the body."

"Hubert had a full set of dentures made when he was a relatively young man due to a virulent gum disease that made extraction of all of his teeth necessary. He usually left them in a cup in the bathroom by the sink," Elsie replied. "It has to be him. Who else would be in his bed?"

"Ms. Dennis, we need to send your brother's body to Madison for the state forensic pathologist to examine," Chief Miller said.

"Why? I believe it is him and that he is dead," Elsie said, her voice quivering.

"The body is needed as part of a more extensive investigation by the state fire inspector," Chief Gilliland said.

"An investigation looking for what?" Elsie asked.

"There is no good way to phrase this, but we suspect arson," the fire chief said.

"No...No...Why would Hubert burn down our

house and us in it? No." Elsie began sobbing.

"Arson doesn't mean your brother set the fire. Someone else may be responsible," Gilliland said.

"And if they are, then your brother's death may not have been accidental," Chief Miller said.

"Are you considering arson and murder because of his earlier poisoning?" Mark asked.

"Yes. All the factors seem to align indicating more than an accidental house fire," the police chief said.

"This is all too bizarre. Of course, do whatever is necessary to get this resolved." She squeezed Mark's hand. "How long will they keep the body? I need to plan his funeral."

"Ms. Dennis, we'll make every effort to expedite the post-mortem. I should be able to answer your question by early tomorrow," Chief Miller said. He stepped outside to phone the morgue to get the corpse on its way to the State Fire Marshall's laboratory. The gentlemen left after apologizing again for the circumstances requiring these difficult decisions.

"Do you still want to go to the funeral home this afternoon?" Mark asked.

"I don't, but I will. If we do all the preliminary stuff today, we'll be able to have the service as soon as his body is available." Elsie began crying again. How could she have any tears left?

"Okay. Polly, would you please call Mr. Ryerson and tell him we're on our way? Thanks." He stood up. "C'mon. I won't leave you until this is done." Mark helped Elsie up from the table and kept an arm around her at the waist. He gently guided her out to his truck.

Elsie didn't say a word on the way to the funeral home. Mark was thankful she had stopped crying. He helped her out of the truck and held her hand as they walked to the door. Elsie stopped. She squeezed his hand, took a deep breath and let it out slowly, then continued into the building.

Mr. Ryerson was very patient and kind—exactly the way someone in his profession should be. He carefully laid out all the options. She maintained a calmness Mark didn't think she had in her until Mr. Ryerson asked about cremation. "No. Please, no. Hubert absolutely did not want to be cremated. He wanted to be buried whole…but he isn't and won't ever be." She burst into tears. Mark let her cry on his shoulder until she was finished. She dried her eyes with the soggy tissue wadded up in her hand. "I'm sorry to be so silly. I can't believe I'm planning my brother's funeral."

"Take your time, Ms. Dennis," the funeral director said. "You don't have to decide anything today. We can discuss it later when you've had time to consider all the options."

She took a deep breath and dabbed her eyes. "No, I'd like to get everything decided now. I don't want it hanging over my head. Given that Hubert knew very few people here and we have no family who will be coming in for the service, I think simple is best. Let's do a short graveside service. I'll talk to Reverend Knox. We can schedule the date as soon as we get him back from Madison."

"Very well," Mr. Ryerson said as he escorted them to the front door. "Thank you for trusting us with this important service. Don't hesitate to call if you have further questions."

Raindrops began to fall as they walked out of the

funeral home. Once they clicked on their seat belts, the skies opened with torrents of rain, gusty winds, rolling thunder, and bursts of lightening. They sat silently for ten minutes until the force of the storm slackened. Then Mark started the engine. "I sure hope they got all the evidence collected in time."

"What?"

"Nothing. I'm just glad we got into the truck before it poured. Have you eaten anything today?"

"No. I am not hungry."

"Elsie, you have to eat something, or you will be sick. Let's stop at Whistler's. It's already five o'clock. I'll call Polly and tell her not to wait supper on you."

Mark punched in Polly's number; after she answered, he said, "We were going to stop for a bite on the way home...Really...You're right...It would be a waste...We should be back in about fifteen minutes. Thanks." Mark ended the call.

"What was that all about?"

"Polly threatened me. I need to bring you home immediately and stay for supper. There has been a steady stream of folks dropping food at her house. Apparently, once the word got out about where you were staying the ladies from the Hearth Tenders committee at church went into action. Polly said she has enough food to feed three armies. She was putting a pot of Mrs. Barrett's chicken and dumplings on the stove and warming some biscuits. So to Polly's house we will go."

"You know this is one of the best things about living in a small town," Elsie said, exhaustion clear in her voice. "Everyone believes in love your neighbor."

I hope she's right. Someone didn't love Hubert

Dennis, but I'm willing to bet it wasn't one of his neighbors. Evil has come here. I can feel the darkness in my soul.

Chapter Nineteen

The next morning Mark walked to Polly's house. Rhett, Polly's ancient Basset hound, ambled over to see him. The low-slung hound rubbed against Mark's leg until the dog got the ear scratching he'd been signaling for. Polly and Elsie were having coffee at the kitchen table. Elsie stood and fixed Mark a cup without being asked.

"Did you get any sleep last night?" he asked.

Elsie nodded. "I was certain I wouldn't, but I believe I was out before my head even hit the pillow. I was physically and emotionally exhausted. It's hard to wrap my brain around the fact Hubert is gone after being with me every single day for the last ten years."

"You didn't live together before you both moved here?" Polly asked.

"What?"

"You didn't live with your brother in Philadelphia?" Mark asked.

"Oh, my brother…no. Hubert and I didn't live together until we came here. I lived with my mom. We'd both had separate lives before our move to the Midwest. I've never lived alone…by myself."

"You don't have to now," Polly said. "I have plenty of room and, frankly, I would enjoy the company. I know Caleb's family is nearby, but it's not the same as sleeping under the same roof with me."

"You have no idea how much I appreciate you opening your home to me," Elsie said. "I'm not sure what I would have done if you hadn't offered the room. And board. Goodness, we're eating well here."

Polly laughed. "Don't get too used to the food. That's the church ladies' largess. It will be gone in a couple more days—especially if Officer Trask continues dining with us."

"Sorry. I can't resist good food I didn't have to fix myself," Mark explained.

The phone rang. Polly answered it. "Elsie, it's for you."

"Hello...okay. I'll let Mr. Ryerson know so we can finalize the service plans...Friday morning by ten...thank you, Chief Gilliland." Elsie hung up. "Hubert will be returned Friday. I need to let the funeral home know."

"Do you want to go over there?" Mark asked. "I was going to drop my truck off at Pop Skelton's to get those dings out of the hood and pick up Phil's car. We could stop at Ryerson's afterward."

"It would be nice to go over everything about the service one more time. I was pretty fuzzy headed yesterday. I need to make sure it is really going to be like I'd hoped. I'll just be a minute getting ready."

After Elsie left the kitchen to go upstairs, Polly said, "I'm so glad Mikal and Elsie are about the same size. We were able to get her clothed without any trouble." She shook her head. "Poor girl cried her eyes out, but I don't think the full impact of the fire has hit her yet. It's going to be hard when it does. Starting from scratch without your own stuff can be paralyzing. I'm glad she was willing to settle here for a bit."

Mark smiled. "Thanks for making things less stressful for her. I'll ask if she'd like to go for a ride along the river to get away for a little while after we're done at the funeral home."

Elsie appeared in the kitchen doorway. "All set. Can I get anything for you while we're out, Polly?"

"Coffee and dog food would get us through the rest of the week. Where is my purse?"

"Don't worry about money. It's the least I can do. Let's go, Mark." She headed out the back door. Mark followed her to his truck.

Elsie sat quietly watching the scenery from the passenger window. Mark glimpsed at her periodically wondering how long it would be before her smile returned and her eyes weren't red from almost constant crying. She'd been through so much and there was still a funeral to endure.

They parked the truck in front of the open bay. Pop Skelton immediately came out of the garage. He gave Elsie a hug and expressed his condolences. Elsie just nodded. He looked at the damage to the truck and promised the body work would be done by Monday. He'd clean the debris out of the back to check for damage in the bed, too. If there was any, he'd fix it as well. Phil's car was tuned up and ready to roll. Mark paid Pop for the tune up and they left.

At Ryerson's, Elsie settled on Sunday afternoon at two o'clock for the graveside service. It would give the mortician time to complete his work and Reverend Knox confirmed he could do the service then. She made a few changes to the order of the service and ordered a large spray of yellow roses and baby's breath for the casket with a banner saying 'Beloved Brother'. She thanked Mark for being with her so that she didn't have to face all of the decisions without any support.

They swung by the Discount Barn and bought Polly's coffee and the largest bag of dog food that would fit in the car's small trunk. Elsie found a prepaid phone and activated it while they were there since her own phone was never found in the debris.

"What about taking the long way home?" Mark asked. "We could follow River Road along the bluffs."

Elsie was more than ready for a ride in the country. He drove the road high above the Mississippi River where they could see for miles to the far horizon. They didn't speak much. They didn't even have the radio on. They enjoyed the companionable silence and the escape from their recent reality. They stopped at a hole-in-the-wall tavern in Rockport for the cheeseburgers they were famous for before heading back to Polly's.

Three hours after they left, they parked in Polly's driveway. Neither of them moved immediately. Elsie reached over and squeezed Mark's hand. "Thank you." She leaned across the seat of the little car and kissed his cheek.

As soon as they got inside the kitchen, Elsie said, "I know I shouldn't be, but I'm really tired. I think I'll take advantage of not being at the shop and take an afternoon nap. Thanks again for all your help, Mark." She kissed his cheek and retreated upstairs.

"Mark, don't forget to come back for dinner," Polly said. "Five-thirty. It's sure to be a feast and there's more deep-dish apple pie and vanilla ice cream."

"Thanks, Polly. You said the magic words. I'll see you then."

****

Elsie was exhausted. Before she could rest, she needed to make one call. Luckily, she knew the number by heart. When it was answered after one ring, she said, "You need to know Hubert Dennis died in a fire yesterday…Oh…He did?…He never told me. I had no idea…Thank you."

After hanging up, Elsie stretched out across the bed on top of the spread. More to think about. *They say bad things come in threes. What else do I have to dread happening?*

****

Mark joined them for fried chicken, mashed potatoes with creamy white gravy, fresh green beans cooked with bacon chunks, and homemade sourdough bread. And, of course, for the promised dessert.

Rhett stayed at Elsie's side when they went into the living room. He sat at her feet resting his long snout on her lap so she could massage his floppy ears. He seemed to know she needed to be comforted.

"If you're all right being left without an escort, I plan to go back to work tomorrow evening," Mark said.

"Oh, of course," Elsie said. "It has been an unexpected gift to have you off the past two days. I think I'm going into the shop in the morning. I'm not ready to see customers yet, but I need to check on the mail and deliveries. I plan to wait until next week to reopen." She offered a weak smile. "I have a lot to replace. I've started a list. I need a little quiet time to figure out what I do next."

"That's totally understandable," Mark said. "Anything I can do to help, don't hesitate to holler. I could probably hear you if you stepped out Polly's back door and yelled."

****

Elsie walked from Polly's to the shop the next morning. A little farther than from her own home but she needed a little exercise, and the sunshine seemed to warm her very soul.

The outside signs for *Sips for You* and *The Book Nook* were mounted over their entrances. They'd followed the style of the *Knitting Pretty* signage. The storefronts were a matched set. She peeked in the window of the coffee shop where the brown paper had fallen down. The counter was installed, flooring and walls complete, and painters were busily at work. She couldn't see anything in the bookstore yet. They were making rapid progress. How on earth had Sully gotten the workmen to come to work and toil so diligently to get their properties ready so quickly? She wondered how the living quarters upstairs were progressing.

She unlocked the front door and quickly locked it behind her leaving the CLOSED sign showing. Cocoa meowed in a scolding tone and jumped down from her perch weaving in and out of Elsie's legs as she moved toward the back of the store.

"I don't know why you're fussing. You have plenty of water and food. You're such a spoiled brat."

Elsie had installed a watering station for Cocoa that she learned to operate with her paw. When she pushed on it, she was instantly rewarded with fresh water. Her food dispenser worked the same way. The only deprivation the feline had suffered was a dirtier than usual litter box, a dearth of special cat treats, and someone to scratch her ears until she purred contentedly.

She went to the back storage area. She had a keypad lock on the door opening to the outside and a small space for deliveries to be made whether she was there or not. The deliverymen appreciated not having to make a second trip to find someone in the store. As expected, it was full. She shoved boxes out of the storage area and into the back of the store. She didn't have the energy to start unpacking the merchandise. She'd just clear out the holding area to be ready for any more deliveries before next week.

There was a knock at the back door. Siobhan Stalatti was peering in the window. Elsie hurried to unlock it. Siobhan pulled her into an embrace. "We have been so worried about you. I saw you peek in the coffee shop. How are you? I'm sorry. What a stupid question. I'm sure you're devastated. Where are you staying?"

"Thank you for your concern. It's all kind of a haze to me. I'm staying with Polly Rogers, a dear friend who lives alone. It looks like you're definitely going to be ready to open soon. Are they making good progress upstairs, too?"

"They are. We have two crews at work—an upstairs one and a downstairs one. Would you like to see?"

Siobhan led the way up the newly installed outside stairs to the second-floor balcony. In the apartments, they had gutted the space over the stores, rewired, and replaced plumbing, all the fixtures and cabinetry.

"My goodness, the apartments are going to be quite spacious and modern looking."

"I'm glad you came in today," Siobhan said. "I need to know what color you want your rooms. The painters will be in by the end of the week."

"I'm fine with white or cream everywhere except for the larger bedroom. I'll paint it myself when I move in."

"Elsie, you didn't say anything about living here."

"That was when I still had a huge house to live in...and a brother to share it with. Seeing this space forced me into a decision." Elsie ran her hand along a window ledge. "I can't live with Polly forever even though she would like me to."

"I'm sorry. I keep stepping all over your feelings. I am delighted were going to be storefront and upstairs neighbors. Sully will be glad to know who will be sharing the second floor with us."

"Is it too soon for me to preview the bookstore and your shop?"

"Absolutely not. I'd love to show them off!"

****

The beginning of the shift was a lot of the usual—barking dogs, teens driving too fast in front of Mrs. Pearl's house, and a teenage girl needing help to change a flat tire. She couldn't call home because she wasn't supposed to be out of the house. Mark convinced her to tell her dad the truth before he saw that the spare had been put on.

During a lull in the evening's calls, Mark logged on the computer to check the license plate number for the black pickup truck. It was definitely an Iowa license plate, but the number did not show as being valid. He would have to check the license plate again. If and when he could get close enough to the truck. Hard to believe he couldn't remember the number for such a short period of time. Of course, he had been practically run over. That could make you misremember.

When Miss Clover's regular Thursday night call came in, Mark volunteered to go. He needed to get back into some kind of routine. She gave him an extra hug for being a hero and rescuing Elsie who she remembered picking up the cookies for the Bike Rodeo.

Chapter Twenty

Ring. Ring. It was a few minutes past midnight when the landline phone rang. Mark stumbled into the living room to answer it.

"Sorry, Mark. Sounds like I woke you. I thought you'd still be awake."

"Phil? Where are you?"

"Where I've been the entire time I've been gone. I was told there was a break-in at your house. Are you all right?"

"Other than losing the answering machine, all the property destruction was confined to your apartment. I tried to clean up the mess, but I'll warn you—you'll have a lot to do when you get home. And your computer and laptop are gone. I had to replace the front door lock and the one at the top of the stairs to your apartment."

"I'll pay you for the damages." He didn't sound surprised. "It was all so unnecessary. They wouldn't believe me."

"Who wouldn't believe you? About what? And how did you find out about the break-in?"

"Sorry. They're back. I need to get off..." Dial tone.

At Domino's whimper, Mark looked at the dog. "You know it was Phil, don't you? At least we have confirmation he's still alive. But that's about all we know. How am I supposed to sleep with all the mystery swirling around in my head?"

Mark turned off the light. Minutes later, both he and Domino were snoring in stereo.

****

The next morning, the landline phone was ringing when Mark and Domino returned from their run. "Hello, Trask here."

"Mark, glad I caught you," Chief Miller said. "Would you have a few minutes this morning to meet me at Polly Rogers's house? Hubert Dennis's body was returned an hour ago. I have some information to review with Ms. Dennis and I would prefer you were with her."

"Sounds ominous, Chief. Want to clue me in?"

"I'd rather do it at the same time as Ms. Dennis, if you don't mind."

"Sure. When?"

"I told her I'd be over at ten this morning. Thanks."

Whatever information the chief had did not sound good.

****

He walked to Polly's house a little before ten. Chief Miller pulled into the driveway at the same time Mark reached the house. Polly opened the door before they knocked and ushered them into the kitchen where Elsie sat at the kitchen table, sipping coffee.

"It's a fresh pot," Polly asked cheerfully. 'Any takers?"

"I'd like some," Mark said.

"None for me," Miller said with a smile. "According to my doctor, I've already had my limit."

Mark sat next to Elsie. The chief pulled out the

chair across from her. Polly parked at the end of the table closest to the coffee pot.

"I didn't know Mark was coming to the meeting," Elsie said softly.

"Would you rather I left?" he asked.

Elsie latched onto Mark's hand and pulled it onto her lap. "No. It must be something bad for the chief to ask you here, too."

"You were together at the fire and I wanted you to hear the news at the same time," Chief Miller began. "Your brother's body is at the funeral home. They are beginning work to be ready for the service Sunday afternoon as you planned."

"Thank you. What else?" Elsie asked.

"It's standard procedure in fires of mysterious origin resulting in a death to perform a total body CT scan. The scan showed three metallic ballistic objects lodged in Hubert Dennis's chest." The chief stopped to let the news sink in.

"Ballistic objects? Bullets?" Mark asked. "Then it was murder with arson to cover the homicide?"

Elsie shook her head. "He was murdered, how can that be true?"

Alarmed at her color, Mark covered her hands with his and gave them a hard squeeze. She took a deep breath, closed her eyes and held it a few seconds, then let it out.

"I'm afraid it appears probable," the chief responded. "According to the report from the state fire inspector, an accelerant was used on the bedding, throughout his room, and down the stairs into the front hall. There were small amounts of the fluid found in every room in the house including yours, Ms. Dennis.

However, the primary focus was upstairs and the steps to the second floor. The bottom line is Mark, you were never going to rescue Mr. Dennis because he had already been shot when you saw the smoke billowing out of the house."

"Who would have done it?" Elsie sobbed. "How did I not hear the shots?"

"This was a professional hit job," Miller said. "No doubt the killer used a silencer. We believe your brother's earlier hospitalization from poisoning was actually the first attempt on his life. Did anything unusual happen right before or after his admission to the hospital?"

Elsie furrowed her brow. "Not that I can remember."

Mark tried to jog her memory. "Didn't someone go to the hospital to see Hubert, insisting he was your uncle?"

"I'd forgotten. Is it important?" She looked at the chief. "He claimed to be a relative but never got into my brother's room. We don't have any other kin, and I didn't recognize pictures of him."

"When you found Hubert unconscious and sent him to the hospital, you saved his life," the chief said. "I think the unknown 'relative' was trying to see him to finish the job. When his plan was thwarted, he turned to a more violent solution. Can you think of any reason someone would want your brother gone?"

Elsie shook her head.

"What about from his past, before you lived in Lansdale?"

"She's been here over ten years, Chief. Do you really think someone would carry a grudge so long?"

Mark asked.

"I'm trying to cover all the bases. You know the drill, Mark."

"From before Lansdale?" Elsie put her head in her hands. "It all happened so long...it can't be anyone from before Wisconsin...it simply can't...I won't believe it is possible...they're all dead." She snuffled trying to hold back tears.

"Ms. Dennis, please think about it. Call me or let Officer Trask know, if you think of anything that may be relevant from Hubert's past. I'll be back in touch." The chief scooted his chair away from the table and left.

Elsie clutched Mark's hand squeezing harder. "It can't be...it is all my fault...he was here just for me...to take care of me." Tears welled again and spilled onto her cheeks.

"Nothing is your fault," Mark said as he peeled his hand out of her grasp. "You need to rest now."

Elsie stared wildly at him. "Where are you going?"

He patted her back. "I was going to leave so you could get some sleep."

Elsie stared straight ahead shaking her head. "I don't want to sleep. I won't be able to." Rhett came over and put his head in Elsie's lap whimpering softly until she began stroking his velvety ears.

Mark hugged her. "Don't worry. I'll stay as long as you need me."

Chapter Twenty-One

Saturday morning the black extended cab pickup was parked on the street in front of Mark's house. No one was visible in the cab. Mark grabbed his phone and hurried to the rear end of the truck, snapped a picture of the license plate, and returned to the house. Just as he opened the front door, a tall, muscularly built man with white-blond hair cut through the neighbor's yard from the alley behind the house and got into the vehicle. Moments later it roared away from the curb.

Mark rushed through the house and out the back door. Domino was relaxing in the sun on the deck. Nothing seemed amiss. Wait. Phil's car looked lopsided. Mark went down the steps to the garage and out to the driveway where the vehicle sat in it's usual spot. Everything was normal…except the right rear tire was totally flat due to a six-inch gash in the whitewall. Now the guy wasn't only a stalker, but a vandal, too. He removed the spare from the trunk of Phil's car, replaced the flat tire then drove to Pop Skelton's garage.

"I was getting ready to call you." Pop tossed him the truck keys. "The body work went a little faster than I expected. Truck's ready to roll. What've you got now?"

Mark showed him the damaged tire.

"Son, you're keeping me in business lately. Take

the truck. I'll see if the tire can be repaired, and I'll swap them back. Mike and I can drop it back at your house after we close at noon today. Okay?"

"Thanks, Pop. Truck looks like new. See you later." He drove home.

When he pulled into the driveway, Elsie met him. She'd been talking to Domino through the backyard fence. Mark had started locking all the doors every time he left the house now.

Elsie walked around the vehicle. "Your truck looks terrific."

"Pop does good work."

"Where's Phil's car?"

Mark explained about the tire vandal's earlier appearance.

"Oh, I was going to ask to borrow the car."

He jingled the keys. "You can take the truck."

She shook her head. "Nope. I never learned to drive a stick shift."

"Where do you need to go? I can play chauffeur."

"I'm going crazy sitting around. I noticed you could use some color in your backyard. You have no flowers or blooming shrubs. I was going to buy some and plant them as a thank you for all your help."

"What a great idea. I intended to plant more colorful things, but my weekends are way too short. And lately, way too exciting. I'll buy the plants, if you'll provide the expert planning and labor."

"Let me buy them."

"Nope. Is it a deal?"

Elsie extended her hand and Mark shook it. "Deal."

"We might as well go now. Do you want to go by The Purple Cow for a little lunch? I'm craving one of their super mocha milkshakes."

"Sounds great. Let me call Polly. I don't want her to worry."

****

A spot at one of the picnic tables by The Purple Cow became available just as their food was ready. They sat down and enjoyed their meals without a lot of conversation.

Elsie dipped her large order of fries one at a time in her super-size vanilla milkshake, then popped them in her mouth making satisfied sounds. Mark savored his mocha milkshake and the double cheeseburger without onions.

Finally, Elsie asked, "Do you have a particular color you'd like in the yard?

"Not really. If we're going to do it, I'd prefer a regular color riot instead of too formal a structure. My mom had hydrangeas that were pretty. My yard is a blank canvas, waiting for your artist's touch."

"A riot of color means our options are limited only by your credit card maximum." She laughed. He hadn't heard that joyous sound for too long.

"Excellent. I'll buy whatever you pick out. I'm good at manual labor and schlepping."

"Good to know. How are you at construction, packing, and moving?"

"I don't like to do it for me, but I'd be happy to help you. Are you planning to rebuild your house?"

"No. I decided yesterday I don't need so much space for just me. I'll have the lot cleared and put it on the market. The renovations the Stalattis are doing include the upstairs space. I had them do the rooms above my shop while they were doing theirs. I'd

157

thought I would rent it out, but I changed my mind. I'm going to move in there. It will be convenient being right at work and if I decide to replace the vehicle I lost in the fire, there is a carport in the alley directly behind the shop's back door."

"Sounds like you've thought this through. I knew you wouldn't live forever with Polly, but I'm a little surprised you'd chose to live alone right now. I can help with minor construction and I'm a good painter. All you have to do is holler when you need me."

Elsie gathered the garbage as she stood. She deposited it in the wire trash basket. "I hope you never get tired of running to my rescue. Are you ready to hit the plant shop?"

"Lead the way."

****

When they returned from buying plants, Phil's car was parked in the driveway as Pop had promised. The key was under the floor mat. Before unloading the truck bed, Mark pulled the car into the second slot in the garage. Now that the vandal knew where it was normally parked, Mark needed to secure it. He still wasn't convinced he was the stalker's target. It could easily be part of the Phil mystery.

They worked most of the afternoon, planting along the perimeter of Mark's yard just inside the fence. It was indeed a riot of color including some light lavender hydrangea bushes. After they finished, the two sat on the deck, enjoying an icy beverage and looking over the results of their labor.

"Thank you. I don't know when I would have taken the time to actually plant flowers and blooming shrubs," he admitted. "You have an eye for landscaping. It's not too surprising. You're a creative person and work with colorful fibers all day."

"Thanks for letting me do it. I needed some physical activity today. I like how it turned out. I think you need to go back to the nursery and buy the birdbath we looked at. It would be perfect in the far corner in the middle of all the impatiens." She pointed to the spot. "Don't you think?"

"Yep. And I'm going to buy the tall shepherd's crook and the hummingbird feeder to put in the opposite corner. All this color is sure to attract some hummers. I've always enjoyed watching them. Did you see the three-foot tall white ceramic rabbit they had in the statuary section? How would he look coming out of the middle of the rosebushes over there?" Mark pointed to the right side of the yard.

"Delightful. You're going to have a little piece of paradise back here. What do you think Domino thinks of it?"

"I'm not certain." Mark laughed. "I hope he doesn't believe it's his new digging area. You notice he stayed on the deck watching all the activity with suspicion in his eyes."

"We should invite Chief and Mrs. Davis over for dinner on the deck one evening to show off your backyard. You can tell him he inspired you."

"We?" Mark laughed. "I guess you and I have started becoming a we. I like the idea. It would be good to return their dinner invitation one day soon."

"I'm beat. I need to head back to Polly's." She stood. "Want to come for supper? We still have goodies in the refrigerator and a cherry cheesecake for dessert."

"I'll have to decline. My waist doesn't need more

sweets and I'm still kind of full from lunch." He held out his hand. "C'mon, I'll walk you home."

They strolled over to Polly's hand-in-hand. When they reached the back door, Mark leaned over and kissed her cheek. Elsie turned toward him and kissed him on the lips. Twice. Then smiled and went inside. It was good to see her mischievous smile where it belonged. He walked home a little faster with a grin on his face.

Chapter Twenty-Two

Sunday's sermon focused on eternal life. Elsie wondered if Reverend Knox was thinking ahead to Hubert's funeral service.

After church, Mark ate dinner with Polly and Elsie. They were joined by Polly's grandson, Caleb Reynolds, and his family—wife Mikal, son Will, and daughter Abbie. It was a quiet meal. Elsie was trying hard not to cry. She was afraid she couldn't stop, if she started.

After a cloudy start to the day with threatening rain, the sun came out brightly as Elsie and Mark made their way to the small tent at the graveside. It had ten chairs beneath it. Elsie hadn't thought they'd need many since Hubert knew very few people in Lansdale.

People began gathering. The ten chairs were full, and people crowded around the perimeter of the tent at least five deep. Polly and her family. Dr. Merrick and his family. Mark's co-workers who were not on duty came in uniform. Chief and Mrs. Davis. Fire Chief Gilliland and half a dozen uniformed firemen. Mrs. Johnson from across the street. Mark's neighbors and Elsie's customers: Mrs. Hollis, Mrs. Barrett and both the Vanoys. Miss Clover. Sullivan and Siobhan Stalatti. The Taylor boys and their father. Muriel and Walt Whistler. Mel Caldwell with his new bride, Beverly, and his sister, Poppy. And people kept coming. It looked as if everyone who'd ever shopped at *Knitting*

Pretty or met Elsie had come to support her in this time of grief. Small town love at its best.

Reverend Knox's service was exactly what Elsie had requested. Afterward, people lined up and filed through the tent to give her a card or a hug or both. Over two hundred people came to the funeral of a man few of them personally knew.

Elsie stepped to the casket and removed three perfect yellow roses from the spray. She'd dry those for the memorial display she had planned for Hubert. The funeral home was going to divide the rest of the spray into individual bouquets and deliver them, at Elsie's request, to the three local nursing homes.

Mark drove Elsie back to Polly's house. She sat quietly sobbing in the front seat of Phil's car. For a long time after he parked in the driveway, he held her hand, unsure what else to do.

"Hubert would have been shocked at the number of people at his funeral. I certainly was," Elsie finally said.

"Funerals are for the living. Those people came to help lessen your grief and to show you they care for you."

"You're right. The funny thing is Hubert never wanted to live in a small town. He thought it was easier to be anonymous in a big city than in a little burg. He was probably right. He told me he almost turned down the opportunity to move to Wisconsin. In the end, he did it because he got along so well with me." She smiled weakly.

"It's a good thing when siblings are actually friends. It's not always true."

"I've been protected and loved. I am blessed. Thanks for not leaving me to face this alone." Elsie leaned over and kissed his cheek. "I'm wiped out. I think I'll call it a day. I need some time to rest and to think about what happens next and when. Thanks again."

Mark came around the car and opened her door. She gave him a brief hug and went in the house.

****

On Monday morning, Elsie shared her plans with Polly about moving in above her shop. It didn't look like it would be too long before the remodeled apartment would be habitable.

"Are you certain you should make the decision so quickly?" Polly asked.

"I need a place to live, and the apartment is being renovated. It seems right to me."

"Well, you're welcome to stay here as long as you'd like." The older woman gave her a hug. "I've enjoyed having your company."

"What are you planning to do today?" Elsie asked.

"My annual snow globe cleaning extravaganza. Once a year I wipe them down and update my inventory log."

"If you don't mind, I'd like to help," Elsie volunteered.

"It isn't necessary."

"I know. It would help me feel less guilty about staying here rent free. Deal?"

"Sure." Polly laughed and stuck out her hand to shake. "The work will definitely go faster with help. My grandson, Will, used to help, but at fifteen he has a very full social life and it's harder to find a time to squeeze this chore in on his schedule."

Elsie had seen the snow globes in the dining room,

but had no idea there were hundreds of them. Polly had a story for each one. She'd written who they were from and the dates she'd gotten them on the bottom of each globe, in addition to listing them in the official logbook. Friends started giving them to her shortly after her husband died when she was fifty-five. She would be ninety-one in November. No wonder there were so many.

****

Monday at work Mark didn't have a chance to check the license plate number for the black pickup. He did look at the paper he had written the number down on the first time—he'd left it under the weight on his desk—and compared it to the picture he'd just taken on his phone. He had originally been off by one number. He had the right one now, as soon as he had time to run the correct number through the Iowa DMV he'd have some answers.

The ballistics report on the bullets retrieved from Hubert Dennis's body showed no matches to weapons in the state data base. Was that another indication the perpetrator was someone out of Hubert's past rather than someone from Wisconsin? The state forensics experts sent the information on the bullets to the national system, hoping it would yield more actionable results.

After reviewing all the reports, the State Fire Inspector confirmed what Fire Chief Gilliland suspected. It was arson, not an accident. The house and contents were a total loss. Finally, Elsie had the information she needed to settle with the insurance company.

****

Elsie reopened *Knitting Pretty* on Tuesday morning. Mark stopped by about one-thirty in the afternoon to check on her. "Do you want me to bring you some lunch before I go on shift?"

"No."

"You have to eat, Elsie, or you'll blow away."

"I have a lot of extra waist to lose before I'd disappear." She patted her middle. "I must look terrible."

"Why do you think so?" he asked.

She walked to the back of the store, popped open the mini-fridge, and pulled out a brown paper sack. "Polly sent me to work with this." She dumped it on the counter revealing a huge roast beef and cheese sandwich, pasta salad, and a large yellow apple.

Mark laughed. "Great minds think alike. We're both trying to take care of you. It's well past lunch time. You need to sit down at the counter and eat while I am here."

"Has anyone ever told you you're bossy?"

"Never..." Mark shrugged. "I'm waiting to see the first bite. Quit stalling."

Elsie pulled a bottle of water out of the fridge. "Do you want anything? Water? Diet soda?"

"Nope. I had my usual big lunch at Whistler's."

Mark leaned on the counter while Elsie sat on the stool eating what Polly had sent. "I was starting to get hungry. Sometimes when I'm in the middle of reading a pattern I lose all track of time." She pointed to the papers on the counter. "I'm trying to figure out if this shawl pattern is too complicated for an intermediate knitter."

"Don't look at me." He threw up his hands.

"Remember, I haven't taken my remedial knitting class yet."

The chime at the front door sounded. Cocoa meowed loudly as Elsie looked at the customer. "Here's someone who can help me."

"What do you need?" Siobhan Stalatti asked as she walked to the back of the shop.

"I need the opinion of an experienced knitter to help me determine how hard this pattern is."

"I'm happy to look at it," Siobhan said.

"Saved by the neighbor. Elsie, please go home at a reasonable hour tonight," Mark said as he rose. "I don't want to see you here when I go home after work." Elsie kissed his cheek as he left.

Siobhan smiled. "Are you and the handsome officer official?"

Elsie hesitated. "We have been seeing more of one another lately. Nothing you could really call official. We enjoy being together. Why?"

"Just asking for a friend. Now let's look at this pattern."

****

At work things were very quiet so Mark finally had time to check the license plate number from his phone picture of the black pickup, but the state of Iowa DMV systems were being updated for the next three nights. No access was allowed except for emergencies.

Chapter Twenty-Three

"Hey, Mark, wait," Elsie hollered as he jogged past Polly's the next morning.

She fell into step beside him. "I decided I need to get back in the morning exercise habit. I want to bask in the sunshine. Do you mind some company?"

Mark jogged in place. "I was planning to take my regular route."

"Okay, where does it go?"

"It goes past the fire." He tried to read her expression. "Do you want to go a different direction?"

She took a deep breath. "I have to go by it again some time. I'd rather it was with you the first time."

They ran down the street staying in step with one another and turned toward the remains of the Dennis home. Elsie noticeably slowed. When they were directly in front of the house rubble, she stopped. She visibly paled. She didn't make a sound. A torrent of tears poured down her cheeks. Mark waited a moment, then took her hand and led her away from the scene increasing his speed with each step.

****

Tuesday, after lunch at Whistler's, Mark stopped at *Knitting Pretty* to check on Elsie after the morning's trauma of seeing her house. When he came into the store, Cocoa jumped down from her perch at the front door. She rubbed against his legs yowling until he bent over and picked her up. He didn't think Elsie had seen him come in. He'd wait until she finished with the customer she was talking to. Cocoa purred contently as he rubbed her ears.

Elsie was shaking her head and frowning. Mark couldn't hear the conversation. Wait. That was no customer. What was that worm Stalatti doing in the shop?

Mark watched as Stalatti leaned closer to Elsie. She continued to shake her head. He kept talking. Then she shrugged and nodded. He turned around with a broad smile on his face and walked to the front of the store. Cocoa's purr switched to a low growl as he passed them. "I feel the same way, Cocoa." Stalatti passed without speaking. Mark put the cat on the floor and walked to the back.

Elsie looked up from the register. "Mark, I didn't expect to see you again today." She walked around the counter and kissed his cheek.

A thousand responses raced through his mind. He tamped down all the jealous ones. He kissed her back. "I stopped to see if you wanted to go on an actual date Saturday night."

She looked surprised. "I'm sorry, I can't."

"Of course, you can," he said. "It's time you and I become an official we, don't you think?"

"Yes, it's time."

"I was going to take you to Harry's Hideaway. Have you been there? They're famous for their prime rib."

"Yes, I know. It's delicious." She spoke without looking at Mark.

"So why can't you go Saturday night?"

"I already have a dinner engagement for Saturday…to go to Harry's."

"Are you giving me a hard time because it's taken so long for me to actually ask you out?"

"No." She hesitated. "I really do have dinner plans Saturday night…with someone else."

"No way." Mark glared at her. "You are not going to dinner with that slime bucket. You would never do that to me."

"I'm sorry. He wouldn't take no for an answer," she said in almost a whisper.

"I'll go tell him you aren't going with him because we have a date." Mark turned to leave.

Elsie grabbed his arm. "I said I'd have dinner with Sully and I'm going to. You do not need to tell him anything. You and I can go another time." Tears welled up in her eyes.

"Right." Mark left without a backward glance.

He sat in the truck seething about Stalatti moving in on his girl. He was a little angry at Elsie for giving into Sully's badgering.

It's my own fault for not telling Elsie straight out how I feel about her. Maybe the situation can be salvaged yet. I have to get Stalatti out of the picture. I wonder if Poppy is willing to do a favor for an old friend.

****

Saturday night Poppy opened the door before Mark rang the bell. She looked very attractive in her frilly, show-a-little-cleavage, emerald-green-like-her-eyes dress. She kissed his cheek, turned and locked the door, then stepped onto the sidewalk and spun around in front of him. "You like?" she asked reminding Mark of an eight-year-old girl showing off her new party dress.

"I like. Perfect. Thanks again." He offered his arm to her. "Shall we?" He led her to Phil's car.

Poppy chattered all the way to the restaurant though Mark could not remember what she said. His mind was already at the hole-in-the-wall restaurant thirty miles away—and he wasn't thinking about their famous succulent prime rib.

"Do you agree?" Poppy asked. "Earth to Mark, hey, I asked you a question."

"I'm sorry. What was it?"

"Boy, you have it bad." She laughed. "What were you going to do if I'd said no to this ruse?"

"I hadn't thought of a Plan B. Fortunately, I didn't need one." He turned into the already crowded parking lot at Harry's Hideaway. "Dang it. Looks like they beat us here. No one else would be driving an Italian sports car with a Pennsylvania license plate on it." He put the car in park. "C'mon. Thanks again for being my date tonight."

Poppy clung to Mark's arm as they walked through the bar into the restaurant. Harry himself rushed over to them with menus in hand. "Officer Trask, so good to see you. It has been too long. What a lovely lady you have with you. I have your table all ready."

He led them to the intimate private dining room in the back of the restaurant. He opened the door to show them in. "What is the meaning of this? How did you get in here?" he questioned the patrons inside.

Harry's son, Peter, excused himself cutting in front of Mark and Poppy, saying, "Dad, I seated the Stalatti party. I took their reservation earlier in the week."

"Well, I took Officer Trask's reservation," Harry

snapped at his offspring.

"Did you look at the book before you promised them this room?" Peter asked rolling his eyes. "Forgive us, Officer Trask. There has been a mix up. I can seat your party in a private corner of the dining room and buy you a bottle of wine as an apology."

Sullivan Stalatti released Elsie's hand and stood. "Please, we know each other…at least some of us do." His eyes never left Poppy. "There is plenty of room for four at this table. Elsie, are you okay with Mark and his date joining us?"

Elsie stared open mouthed at Mark and Poppy, then swallowed hard saying, "Sure, the more, the merrier."

Sully walked to the door and extended his hand to Poppy. "I don't believe we've met. I'm Sullivan Stalatti. You are?"

Poppy took his hand smiling broadly. "I'm Poppy Caldwell. Nice to meet you, Mr. Stalatti. Good evening, Elsie."

"Please call me Sully." He pulled out the chair across from Elsie and next to him.

Peter handed Poppy a menu and excused himself.

Harry said, "Sorry for the confusion. It looks like it is working out." He handed Mark a menu as he approached the door and palmed a twenty-dollar bill.

"Yes, it is. Thanks, Harry," Mark said.

Mark sat down across from Sully and between Elsie and Poppy. He'd gotten exactly what he wanted. Now what?

****

By the end of the meal, Mark and Elsie were able to meet one another's eyes without embarrassment. Poppy and Sully proved to be such great conversationalists that no one noticed the other two people in the room were amazingly silent. Mark thought Poppy laughed a little too loudly and frequently at Sully's quips and leaned far too close to him providing the man a bonus view of her cleavage. Sully didn't appear to think there was a problem on either count.

The check arrived and the server handed it to Sully along with a credit card Mark had never seen him give to the woman. "Just a minute, miss. This was supposed to be two checks of two each," Mark protested.

"It's not her fault, Mark. I made arrangements earlier," Sully explained.

"Which was fine for the two of you. I'll pay my own way and Poppy's, too."

"It is done. We have no reason to make it more difficult for this young woman to do her job. You may leave." Sully dismissed the server.

"You do that as if your word is final. You're in a strange place. Not a good way to start out, if you're trying to make friends," Mark said through clenched teeth.

"On the contrary. Most people would think being treated to dinner by the new kid in town would be a great beginning to a new friendship," Sully countered.

Elsie said, "We can agree to disagree about the approach."

"Fine. The next dinner for four is on me. Will that suit you, Mr. Stalatti?"

"Absolutely. I'd love to do this again." He winked.

Not at Elsie.

At Poppy.

Elsie pushed away from the table, then everyone

else stood and filed out into the parking lot. The men shook hands. Poppy and Elsie briefly half-hugged. Everyone left with the date they had come with.

After taking Poppy home, Mark began to think about the disastrous date. He sat out on the deck in the dark, nursing an initially ice-cold beer until long after midnight. Domino kept walking in and out of the house confused by his master's behavior. Finally, the dog laid across Mark's feet waiting for him to come to his senses and into the house.

Mark told his four-legged companion everything that had happened during the evening. Occasionally, Domino would whimper or thump his tail in response. Mark kept talking.

"I'm not sure what I accomplished tonight. I'm even less certain about what I wanted to have happen. I guess I was trying to make Elsie as jealous as I felt when she agreed to go out with Stalatti. Then he showboats and pays the entire bill. What a hot dog. He openly flirted with Poppy as if one of my...my what? Women? Dates? Was not enough for him. How do you think he made Elsie feel when he did it right in front of her?"

Domino whimpered. Mark started again, "I'm as big a jerk as Sully. I did the same thing flaunting Poppy in her low-cut, green dress right in front of Elsie. Yep, I'm as much of an uncouth pig as Stalatti is. Maybe more so. I orchestrated the whole thing. He just saw an opportunity to date a beautiful woman and pounced on it. What a mess I've made. C'mon, fella, time for bed."

****

Church service on Sunday was an icy affair. No one sat together or in their *usual* seats. They nodded hello to one another across the sanctuary. No smiles. No touching. No discussion of where to have dinner after the service. Even the singing seemed less spirited than normal. Reverend Knox's sermon was on jealousy—an evil sent directly from Satan to ruin relationships and cause people to doubt the ones they used to trust. Wonder who clued him in on Mark's situation. It wasn't the first time it felt like the sermon was specifically written for his mental state. Lots of food for thought. Too much.

He needed to go on a mental diet.

****

Mark opened the garage door and pulled his truck in next to Phil's car. He ran the door down and unlocked the door to the yard, then relocked it when he closed it. Domino didn't run down the steps to meet him. Mark got to the top of the stairs and saw the reason why. Phil was sitting in a chair on the deck cooing at the dog and scratching his ears.

Mark approached him with open arms. "Man, am I glad to see you. Where on earth have you been?"

Phil gave his landlord a hearty bear hug. "It's a long and tragic tale." He laughed. "Looks like you have some things to tell me about, too. My keys didn't work, and everything is locked up tight. I had to scale the fence to get in the yard. Then I landed in the middle of a rosebush that hadn't been there when I left. I hope I didn't damage it. I love the rabbit. The yard looks great. I didn't know you had the creative landscaping gene."

"I don't but you're correct. A lot has been happening here in the last almost month. I have new keys for you on the desk. I expected you'd come home eventually. I'll make us some sandwiches and we can catch up."

As they walked into the kitchen with Domino close behind them, Mark said, "I need to change clothes before we get into things. Say, where is your luggage?"

"It's still with my wife," Phil said.

"Your wife? You do have a lot to tell me."

Chapter Twenty-Four

Mark and Phil carried their paper plates and drinks out to the picnic table on the deck. Mark said. "You go first."

"I'm pretty embarrassed about the whole adventure," Phil began. "I met her online—in a sci-fi chat room. Her name is Arianna Joy Moonstone. We hit it off from the first message." Phil took a drink of water and a bite of his sandwich. "Her mom had a medical episode the second week of our relationship. Arianna could only scrape together half of the five thousand dollars needed for her Mom's urgent surgery. I wired her the other half."

"You've got to be kidding, Phil. That's the oldest scam in the book. Where was she?"

"Philadelphia. After I wired the money, I didn't hear from her for almost a week. I figured I probably was the victim of an online scam and felt lucky I hadn't been taken for more. Then she called. We spoke or texted every day after that." Phil took another bite. "You hadn't been gone an hour when the doorbell rang. I opened the door and there stood Arianna Moonstone in the flesh with her two brothers and sisters-in-law, and the chauffeur who drove their limo.

"They came to take me to Pennsylvania so we could be married where her mother could attend our wedding. When I couldn't leave until you got back, they stayed, and we had an all-week party. Arianna and I got to know one another better. Her brothers grilled me about money. I had nothing to hide so I had my financials sent here."

"Was that the package Nico retrieved?"

"Yes. We left for Philadelphia the day before you were due home and drove straight through."

"Okay. You got there on Monday in the wee hours. Nico didn't retrieve the package until Thursday." Mark counted the days on his fingers. "Did you wait to get married until they could bless your financial situation?"

"No. Tuesday morning we went to the courthouse for our marriage license. Then we drove to the rehab center. I met Arianna's mother, and we got married in the small chapel there."

"Wow, that was fast. What did you really know about Arianna? Maybe I've been a cop too long, but there are all kinds of red flags popping up."

"None of that matters. I love Arianna and we are legally wed," Phil growled.

Mark leaned back trying to be less intense. "Where is your bride now?" No response. "You got married on Tuesday. On Wednesday you called about the package. Thursday, Nico retrieved the package. Friday, we had the break-in. Why?"

"Her brothers did not believe the financial statements. They were certain I was hiding my true wealth from them. They sent Nico to toss the apartment and make certain I was telling them the truth."

"Why should it matter to them what assets you did or didn't have?"

"I'm getting to that. I was an idiot. We came back from our one-day honeymoon to Arianna's place."

"I thought you said they all lived together in her mother's house."

Phil downed a large gulp of water. "Arianna and her mother lived together in a rundown apartment building in west Philadelphia." He hesitated. "Almost all of what I believed about her was a lie. She's an only child. Gino and Al are neighborhood thugs, not her brothers. Since I wired the twenty-five hundred dollars, they assumed I had a whole lot more money than I do. After I married Arianna, they planned to force me to give them money on a regular basis. She only did what they demanded because they had threatened her mother…and because she loved me."

"What did you do when you found out the truth?"

"Arianna and I went to the police. Arianna wore a wire and got everything recorded about the whole scam. Gino, Al, Maria, and Vicky were arrested. I bought two airline tickets to bring her back to Wisconsin with me. Yesterday morning when we were due to leave, I found a note. She was gone. I didn't know what else to do other than come home. We are still legally married. I love her with all my heart. I don't care about any of the rest of it." Phil took a deep breath. He looked on the verge of tears.

Mark patted his back. "What an adventure. Hey, does your mom know you're home? Or about Arianna?"

"Not yet. I'll call her later today. Promise."

Mark told him about all the dramatic events that had happened since his return from vacation. He hesitated a moment.

"Seems like things have been hopping here, too," Phil said. "No wonder everything was locked up tight while you were away from home."

"Yeah. You probably don't care, but I have to talk to someone about Elsie and me."

"Of course, I care. Didn't you date her a long time ago?"

Mark nodded. "A real long time ago. I'm almost as dumb about women as you are."

"Not a good way to be." Phil smiled weakly.

"Sullivan Stalatti, the new bookstore owner in town, is more than a little interested in Elsie, even though he knows we have been seeing one another regularly. I made a mess of things and long story short she isn't talking to me now."

"Sounds to me like you're as enamored of Elsie Dennis as I am of Arianna Moonstone—speaking as someone who knows all the symptoms."

"I'm afraid you're right. She's been staying with Polly Rogers one street over since the fire."

"Maybe you should casually jog by. You are still running?"

"I am. Usually in the morning. Maybe I should cry 'uncle' and just call her and beg for her forgiveness."

"You know the lady in question better than I do."

Mark pulled out his phone and hit the speed dial for Elsie's number. It went straight to voice mail. He almost hung up but decided to leave a message.

"Elsie, I'm leaving a message in case you don't automatically delete all my calls. First, I'm sorry for acting all junior high school about Sully asking you out. We can talk more about it later, if you're interested in knowing my reasons. Are you still planning to move soon? Do you need me to help move anything with the truck? Or any general muscle and painting help? You

know the number. I'm hoping you'll give me a holler."
Mark hung up.

"I sure hope she listens to the message."

****

Phil was glad to be home. He called his mom before he turned out the light. She was relieved he was home, but he didn't tell her she was a mother-in-law yet.

****

Monday morning Mark and Domino went on their pre-breakfast run on the route going past Polly's house first. He intentionally ran slower than normal as they passed the three-story white house on the corner. Footsteps fell in behind them.

"C'mon, Trask. Cut me some slack. Slow down," Elsie said struggling for her breath.

"Good morning, Ms. Dennis. Lovely day isn't it," Mark said jogging in place. Elsie caught up. Domino licked her hand. All three started off again...slowly. "Did you get my message?"

"Yep."

Mark took a few more strides, then stopped. "Well?"

Elsie stopped and gulped air. "I am moving. Today. I don't need a truck because all the big stuff is coming directly from the furniture store. I have a couple of suitcases of clothes I've bought since the fire."

"Right. You lost everything." He tapped his forehead with his hand. "Stupid question."

"No. I thought it was sweet. Oh, maybe the truck is a good idea. I will have a couple of boxes of household stuff. Polly has been doing major downsizing. She swears she's intended to get rid of her excess dishes, pots, and linens for years, but hadn't done it yet."

"Glad to load and unload the boxes any time."

"Do you have time later this morning before you go on shift this afternoon?"

"Sure. What about ten o'clock?"

"Perfect. I'll see you then." Elsie started back toward Polly's.

Mark scolded, "You didn't do much of a run this morning."

"I did enough to get some moving help." She winked and left.

"Well, Domino, guess I'm on my way out of the doghouse." Domino barked and they both continued on their original route.

****

Promptly at ten o'clock, Mark pulled into Polly's driveway. Boxes were stacked in the carport waiting for his arrival. Will and Caleb came out with two more large cartons and sat them directly in the bed of the truck. They handed boxes to Mark standing in the truck bed and he stacked them low and close to the cab. The truck bed was full by the time the last box was loaded.

Thankfully, Will and Caleb piled into the cab with Mark. Elsie was already at the apartment. There were stairs to navigate to get the boxes to their final destination. Mark handed a box out of the truck to fifteen-year-old, Will. He quickly scaled the steps and handed it to his dad, Caleb. They continued the process until the truck bed was empty. It worked well to give the most strenuous work out to the youngest member of the trio.

Elsie was delighted they had finished so quickly. She offered to buy them all lunch over at Whistler's.

They declined, but did accept a hug and a kiss on the cheek all around.

"Are you sure you don't need painting help?" Mark asked.

"No. Everything is done except my room. I'll be able to do it today. The living room furniture and appliances are coming this afternoon. My bedroom suite won't be here until tomorrow." She gave him another peck on the cheek. "Thanks a million. Couldn't have done this without your truck and the trio of musclemen. See you later."

Mark dropped Caleb and Will at home, then ran over to Bob's Market. He had a long grocery list. Seemed like all his staples ran out at the same time. Mark rolled a heaping cart out of the store thirty minutes later and was halfway to his truck.

Vroom! Vroom!

He whipped his head around. A black pickup truck was bearing down on him traveling much faster than normal parking lot speed. He pushed the cart between two nearby cars and dove between them.

The unmistakable sound of a shotgun blast rang out. The squeal of tires. The truck sped out of the lot's side exit. Mark pushed the cart back into the lane and ran toward his truck. Windows on both the driver's side as well as the passenger side had been shattered. Shards of glass littered the seat and the parking lot.

He called 911 to report the incident then loaded his groceries in the back of the truck and returned the cart, He swept the area around his vehicle with a broom and dustpan the store manager provided. He had just finished cleaning up when the police cruiser pulled in.

After delivering the basics, Mark shared his

thoughts with his colleague. "I don't think the driver intended to hurt me. With a little more speed he could have easily run me over in the parking lot. It was more terrorizing and a warning. I want to talk to my boarder. He got home yesterday from a mysterious absence. The incidents might be related. I'll let you know when I come in tonight." He showed them the picture on his cell phone with the correct license plate number for the vehicle.

It was a breezy trip home with no windows on either side of the seat. Mark parked in front of his house to take the groceries in the front door—bypassing the stairs from the garage. He got everything put away and went to Phil's apartment. His boarder was in his office, sorting through the tubs Mark had filled.

"Look out the window," Mark directed.

Phil stood and gazed out. "I see your truck at the curb. Am I supposed to see anything else?"

"Look at the driver's side window."

"Do you have a broken window? Hit a rock?"

"Nope. Shattered windows. Both sides. Shotgun blast from the driver of a black pickup truck."

Phil peered out the window again and shrugged his shoulders. "Why are you telling me this?"

"Are you certain the Philadelphia scam artists are still safely behind bars? Where does Nico live?"

"I'll double check about Philly. They shouldn't be released yet. I don't know where Nico lives. I've never seen him. Why ask about him?"

"He was driving a black pickup the night he was here. I'm wondering if they are trying to harass you through me. This truck didn't appear here until you disappeared. You're back and it's still here and getting bolder."

"I can see why you think there might be a connection. Let me make some calls."

"I'm going to change for work and run over to Pop Skelton's. I hope he can order new glass for the windows and fashion some kind of stopgap measure for the interim."

****

Pop Skelton walked around the truck. "You sure are hard on this old girl, Mark. You're lucky she was built when we knew how to build things to last. Your grandpa took great care of her. I'll have Mike get online and see what we can scavenge up to fix her."

"Thanks. Gramps always babied her. I've tried to follow his lead, but forces beyond my control have been conspiring against me lately. Do you have some plastic we can use temporarily?"

Mike Skelton had made this type of repair often enough to be very proficient completing the job. Mark made it to work exactly on time.

Chapter Twenty-Five

Thankfully, it was a quiet shift. First thing, Mark sat down at his computer and ran the truck license plates with Iowa DMV.

The pickup belonged to a company in Dubuque, Iowa called The Rock and Lawn Landscapers owned by a man named Chester Stephens. The name didn't ring any bells for Mark. There was no lettering on the side of the truck that harassed him or landscaping equipment in the back. He wrote down the business phone number.

Mark made the call. He got a recording that related usual business hours and to call back when they were open. He kept wracking his brain. Did he know a Chester Stephens? Ever?

****

The kitchen appliances were delivered immediately after Mark and company left Elsie's apartment. She went to work unpacking, washing, and putting away her dishes, pans, and small appliances.

She leaned against the kitchen counter nibbling on one of the cookies Polly had sent with her this morning. Perfect. One room complete. There was a knock at the door. The living room furniture and dinette set had arrived.

The delivery guys groused about the long climb to her apartment. She assured them the steps were brand new and completely safe. They had to lift the sofa over the railing to make the turn into the apartment. Luckily, everything else could make the turn without being hoisted over their shoulders. Another room complete.

About four o'clock, the hardware store delivered the pale lavender paint Elsie needed for the bedroom along with brushes, rollers, a pan, and drop cloths.

Elsie liked the peaceful rhythm of painting. After spreading the drop cloths and putting on an old shirt of Polly's late husband, she prepared to start. A knock at the door stopped her.

Siobhan Stalatti was at the door holding two bags. "I've heard the comings and goings all day. This is the first chance I've had to drop in. Looks like I interrupted you in the middle of something."

Elsie opened the door wider. "Come in. I'm preparing to paint the bedroom. I haven't started yet. What have you got there?"

"If you haven't eaten yet, I'd like you to be my guinea pig. Did I tell you we're having our soft opening of *Sips to You* later this week?"

"I haven't had supper. What wonderful news." She led Siobhan to the kitchen. "I know you're excited. Grand opening next week?"

"Yes, if all goes well on the soft opening. Sully will do the same with *The Book Nook*. I'm going to offer light meals, sandwiches, small salads, cup of soup—that kind of thing. I brought some samples for you to try, if you're game."

"What fun. I'd love to taste test for you. What do we have?"

Siobhan opened the bags and sat the selections on the counter. "Soup, salad, sandwiches and desserts. What would you like to try?"

"Goodness. How am I supposed to choose? It all looks and smells marvelous. What about we each pick a soup and split the sandwiches, salad, and desserts between us? I even have real plates and silverware courtesy of Polly Rogers we can use. I have diet cola for drinks and the ice maker has been running most of the day."

"Perfect. Shall I plate our food?"

"Yes, please."

The women sat down at the small table to their impromptu feast and enjoyed it amid much conversation and laughter. Two hours later, Elsie pushed away from the dinette. "I am so stuffed I can hardly move," she said. "If your lattes are as good as this food, you're going to have a booming business. I didn't realize you'd put in a full kitchen."

"It's a small one," Siobhan said. "Thanks for being my guinea pig. I love how your apartment is taking shape. We're all moved into our apartment, too. Downstairs will be complete tomorrow. I'm hoping to be open Wednesday morning for coffee drinkers."

"I'll plan to be one of your first customers. I hate to rush you off after you fed me so well." Elsie began clearing the table. "I need to get the bedroom finished before they deliver the furniture tomorrow afternoon."

Siobhan gave her a hug and left.

By the time the dishes were loaded in the dishwasher, the ladder set up, paint stirred and poured, it was almost eight o'clock. Elsie carefully taped around the baseboard and door and window frames. Then she painted the edges of the walls. She was ready for the roller.

Knock. Knock.

Had she locked the door after Siobhan left?

"Come in," she hollered. "I think it's open."

"Indeed it is," Sully said as he came through the door.

"Oh." Elsie looked at him. "I'm glad it's you."

Sully grinned. "I'm happy to hear you say that."

"Let me be clearer." She put down the paint roller. "I'm glad you weren't Mark."

"Even better." Sully never stopped smiling.

"What I meant was Mark is always scolding me for leaving doors unlocked." Elsie carefully came down off the ladder. "I'm glad he didn't catch me doing it again. Understand?"

Sully looked a little hang dog. "You can't blame a guy for trying." He walked into the bedroom. "Beautiful shade of lavender. Should be calm and peaceful for sleeping…if you also bought room darkening shades. Those streetlights put off more of a glow than you realize."

"I hadn't thought of the lights. Where did you get shades?"

"I couldn't find them locally. I ordered them online. I'll give you the website." He pulled out his phone and sent her a text with the site. "Do you need any help painting?"

"I only have the one roller. It won't take too long for me to finish—if I get back to it."

"Fine. I can take a hint. What do you say I give you an hour to finish and I'll bring back a bottle of wine to christen your new home?"

"Nice of you to offer, but it's not necessary," Elsie protested.

"I won't take no for an answer." He walked out of

the room. At the door, he said, "See you in an hour."

She was certain Sullivan Stalatti did not understand the meaning of *no*.

After Sully left, Elsie climbed back on the ladder. "I think I'm going to enjoy living here. Of course, it's making me talk to myself. Out loud. Maybe I should be worried." She laughed to herself and got lost in rhythm of the painting.

When she was finished, she slipped into the bathroom, out of her paint clothes, and back into comfortable sweats. She heard a knock at the door and it open and close.

"Have you got a corkscrew?" Sully was in the kitchen opening drawers and rifling around in them.

"I don't think so. Sorry."

"I have one. I'll be back in a flash." He returned with the corkscrew and two wine glasses.

"I should have asked. Is red okay? You drank some the other night so I assumed it would be."

"Sure."

Elsie wandered into the newly painted bedroom. She stood with her back to the windows admiring her handy work. Sully brought two glasses of wine in and handed her one.

"A toast. To much happiness in your new home." They clinked glasses and each took a taste.

She closed her eyes to savor the smooth taste of black currants with a subtle hint of mocha. "Thank you, Sully. To new neighbors." Another sip. She felt the tensions of the past month slipping away and her shoulders relaxed for the first time in days.

He raised his glass again. "To us."

Elsie didn't raise her glass. Tension flew back into

her body.

"You can't drink to us? Why not?" He frowned in an exaggerated way.

"There is no *us*." She rubbed the back of her neck. "We're friends, Sully. Platonic friends. I'm afraid I may have given you the wrong idea by accepting your dinner invitation."

"I don't believe I've misread any of your intentions." He sat his wine glass on the wide window ledge. "If you would be a little open minded, there could be an *us* and so much more." He put his hand under her chin, tipped her head back, and kissed her while pulling her tightly to him.

Elsie pushed against his chest with her empty hand. "No. You are totally mistaken about my feelings." She extracted herself from his embrace. "It's time for you to leave. Take everything with you."

Sully laughed. "I don't understand why you have such loyalty to a hick cop. You'll get over it. And I'll be here when you finally come to your senses."

"Leave, Sully." She pointed to the door. "Now." She walked into the kitchen and dumped her remaining wine down the drain, put the corkscrew in the glass, jammed the cork into the top of the bottle, and shoved it into Sully's arms.

"I will…this time." He smirked. "You'll soon learn it won't be so easy to get rid of me the next time."

She walked ahead of him and opened the door. As soon as he cleared the jamb, she closed the door, locked the knob, then got the key off the hook and locked the deadbolt. Sully stood outside staring in the window as if he couldn't understand what had happened. She wasn't sure she did either.

****

Domino met Mark on the deck. The dog wagged his tail and licked the toe of his boot. "It's nice someone is glad to see me." He opened the back door and continued talking, "There's a reason you're man's best friend. I don't come home and find you in the arms of an out-of-town Romeo."

"I guess I left you alone too long," Phil said as he finished drying the last plate in the dish rack.

"I've always told Domino my problems. Usually you were already lights out by the time I came home." Mark laughed. "Glad to see you've learned to do dishes."

"Go ahead and rub it in. I deserve the abuse for the mess I left for you. What do you think about going halfsies on a dishwasher?"

"You want to invest in my property? Does that mean you're not going to chase Arianna to wherever she decided to go?"

"I have great confidence in the power of true love. There's a saying about loving someone enough to let them go and they'll come back to you, if it is meant to be. I'm here…at least until Arianna returns to me. She is my wife. Enough about my woman troubles, what were you fussing about to the fur ball?"

"I can't figure Elsie out. Just when I think we're back on track I find her falling into Sullivan Stalatti's arms again. I'm not sure how to combat the growing attraction between them."

"Why not ask the lady in question? Only a thought. You know my track record so take it for what it is worth." Phil hung the dish towel on the rack. "I'll see you tomorrow. I have a lot of work to get done. Good night."

Mark wasn't sleepy. He was mentally exhausted. Maybe life would be easier if he gave up on the idea of a happy-ever-after, but somehow that didn't sit right with him.

He flipped on the TV with the volume on low. The news crawl wasn't the least bit uplifting. He turned it off. When was the last time he'd actually sat down and read for pleasure? Months at least. Why did he buy so many crime mysteries? Wasn't his real life full of enough of those? The cell phone in his pocket vibrated.

"Hello. Trask here."

"Good since that's who I was hoping to talk to," a feminine voice said softly.

"Elsie? I thought you had company tonight." It popped out of his mouth without a thought. Too late to take it back.

"I'm sorry. How would you know whether I had someone visiting or not?" There was a hint of irritation in her tone.

He'd might as well tell her all of it. "When I drove past your place on my way home your light was still on. I was going to stop to see you. When I got out of the truck and looked up at your window, I saw you wrapped in someone's arms. I assume it was Sully." He spoke slowly—trying to keep his anger at bay.

"Mark Trask, you sound jealous."

"No…What the heck?" He stopped. "Yes. I confess. I'm pea green—I'm so jealous. Every time I think we're getting somewhere with our relationship there's always Sully lurking in the background trying to weasel his way in between us. You probably think I'm acting childishly."

"No." She laughed softly. "If I'm as truthful as you are being, I'm delighted you think I'm worth being jealous over."

"If that's the case, why were you in Sully's arms tonight?"

"Apparently, you only saw the beginning of the embrace, not the end."

"You're right. As soon as it started, I drove off in a hurry to lick my wounds and feel sorry for myself."

"It was completely one-sided. I immediately pushed him away, poured out my wine, and sent him packing. I clearly communicated he and I are not an us and will not ever be. Any questions?"

"No, ma'am. I read you loud and clear." Mark couldn't stop grinning. "Did you see my truck in the street? Is that why you called?"

"No. I was thinking about you and wanted to tell you good night and wish you sweet dreams, Officer Trask."

"Same to you, Ms. Dennis, mine will be a heck of a lot better now than they would have been fifteen minutes ago."

Chapter Twenty-Six

The envelope was face down on the floor below the mail slot in the door. It was addressed using a label maker on clear tape. No postmark. No stamp. No return address. Exactly like the last one. Inside was another threatening anonymous message.

Morgan thrust the single page into the manila envelope with the others. It was foolish to think this could be handled without help. No. It was stupid—in the way that could get you killed. The descending darkness was palpable.

Lord, where is the daylight? Please take me there.

****

On Wednesday morning, Domino and Mark rounded the corner of the last block of their run. The black pickup tore off down their street in the opposite direction, passing them at high speed. Mark increased his pace and cautiously circled the house. Nothing seemed to be amiss from the perimeter review. He unlocked the front door. Domino scooted into the house the moment the door was ajar.

"Yoo hoo! Mark!" Mrs. Hollis called from her front yard. She was in her gardening hat and waving gloved hands.

He walked over to the fence.

"There was a young man here, well not really young, older than you, but younger than me. Anyway, he dropped this package off and asked me to give it to you as soon as I saw you. You just missed him. He was in a big, black truck." She handed an oversized shoe box wrapped in brown paper tied with string across the fence to him.

He immediately sat it on the ground six feet away from him. "Mrs. Hollis, call 911. Tell them we have a possible bomb." She stared at him, her mouth open in a huge O. "Go. Now! Hurry!"

She ran into her house, screaming at the top of her lungs. A few minutes later three emergency vehicles came down the street. One parked in front of Mark's house and the other two across the road at each end of the block. They sent him behind a shield on the far side of the street and using a bullhorn cautioned all the neighbors to stay inside their houses.

A man in protective coveralls and head covering sent a drone equipped with a special x-ray device to hover over the box. It sent pictures back to the tablet a second technician held.

"It's a pipe bomb. We need the robot," the technician with the tablet said.

A few moments later a crazy looking metal device that appeared to be half go cart and half telescoping arms rolled from the street across the lawn to the box. A large metal container was placed next to the shoebox. The robot took the box with its telescoping arms and carefully put it in the container. Everyone stepped back. The automated arms went to work. After fifteen minutes—while all those present collectively held their breath—the dismantling was complete. All of the components were collected and sealed in bags to be analyzed as evidence.

The police wanted to know how Mrs. Hollis got the box. She was sitting on her front steps. Mark walked over to his neighbor's house with the policeman. He sat next to her on the stoop. She fell against him with tears streaming down her cheeks. He gave her a brief hug.

"I assumed the man was a friend yours," she said to Mark. "He was driving the big black truck I've seen parked in front of the house multiple times in the past month. He said I should give the package to Mark Trask as soon as I saw him. I hadn't had it five minutes when you and Domino came jogging to your front door."

"Could you describe the man who gave you the package?" the police office asked.

"I thought he was Mark's friend. He was a quite a bit taller and broader than Mark. A dark colored baseball cap covered all his hair. I don't know what color it was. He wore sunglasses—those super dark ones so no one can see your eyes—the really expensive kind of shades they advertise on TV to block out all the glare. He was wearing a blue polo shirt with some kind of a business logo on it. I couldn't read it. He had on khaki-colored work pants, like my dad used to wear. You know, the real durable kind they advertise that wear like iron. He was very polite and surprisingly soft spoken for such a large man. He had a nice smile, but I think he had bad teeth. He never let them show."

"Thank you, Mrs. Hollis. This is very helpful. If you think of anything else, please call me." The officer handed her a business card. He turned to Mark and said, "Check in with me when you get to work. I may have more information." He started toward the patrol car.

Suddenly, she jumped up. "Oh, officer, I don't

know if it's important," she called hurrying toward him. "He had a problem with his right leg. He walked without bending it—you know, like the deputy on the old western TV show."

"Thank you. More very helpful information." The policeman made a note and got into the patrol car. The police and bomb disposal unit returned to their vehicles and all left.

Mrs. Hollis began crying again. Mark walked next to her and helped her into the house. "Why are you crying now?"

"You could have been killed. I could have. Phil could have. Domino could have. Things like this aren't supposed to happen in a little town, like Lansdale. They just aren't." Mrs. Hollis shook her head.

"You were great." He left her on the sofa in the living room and got her a glass of ice water. "You did exactly what needed to be done. Thank you. Get some rest."

Phil.

Mark unlocked the front door and took the stairs to the second floor two at a time. He knocked loudly on the door. "Hey, Phil. I need to talk to you. Now."

Phil opened the door and stood back. His landlord barreled past him. "Didn't you hear the sirens?"

"No. I was on a conference call. I wear earpieces to hear better. I'm lucky if I can hear the participants, much less what's going on outside. I listened to too much loud music as a teenager."

"They just dismantled a bomb in our front yard. A gift from our friend in the black pickup truck. It's owned by a Chester Stephens. Is the name familiar to you?"

"I don't think so. You still believe this guy is somehow related to my whole Arianna and the Philadelphia thugs episode?"

"I don't know what to think. Things are getting stranger and stranger. Try and keep an eye out for anything unusual while I'm at work today. I haven't even had my breakfast yet and I could have been blown apart. I need a shower and some coffee. I'll let you know if I learn anything else. Stay safe."

Mark went back downstairs and straight into his room. He stood under the shower until the water went from hot to tepid to downright cold. What a crazy way to start the day.

****

Sips To You and *The Book Nook* had their soft openings on Wednesday morning. Siobhan had customers lined up out the door at seven-thirty getting coffees, lattes, and pastries before going to work. The bookstore opened at ten o'clock and had a steady stream of parents and kids coming in to get their free books. Lots of people were cashing in their coupons from the Kid's Bike Rodeo in both places.

Elsie had heavier than usual traffic for a Wednesday in the summer. People she'd never met stopped in saying they didn't even know *Knitting Pretty* was downtown. And they didn't just look. They were buying. One woman new to the shop made a two-hundred-and-fifty-dollar purchase. She was a spinner who'd only lived in town a month. She was delighted to know she could buy her fiber or special order it at Elsie's store. She liked supporting local businesses.

By late afternoon, it was obvious the new tenants were a great draw for everyone's business. Elsie, Sully, and Siobhan compared notes after five o'clock. They were very pleased.

****

The station was still buzzing about the pipe bomb when Mark got to work. The bomb disposal experts said it wasn't large enough to have done structural damage, but it was big enough to have blinded him or caused the loss of hands and/or arms—if he had opened the box. It was another warning from the black pickup driver.

The forensics team hadn't found any definitive information about who the bomber was. No visible prints yet. It could take another day or two to finish combing through the evidence.

Mark sat down at his desk and called The Rock and Lawn Landscapers again. Even though it was three forty-five and after their normal business hours, a man answered the phone. "This is Chester Stephens. What can I do for you?"

"Thanks for answering," Mark said. "I was afraid you'd be closed for the day."

"We are. I always answer the phone, if I'm here, regardless of the time. Being the boss means I never want to pass on an opportunity for more business. What do you need?"

"Do you own a black extended cab pickup truck with license number RJP9980?"

In the time it took for Mark's heart to take another beat, the man's tone went from friendly to ice. "Who wants to know?"

"Sorry, I'm Officer Mark Trask in Lansdale, Wisconsin. This vehicle has been spotted in town recently."

"It was my truck. It was stolen a little over a month ago. No idea who took it. I filed the report with the Dubuque police, if you need to verify it. No wonder they haven't found it if it is in Wisconsin." He sounded frustrated.

"Was it a company vehicle?" Mark asked.

"Yep. Why?"

"It must have been repainted. There's no signage on it at all. Only a solid black truck."

"All of my vehicles bear those magnetic signs with the company logo on the door panels. It's much easier to move to a new vehicle and a lot cheaper than custom painting," Mr. Stephens explained.

"And easier to remove to hide a stolen one," Mark said.

"You're right. It's never happened before. I never thought about it working in reverse. Has my truck been in an accident?"

Mark hesitated. "Yes, but it wasn't damaged. We haven't arrested the driver yet. As soon as we do, I'll be in touch. Thank you."

Mark brought the rest of the team up to speed on his findings about the mysterious black pickup.

Chapter Twenty-Seven

There were no signs of the black pickup near the house when Mark and Domino went for their run on Thursday morning. But the feeling that all his moves were being observed made him shiver. These attempts on his life, or indirectly on Phil's, were beginning to wear on him. Waiting for the next misdeed was infinitely more agonizing than dealing with the actual mayhem when it finally occurred.

Work was typical for a Thursday. A few minor calls about domestic disputes, kids who failed to come straight home from a social engagement, and, of course, Miss Clover's sugar cookie reward.

Mark drove home past *Knitting Pretty*. The apartment lights weren't on but the store lights shone bright, as if the shop was open for business. He parked the truck at the curb and walked across the street. He saw Elsie pushing a large box across the floor toward the shelves on the far wall. Cocoa was making a nuisance of herself jumping on top of it. Mark reached for the doorknob and found it locked.

Good. She finally did what he had been asking.

He knocked.

Elsie looked over at the door, smiled, and waved. She pulled the keys out of her pocket while crossing the room. "Good evening, Mark. What brings you here at this time of night?" She relocked the door once he was inside and left the key in the lock.

"The better question is why aren't you upstairs in bed? Isn't it kind of late for stocking shelves?"

"I couldn't sleep. One of the things about living in the same place as your work means it's a short trip to come down and stop in for a bit. I'm finding it is both a good and bad thing at the same time. I never would have crawled out of bed at the house to come to the store in the middle of the night. Tonight, I couldn't make myself stay in bed upstairs."

"Do you want some help?"

"You know me, I'll always take some assistance from a tall, good-looking police officer. This box needs to be opened, and the yarn stocked on the shelves." She pointed to a small nearby table. "The box cutter is over there."

Cocoa lay sprawled across the packing tape line on top of the box Elsie wanted opened. Mark tried to scoot her out of the way. She hissed and swatted him with her paw. Elsie reached down to move her off the box. She hissed again. "You silly cat. What is wrong with you?"

The cat pounced on Elsie's arm and bit her hand hard enough to draw blood. Mark handed her his handkerchief to wrap around the bleeding wound. "You'd better clean it and put some antibiotic on it immediately. Has she been this way all night?"

"No. Most of the time she's been on her perch totally ignoring me. It's only this particular box she's interested in. I have a first aid kit behind the counter. I'll go wash this off and get the antibiotic ointment. I'll need your help to put a bandage on."

While Elsie tended to her puncture wound, Mark went to his truck. He returned with a pair of heavy duty, leather work gloves. He got Elsie's hand bandaged and put on the gloves. "I'll pick her up. Her teeth won't get through these. You can open the box while I hold her."

"Watch her back legs, they still have claws, and she knows how to use them."

Mark successfully captured Cocoa and held her close against his torso. He immobilized her back legs with one hand. She let out a deafening, angry yowl and kept crying. He'd never heard an animal sound so frantic or unhappy.

Elsie grabbed the box cutter and slit the top of the box. She opened the flaps. As expected, it was full of flat plastic bags with six skeins of yarn in each bag. She reached down and lifted the top bag out of the box.

Cocoa managed to free one back leg, twist around upside down, and strafe Mark's face. He dropped the cat. The feline ran straight at the box yowling and thumping against the side of it.

Elsie screamed.

And kept on screaming, all the while pointing a shaky finger at the box.

A hissing rattlesnake as big around as Elsie's wrist coiled on top of the next plastic bag of yarn in the box. It slowly raised its head with its tongue darting in and out until it was even with the top of the side. Cocoa continued taunting it by hitting the side of the box and yowling. The snake's tail rattled. Elsie screamed so much she began coughing and retching.

Mark tried to close two of the flaps. The snake was too high. In one swift move he flipped the box over, trapping the snake underneath the pile of yarn. He upended a small table and put it on top of the box hoping to weigh it down sufficiently to keep the snake confined inside. Cocoa stopped yowling, but continued circling the box, and finally, leaped atop the table adding her weight to hold it in place.

Mark called 911 for Wildlife Management assistance, then went to Elsie's side. "Please stop screaming. You're all right."

She began sobbing. He held her to his chest. Then she screamed and pointed. The snake's head appeared in a small crack between the box and the floor. It wasn't all the way out of the overturned carton yet. Cocoa jumped off the table and charged at the reptile batting its head with a paw. The rattle sounded from inside the overturned box.

Mark ran over and grabbed the cat by the scruff of its neck. The back door slammed opened. Sully and Siobhan rushed into the store.

Sully hollered, "Elsie, what's wrong?"

Mark signaled for him to look at the floor. "Stay where you are. I'm going to try and reposition the box so that it's trapped again." He thrust Cocoa toward Sully. "Take the cat."

Cocoa hissed loudly, jumped out of Mark's hands, and onto Sully's chest. Her back claws were fully extended refusing to retract no matter how hard Sully tugged at her. Elsie went to his side and they both headed to the back of the store to give Mark more room to trap the snake again. As soon as Cocoa was extracted from his chest and held tightly by his mistress, Sully charged to the front of the store.

The snake had slithered farther out of the box and seemed determined to reach Mark who was holding an empty box at his side trying to determine the best way to recapture the reptile. Suddenly, the rattler darted toward Mark.

A shot rang out. The snake crumpled dead only inches from Mark's boot. Sully stood nearby holstering a revolver inside his jacket. "No need to thank me, Officer Trask."

"Don't worry, I won't be." Mark glared at him. "You are an idiot."

Sully gaped at him, then smirked. "I just saved your life."

Mark shook his head. "No, you didn't. I have on my work boots. The snake's fangs couldn't have gotten through them. The Wildlife Management people, who would have *captured and relocated it*, are on their way. Do you have a permit for that weapon?"

"Of course, I do."

"A *Wisconsin* permit?"

"What does it matter? Why didn't you shoot the snake when you had the chance? You have your service revolver."

"I wasn't going to discharge my gun in here, if it wasn't absolutely necessary. If I could have trapped the snake, Wildlife Management would have disposed of it somewhere other than in the middle of Elsie's store."

A knock at the front door sounded. Mark walked over and let the Wildlife Management team in. "Sorry, the emergency has passed. Mr. Stalatti killed the reptile."

The agents walked over to the snake and stretched it out to a full seven feet. "Lucky for you, Mr. Stalatti, this isn't the Timber rattler or Swamp rattler we have around here. They're both protected. You could serve time for killing one of them. The question is how did an Eastern Diamondback get inside a package delivered to a yarn shop in Lansdale, Wisconsin?" the senior agent said. "May we take the body?"

"Sure," Mark said. He leaned close to the agent and kept his voice too low for anyone else to hear.

"You got it. I'll drop it by the station tomorrow," the agent said.

The agents took the snake's body and left.

Siobhan and Elsie got out the cleaning supplies and tackled evidence of the death scene on the floor. Mark signaled for Sully to follow him to the front of the shop. "How did you get in the back door?"

"It was unlocked. We heard screaming and assumed Elsie needed help," he said defensively. "You would have done the same,"

"Probably." He pointed to Sully's holster. "Do you always wear a gun?"

"No, I grabbed the holster and put it on coming down the steps."

"You need to come into the station tomorrow and get your weapon registered with the state of Wisconsin. I'll let them know what the situation is ahead of time. "

"Sure. I don't want to get in trouble with the local authorities. Is there going to be a problem with what happened here? With the shooting?"

"I don't know. Those determinations are way above my pay grade. The Wildlife Management agents will file their report, and I'll explain you have an unregistered gun. Someone else will decide what the penalty will be, if any."

"Fair enough. Do you need anything else from me?"

"No."

Sully walked over to Elsie and gave her a hug. "We

will be going unless there is anything you need…from me." The guy apparently didn't understand this wasn't the time to be making a play for her.

Elsie glanced over at Mark who was glaring at Sully. "I'm sure I'll be fine. Mark is here. Thank you."

After the Stalattis left, Mark embraced Elsie. "I was so glad when I stopped tonight that you had the front door locked. I don't want to fuss at you after all this excitement, but it's important you keep the back one locked, too—especially when you're alone in here before or after hours. You should probably keep the back door locked even when the store is open. You never know who may decide to come in when they find an opportunity." He gave her a squeeze.

She stayed in his embrace. "Are you saying this because it was Sully who came in?"

"No. I'm telling you what my concerns are. It wouldn't matter who came in tonight."

"I think you're jealous."

"I haven't made any secret of it. My feelings for you have absolutely nothing to do with this discussion. We're talking about safety, not your neighbor."

Elsie stood on tiptoe and kissed Mark's cheek. "Thanks for being here tonight. You need to put some antibiotic on that scratch on your face. Then it's time for us both to get some sleep."

"You're right. I'll treat it before bed. You lock up and I'll walk you home. I can walk around the block to get my truck."

"Not necessary. I promise to lock everything tight, march right upstairs, and straight to bed. Go out the front door. Please. I'm too exhausted to battle about it."

He bent down and kissed her. "Has anyone ever

told you how stubborn you are?"

"Never." She pointed to the front door. "Now go!"

He complied.

Chapter Twenty-Eight

On arriving home after his Friday morning run, Mark heard the landline phone ringing as he opened the door. He answered it out of breath.

"Did I wake you?" a voice asked softly.

Elsie.

"No. Just got back from my run. I couldn't sleep in this morning. I was still too keyed up from yesterday. How about you? Did you get any sleep?"

"I went out like a light. My body had exhausted its supply of adrenalin. There was nothing to keep me awake. I'm sure you have things to do. Domino is probably staring pathetically at you because you haven't gotten his food yet."

"Do you have a vision phone? Pathetic is the perfect description of his expression." Mark chuckled. "Did you need something?"

"No. I was thinking about you and wanted to hear your voice."

He couldn't suppress a smile. "I like hearing that, talk as long as you want."

"Thanks again for last night. You seem to know when I am going to need rescuing. Talk to you later."

"Goodbye."

Nice to know Elsie liked his voice.

Ring.

Mark answered the phone. "Did you want to hear

my voice again?"

"Not really."

Pop Skelton, not Elsie.

"Oh, Pop, I thought you were someone else."

"Better check caller ID before you start cooing into the phone. You might get yourself into deep trouble." Pop laughed. "We've got the window glass in for your truck. Could you bring it by this morning?"

"Yep. Let me hop in the shower and I'll be over in about an hour."

He called Elsie back. "Could you meet me at Pop Skelton's in about an hour? They have the glass for the truck."

"I'd love to see you, but remember, I don't have a car."

"I'm an idiot. I'll talk to Phil. See you later."

Mark popped in the shower, got dressed, and called Phil.

"Do you have time to bring me back from Pop Skelton's in a few minutes? I need to drop my truck off to get the windows replaced."

"Sure. Can I follow you over there? I'm not exactly certain where it is," Phil said.

"Can you leave now?"

"On my way."

****

A little later, Phil dropped Mark off at work. Thankfully, it was a quiet shift. He wasn't certain he could handle more drama.

Pop and Mike Skelton delivered Mark's truck to the station with its new windows installed and sparkling clean. He'd put so much money in the old girl recently she looked really good. His grandfather would be

210

pleased.

Mark hadn't talked to Elsie since this morning. He left work planning to drive by the shop and see if any lights downstairs or in her apartment were on.

Two blocks from the station headlights zoomed toward him. At the last second, the black pickup fell back into its own lane. The vehicle made a rapid, two-wheel, U-turn, and it approached fast behind Mark. It thumped hard into Mark's back bumper, then eased off preparing to hit him again.

Mark increased speed and checked for oncoming traffic. When the pickup had almost overtaken him, he pulled the steering wheel as far to the left as possible, executing an unexpected U-turn leaving him hood-to-hood with the rogue truck.

The black pickup immediately shifted into reverse increasing speed and turned right at the corner while still moving backward. Mark pulled in front of him blocking his exit. He tried backing up farther but hit the retaining wall at the end of the street—he'd turned down a dead-end street. Mark called 911 for backup and stayed in his idling truck, blocking the way out.

Within minutes, two patrol cars joined Mark at the end of the street. The officer from one cruiser got out and advanced toward the pickup. The driver revved the engine threatening to run down the officer and/or the barricade blocking him. A third police car drove over the curb and down the street then set crossways in front of the dangerous vehicle. While staying behind his cruiser as a shield, the officer drew his revolver and ordered the driver to get out of his vehicle. The truck's engine roared loudly again. The officer fired into the air above the driver. The engine sound immediately silenced, and the blond-headed driver stepped out of the truck with his arms extended and hands over his head.

He was a large man, had at least six inches on Mark. A sleeveless T-shirt stretched tightly across his chest. He was broad across his shoulders and was in good physical shape, except for a developing beer gut. His left arm was covered with tattoos of devils and dragons. His right arm had a heart tattoo with 'Sweet Adeline' written inside it.

Who had been menacing him for more than a month using a stolen vehicle? Mark got out of his vehicle and recognized the man immediately.

Elmer Claridge.

Mark had been called out on a domestic dispute shortly after he joined the force. At the house, he found Elmer in the yard brandishing a shotgun. Periodically, he fired in the direction of his wife of five years who stayed on the porch despite Mark warning her to go inside the house. One of the random shots nicked her shoulder. In the confusion after she was hit, Mark was able to get Elmer to the ground and hold him there until backup arrived.

It wasn't the first time the Lansdale police had been dispatched to the Claridge home for a domestic dispute. There had been four other situations in the past eight months. The violence had escalated from fists and bloody noses to shotguns and injuries requiring medical attention.

Adeline Claridge finally had had enough. She filed charges against her husband. And she didn't cave and drop them, like Elmer had convinced her to do the two other times she'd filed a complaint. Mark arrested him. He was convicted on felony battery and sentenced to eight years in state prison. While he was incarcerated, Adeline filed for divorce and moved to Montana where the rest of her family lived.

The officer finished handcuffing Elmer Claridge. The prisoner spit on the arresting officer's boots. As Mark approached him, he broke free of the policeman's grasp and charged at Mark roaring like a raging bull. "You S.O.B.—you're the reason my sweet Addy left me. You talked her into it."

Mark sidestepped the man barreling toward him and another officer tackled him.

Claridge kept screaming. "You don't deserve to be happy after what you did to me." He spat at Mark but missed. He continued screaming as they loaded him into the back of the cruiser.

Could this nimrod be responsible for Elsie's woes? Because Claridge knew she was important to him? He followed the police cars back to the station and talked to the arresting officers about the unsolved crimes at Elsie's house and shop.

No one could get Claridge calmed down enough to ask him about other crimes. They booked him for assault of a police officer—multiple counts which included attempted vehicular manslaughter. Tomorrow they would interview the prisoner in more depth.

Mark drove home by way of Elsie's. He was glad to see her place dark. He'd call her in the morning and tell her about Elmer Claridge. At least the mystery of the black pickup truck had been solved. And maybe more.

****

When Mark came in from his morning run, he called Elsie and invited her for lunch at Whistler's after

Knitting Pretty closed at noon. He told her he had important news.

Mark parked in front of the shop. He was a little early and Elsie was with a customer. He walked down the street to peek in the windows of *Sips to You* which looked to be at least half full of patrons seated at the small tables scattered throughout the coffee house. He walked a little farther and looked in the front window of *The Book Nook*. People were milling around the store and lined up six deep to check out.

It looked like the Stalatti siblings had found two unfilled niches in the downtown Lansdale business landscape. He wished their success wasn't right at Elsie's doorstep. He would prefer a little more distance between Sully and the woman he was beginning to wonder how he could ever live without.

About ten after twelve, Elsie walked out of the shop with her last customer and locked the door behind her. She waved at Mark. "Sorry to be late. I hate to rush people even when they come in at the absolute last minute. I know there are very few true yarn emergencies, but I'm the one to fix them if there are."

"I guess that makes us both first responders, right?" Mark laughed and Elsie joined him. "Is Whistler's all right? I'm kinda craving one of their fried green tomato BLT's."

"I haven't had one of those in years. It sounds wonderful." She grabbed Mark's hand smiling. "Lead on."

Muriel Whistler asked Mark quietly, "Is Poppy's section okay?"

"Sure." Mark winked. "We're friends again. Thanks for asking."

Poppy brought two ice waters to the table moments later. "Just the two people I wanted to see today."

"Why did you need to see us?" Mark asked.

"To thank you. After the let's-all-make-each-other-jealous dinner, Sully called to ask me out. We're having dinner tonight. I'm not telling you where—I want to be alone with him." She laughed. "He said if we hadn't met the other night, he never would have wanted to go out with me. He said I was charming in a small-town girl kind of way. Isn't that rich?" She batted her eyes mockingly.

"Sounds like things worked out very well," Elsie agreed.

"I think we'd both like the fried green tomato BLTs with French fries, right?" Mark looked at Elsie. She nodded.

"I'll put the order right in," Poppy said and left.

"So, what is the important news you couldn't wait to share?" Elsie asked.

Mark told about the truck chase last night, the arrest of Elmer Claridge, and his ranting about payback for his wife leaving him while he was in prison. "He didn't want me to be happy since he believed I was the cause of all of his unhappiness."

She raised her eyebrows. "And you think he is the one behind all the mayhem in my life, too?"

"I think it might be possible. The guy is clearly unhinged. He only got out of prison three months ago. Six weeks ago he stole the truck. The timing seems to point to him. We'll have to find some proof that links him to more than the vehicular threats to me. I'm so sorry I inadvertently pulled you into this mess."

"You have nothing to apologize for. I'm not

convinced it was all this Claridge guy." She took a deep breath. "I'm not a cop so I don't have the same instincts as you, but Hubert was murdered, and he wasn't directly linked to you. That's a pretty big escalation from threats and driving recklessly to murder of a stranger. Don't you think?"

"Maybe. Maybe not." He shrugged. "Like I said. The guy is totally nuts. We will wait and see what they find when he is questioned further. I'd be a lot more comfortable leaving you alone, if we've found the person harassing you. If it was the same man who had me in his sights, I'd consider it a bonus."

Poppy delivered their sandwiches and refilled their drinks. "Enjoy. I know I will tonight."

The BLT was as scrumptious as Mark remembered. Elsie enjoyed every bite.

"What have you got planned this afternoon?" she asked.

"I will be doing whatever Elsie says."

"Yea. I hate to ask for your help, but I haven't finished restocking everything we got in this week. After the other night, I'm a little reluctant to do it alone. I may need more protection than a hissing Siamese cat can provide." She gave him an exaggerated smile. "And Cocoa's muscles aren't nearly as well-developed as yours."

"My lady, your wish is my command," Mark said as he slid out of the booth. "Let's pay the proprietor and get to work." They walked back to her shop holding hands.

Chapter Twenty-Nine

Elsie was right. There was a lot to do. Fortunately, none of the parcels caught Cocoa's attention. The feline slept on her perch the entire time they were working.

Elsie stood with her hands on her hips surveying the store's full shelves, overflowing bins, and new product displays. "I feel like I should be paying you. You're helping me make the shop look better than it ever has." She walked over and kissed Mark's cheek.

"Hmm…that's a pretty good start."

The radio playing overhead started an old Frank Sinatra song. Mark swept Elsie into his arms and danced through the middle of the store. The song ended. Mark collapsed onto a nearby folding chair pulling Elsie into his lap. "Now, where were we? Oh, I remember." He gently turned Elsie's face to look at him, then he softly, tenderly kissed her. She quickly returned the favor.

"Has anyone ever told you what a good kisser you are, Mark Trask?"

"Of course, legions of women—my smooches are legendary."

She cuffed him. "You are totally incorrigible."

"Would you rather I were corrigible?"

"No. I'd rather you say yes to staying for supper. I have the fixings for a delicious pasta dish and the perfect bottle of Italian red wine to go with it."

"You had me at say yes. What can I do to help?"

"Run next door before Siobhan closes and pick up some cannoli. Hers are freshly made and so delicious. They'll be perfect for dessert."

"And if she's out of cannoli?"

"The tiramisu."

"You got it. I'll be back shortly."

"Bring it upstairs. She can let you out her back door to come up to the apartment."

Mark ran over to Siobhan's shop and bought both desserts. The pasta was every bit as flavorful and delicious as Elsie had promised. After the delectable meal, they were both too full to sample either dessert.

"You can bring the desserts over to my house tomorrow. I was going to grill after church. I'd love for you to come. I'm trying to cheer Phil up. He's been depressed since he got home. I'm sure he'd be happy to help solve our excess desserts problem."

"It's a date. Speaking of which, I wonder how the Poppy and Sully date is going?"

"Probably swimmingly well. I think they're well-suited to one another."

"You aren't jealous because Sully made a play for Poppy?"

"Not in the least. I'm delighted his attention has gone in a different direction. He's apparently gotten the message you are not available."

"I'm not available?" She batted her eyes.

"Darn tootin'. You are spoken for ma'am…I hope you think that's a good thing," Mark said a little sheepishly.

"Don't worry. This lady believes it's a very good thing."

"It's getting late. Do you need help with the dishes?"

"No. Will you pick me up for Sunday school?"

"Yep. Be in the alley about eight forty-five." He kissed her. "Good night."

"Have sweet dreams."

"You, too."

****

Reverend Knox's sermon was on taking all your problems to Jesus, large and small. Elsie held Mark's hand through the entire service, sometimes squeezing it a little harder. Was she worrying about something specific?

Mark parked in the alley behind Elsie's building. They went upstairs together to retrieve the desserts. When they came out of the apartment, Siobhan was pacing across the balcony. She had a worried expression and was smoking a cigarette.

"Good morning," Mark said.

"Morning," Siobhan said.

"I don't think I've ever seen you smoke," Elsie said.

"I only do it when I need to calm down."

"We missed you and Sully at church. Come to think of it, Poppy wasn't there either. Are they the reason you need to settle your nerves?" Elsie asked.

"Sully didn't come home last night. I wonder if Poppy did."

"I have her number. Do you want me to check?" Mark asked.

"Please."

Mark tried her number. No answer. He left a voice message saying Sully needed to contact his sister, if

Poppy saw him.

"Would you like to come over for dinner? I'm grilling," Mark offered.

"Thanks. I'd better stay close to home. I'll take a rain check." Siobhan returned to pacing.

Elsie set the desserts on the floorboard behind her seat in the truck. "They must have had some date if Sully isn't home, and Poppy isn't answering her phone."

"No kidding. I hope they're both all right. Poppy is a major flirt, but I wouldn't have pegged her as a girl to stay all night with someone on the first date. She certainly didn't make me any offers like that."

"Maybe you're not as charming as the sophisticated Mr. Sullivan Stalatti." Elsie smiled and raised her eyebrows. "I do find it interesting that Poppy's number is still in your cell phone."

"Ms. Dennis, I think you're a little jealous and way too frisky this morning."

They didn't speak during the remainder of the drive to Mark's house but harmonized beautifully when the radio played a familiar hymn.

Mark opened the garage door and pulled in. It wasn't really necessary with Elmer Claridge in custody. He couldn't imagine anyone else who would vandalize his truck. All the same, it seemed like a good deterrent measure. He and Elsie each took a dessert and started up the stairs to the deck. He stopped when he heard peals of laughter. They continued to the top of the stairs.

A lovely woman with ebony, shoulder-length hair and sparkling eyes sat on the chaise lounge with her long legs extended the length of the cushions until they crossed at the ankles. Phil was in the chair next to her, leaning toward her listening intently and holding her hand.

Mark walked across the deck and extended his hand. "I have to be in the presence of Arianna Moonstone. I'd have known you anywhere from Phil's description. It's a pleasure to meet you. I'm Mark Trask and this lovely lady with the tiramisu is Elsie Dennis. It looks like dinner will be a homecoming celebration."

Mark shook hands with Phil's beaming bride, then Elsie did. He took the desserts into the house and came back out with a *Kiss the chef* apron on. "The steaks are marinating. Glad I had four. I know Elsie and Phil are medium rare steak eaters. What about you, Arianna?"

"Sorry, Mark. I don't eat steak except once in a blue moon. I will try everything else."

"Arianna, are you here to stay?" Elsie asked. "Oh, I'm sorry. It's really none of my business."

"Please don't apologize. First, it depends on whether Phil wants me to stay after all that has happened." She smiled, her eyes never leaving her husband. "If his answer is yes, then I will."

"Arianna only arrived five minutes before you got home. I'll answer her first question. Yes. Yes. Yes. Stay with me forever." Phil leaned over and kissed her.

"The grill is preheating. Would you come in the house and help me with the salads and potatoes?" Mark led Elsie into the kitchen.

The whole time Elsie and Mark were working in the kitchen, Arianna and Phil had their heads together. There was laughter. There were tears. After half an hour, Phil came in the kitchen. "It's okay to start dinner. We still have a lot to discuss, but we've gotten a good start on the important things. Come back outside."

Mark started potatoes in the microwave, grabbed the marinating steaks, and made his way to the grill. Elsie set the picnic table.

"Mark shared a little about you, but I'd love to hear the story of how you two met and married. I'm a sucker for a good romance," Elsie said.

Over the perfectly grilled steaks, Arianna shared their love story. Finally she said, "Phil left Philadelphia without me because of my mom. I got my mom moved to upstate New York to her sister's and she told me to go find Phil to write the happy-ever-after ending for our tale. Once I knew she was safe, I caught a plane for Wisconsin."

"And I couldn't be more delighted," Phil said.

"You have a beautiful name perfect for a fairytale princess—Arianna Moonstone—it fits you. I should have chosen better. Mine is a cow's name," Elsie said.

"She is as exquisite as I thought she would be when I first heard her name," Phil said.

Arianna's eyes filled with tears.

"Darling, what's wrong?" Phil asked.

"Arianna Moonstone is a make-believe person. My real name is Hazel Eunice Hazzard. I hate that name." Tears slipped down her cheeks. "When I am with you, I feel like I truly am Arianna Joy Moonstone."

"Then you shall continue to be with one minor addendum—Arianna Joy Moonstone Hughes. I want you to love your name as much as I love the woman who has adopted it."

"Thank you, Phil." She laid her head on her husband's shoulder.

Elsie and Mark left the newlyweds alone to sort out

the rest of their combined future.

When cleanup was done, Elsie and Mark went into the living room and sat side-by-side on the sofa. He put his arm around her shoulders and hugged her closer. "I'm happy for Phil. I'm so glad it is working out for him."

"What a romantic story they'll have to tell their children," Elsie said dreamily.

"More romantic than 'Kids let me tell you how your dad's skill with a screwdriver made me positive he was the one and only guy for me.'?"

"The Hugheses will have a romantic story, but ours will be sweet and heroic, too."

"Heroic?"

"How many mothers can say 'Your father pulled me out of a burning house'?" Elsie said softly.

"Sounds like you're already thinking about our mythical children."

Elsie didn't say anything. She leaned closer to him.

Mark stood, then got down on one knee in front of Elsie. "I think those wonderful children need to know how I proposed to their mother." He clasped her hand in his. "Nothing would make me happier than for you to say you'll be my bride and the mother of my children."

"You mean if you actually ask me?" Her eyes twinkled.

"You drive a tough bargain." He stayed on his knees. "Ms. Elsie...I don't know your middle name."

"Joyce."

"Ms. Elsie Joyce Dennis will you, please, marry me?"

She blinked trying to stem the flow of tears.

"I hope those are happy tears."

"Yes, they are. I would be delighted to marry you, but…"

"Hooray…what do you mean but?"

"You need to know what you're getting into. We need to talk."

He sat next to her. "Okay. Talk. I'm listening. What do I need to know?"

"Not tonight. Let's savor the pure romance of this moment until tomorrow. Or even the next day. I love you, Mark Trask."

"And I love you, Elsie Joyce Dennis."

Elsie smiled. "Please remember that no matter what else happens."

"There's nothing you can say that will change how I feel about you one iota."

Phil and Arianna walked into the living room.

"Did we infect you?" Phil asked.

"I think we were already bitten by the love bug. You only hastened the progression of the disease." Mark laughed. "Looks to me like there are lots of changes on the horizon around here."

Chapter Thirty

Whistler's was buzzing when Mark arrived for a late lunch. Poppy had not come in to work, nor had she called, and no one could raise her on her cell phone. Susie and Doris were worried as they knew she'd been out with Sullivan Stalatti on Saturday night.

Susie came to take Mark's order. "You having the meatloaf special?"

"With mashed potatoes and green beans. I'd like a small salad with French dressing. No tomato," he added.

"You got it." Susie went to the back, put in his order, then returned to Mark's table and plopped down in the seat across from him. "Do you think Poppy is all right? She's never missed a shift at work unless she was so sick she couldn't get out of bed. Even then she'd call so we could get a sub for her."

"You're right," Mark said. "It's very out of character for her. I heard Muriel talking when I came in; she was wondering if Poppy and Sully eloped. I can't really see it. I guess we won't know for certain until one or both of them reappear."

A *ding* sounded from the back. "Your food is ready."

Susie delivered Mark's meal and left him in peace to eat. Would Poppy have run off with Sully in a moment of passion? Even if she was willing, he couldn't imagine Sullivan Stalatti being swept away…by anyone. He was way too self confident to give into any woman's whim.

Mark stopped at *Knitting Pretty* before he went into the station. Elsie was with a customer. He stood by the front door and scratched Cocoa's ears as she lolled on her lofty perch. Soon he had her purring like a little motor. He looked around at the shop. The myriad of colorful yarns blended together in a peaceful, calming mosaic. He had a little burst of pride at his part in creating the beauty around him.

Elsie walked the customer laden with three large-handled bags to the door and opened it for her. She closed the door and stepped into Mark's waiting arms. He kissed the top of her head.

"What's your day been like?" he asked.

"Surprisingly busy. I think it's mostly nosy people stopping by after they've been to grab a latte and wander around the bookstore. They're hoping I have the inside skinny on Poppy and Sully's possible elopement."

"Whistler's is buzzing with the same rumor. How is Siobhan doing?"

"Soldiering on. She opened both the coffee shop and the bookstore this morning. She has some help and is supervising both operations. She told me when I went in to grab a latte that she was glad they put the opening in the wall between the stores to make it easier for one person to manage both. She hasn't heard a word from Sully. He's not answering his cell either. She called the state police to see if there'd been any auto accidents. Nothing."

"Poppy didn't call in and isn't answering her

phone. There's really nothing to do until they come home or contact someone," Mark said. "They haven't technically been gone long enough to file a missing person's report. I came to check and see how you're doing. Holler if you need anything." He kissed the top of her head again, appreciating the floral scent of her shampoo.

She kissed his cheek and opened the door for him.

****

Mark looked at the large man slumped over the table behind the one-way glass. The two detectives across from him continued to pepper him with questions. No matter what he confessed, one thing was certain. Elmer Claridge was headed back to prison. Stalking a police officer with the intent of vehicular manslaughter was definitely a parole violation. The man was totally unhinged. He emphatically denied having anything to do with any of Elsie's woes—or even to knowing who Elsie and Hubert Dennis were. He became almost hysterical when they questioned him about the rattlesnake. He couldn't hardly look at a snake, much less capture one and pack it in a box for someone to find. Mark decided he was no longer in danger from Elmer Claridge's long-festering delusions put into action.

Unfortunately, whoever was menacing Elsie was still out there. He no longer believed Hubert was the primary target. The evil behind this trail of chaos was after Elsie Dennis—for reasons he didn't understand. Yet.

Could Elsie have known all along who was responsible and not have told him or asked for his help before now?

A call came into the station at ten-fifteen p.m. from Siobhan Stalatti. There had been an accident. Elsie was asking for Mark to come right away. They were both in the Stalatti apartment.

The sergeant told Mark to take his truck to the scene and he would follow in a cruiser so Mark could stay with Elsie. They wasted no time getting there. Mark and the policeman parked in the alley on the Stalatti side behind the stores. There was a pile of iron and cement debris in the alley directly under Elsie's second-story doorway, blocking the rear entrance to her shop.

Mark took the stairs to the balcony outside the Stalatti apartment two at a time. He pounded on the door. An ashen-faced Siobhan Stalatti answered. "She's in here on the sofa in the living room."

Mark and the sergeant followed Siobhan through the kitchen into the living room where Elsie sat on the gray plaid sofa. Tears tracked down her cheeks. Mark went and sat down beside her. She grabbed his hand and held it without speaking.

"Elsie, what happened?" he asked.

She shook her head. She couldn't speak.

"Maybe I can tell you," Siobhan said. "After we both closed for the night, Elsie and I had a bite to eat in my shop."

"What about the railing?" the sergeant asked a little impatiently.

"Thanks, Siobhan. I think I can talk." She squeezed Mark's hand. "After dinner we went to Siobhan's apartment for a nightcap. Then I walked across the balcony to my place. I leaned on the railing looking at the stars and the full moon. When I turned to unlock my door, I heard a loud crack. The railing started to fall. I jumped away from it. The railing tore away from the wall and fell to the ground taking part of the concrete balcony with it." She hesitated. "If I'd been two seconds slower, I would have been on the ground, too. Probably under the debris...dead...or at least severely injured." Tears streamed down her cheeks. "I can't take much more." Mark held her closer gently rocking her back and forth.

The sergeant asked, "Was there any damage on this side of the balcony?"

"I didn't see any cracks," Siobhan said. "The stairs leading to her apartment are intact. It's only the area directly outside her door which seem to be affected."

"Did you see anyone out here earlier today?" the sergeant asked.

"We were both so busy, there could have been an army of people out there and we'd never have noticed," Siobhan said.

"I'm going to have a structural engineer come out first thing tomorrow and investigate things in the daylight," the sergeant said. "Where are you two staying tonight?"

"Elsie's welcome to stay in our guest room," Siobhan offered.

"I'm not comfortable with either of you staying here," Mark said. "Polly Rogers is a night owl. Let me see if she could stand some overnight guests." He went into the kitchen and called Polly.

A few minutes later Mark returned. "Polly has two rooms ready and waiting. Siobhan, pack a bag. Elsie, Polly said you left a few things there earlier so you're all set for tonight."

Mark herded the shocked women down to the police car and followed them to Polly Rogers's house. Polly opened the door as soon as they pulled in the driveway.

"Mark, I'm glad you remembered how late I stay awake. I'm happy for the company. Elsie, you can take your old room; Siobhan can have the room across the hall. There are toiletries on the shelf in the bathroom. Help yourselves." Polly led them to the stairs, then returned to the kitchen.

"Thanks, Polly. They didn't need to stay at a possible crime scene and I didn't think they should be alone," Mark said. "You've got my number. If you need me, I can be over here in a couple of minutes. We'll get out of your way. Have a good night."

Mark and the sergeant left. They briefly compared notes standing in the driveway, then Mark went home and the officer back to the station.

Elsie wasn't the only one who couldn't take much more. Mark was right there with her.

****

Mark and Domino jogged past Polly's house on Tuesday morning.

"Hey, wait!" Elsie called as she ran down the driveway. "I hoped I'd see you this morning."

"I'm surprised you're already awake." Mark slowed the pace a little to allow for conversation while in motion.

"I hit the bed and didn't move until about an hour ago. I'm beyond exhausted, mentally and emotionally."

"How is Siobhan doing?"

"I think she was down at her store by six-thirty to open for the morning regulars. She's managing both stores because she doesn't want to lose momentum after yesterday's grand opening. She's more than a little miffed at Sully for leaving her holding the bag."

"I hope he is just being inconsiderate and there isn't a problem somewhere."

When they reached the park, Mark sat down on a bench and Elsie happily plopped down beside him panting heavily. Domino sprawled out on the grass with his tongue lolling out of his mouth.

"I know it's crazy with the investigation going on about the balcony collapse, but tonight is the date we invited Chief Davis and his wife to come to dinner at my house to see our landscaping work. I already planned to take a personal day today to get some other things done."

"I'd completely forgotten about the invitation," Elsie said. "Let's go ahead with it. What do you think about adding Phil and Arianna, and Polly and Siobhan to the invitees?"

"Great idea. They should all meet one another. Maybe getting to know some more people in Lansdale will help Arianna decide she wants to stay here. I'll get more brats and hamburger out of the freezer."

"I'll fix potato salad and coleslaw before I open the shop. I'm sure Polly won't mind me using her kitchen—especially if she is invited to eat with us. Do you like baked beans?"

"Sounds great. Is that too much for you to get done?"

"No. What about getting one of the cold watermelons from Bob's Market for dessert? And maybe some of their chocolate lava brownies? I'll let Siobhan and Polly know they have a dinner date."

"Perfect. I'll go to the grocery store later this morning. I'll call the Davises to tell them we're going to be a bigger party. Sounds like a good plan. I better get home to get it done!"

They returned the way they'd come. Domino whimpered, but finally got off the grass and slowly followed behind them.

Mark swung by the station on his way to the grocery store. The building inspector had signed off on the balcony at Elsie's when it was first completed. He and the state inspector were there now with a structural engineer to determine how the railing and half the balcony had crashed to the ground. Chief Miller promised to call Mark as soon as they had any definitive news.

He also learned Elmer Claridge's hearing was scheduled for next month. Until then, he'd remain a guest of the county for violation of his parole.

Chapter Thirty-One

Polly and Siobhan arrived with Elsie about six o'clock carrying the food they prepared from Polly's house to Mark's. The Davises arrived on the dot at six-thirty, bearing a huge bowl of colorful fruit salad.

Phil and Arianna came out on the deck a few minutes later. Elsie introduced them to everyone. They visited on the deck drinks in hand enjoying an appetizer tray and the beautiful flowers in the newly landscaped yard.

"You did a wonderful job placing the plants, so they show off the best," Mrs. Davis said. "Did you have professional help?"

"You're looking at my professional help. Elsie has a gift for putting together colors," Mark said as Elsie blushed.

"All you have to do is look around *Knitting Pretty* to see her artistic abilities," Polly said.

"Glad I could inspire you," Chief Davis said with a smile and a wink. "Honey, we need to get a birdbath like that for our yard."

"I like the hummingbird feeder, too," Mrs. Davis said.

Soon perfectly charred brats and juicy hamburgers were ready to eat. Everyone took their plates to the grill and selected their first helpings.

Soon laughter echoed through the yard. There was

lots of discussion about living in a small town versus the big city between Siobhan and Arianna. No one mentioned Sullivan Stalatti being missing or Elsie's recent near accident. Everyone stuck to less controversial, more pleasant topics like weather, the high school football prospects for the coming school year, and the beautiful surroundings.

After the Davises left for home, Arianna and Phil helped clear the table and clean up, then said their goodnights and retired to their apartment upstairs. Mark was pleased with the impromptu dinner party. He and Elsie made a good team. He realized it more every day.

Polly and Siobhan were about to leave when Mark got a call. He held up his hand signaling them to wait. When he ended the call, he asked the ladies to sit back down a moment. "That was Chief Miller. He apologized for calling late, but thought we'd want to know what the inspectors and engineers found today when they evaluated the balcony outside Elsie's apartment."

"Did the workmen use sub-standard materials or something?" Siobhan asked.

"No. Nothing like that. The state building inspector said all the material seemed to be premium grade which is the same thing the local guy said when he initially approved the job."

"What was it then?" Polly asked.

"The bracing below the balcony had been tampered with as well as the point where the railing met the wall and the stair steps on Elsie's side of the balcony. Bolts had been removed or severed so they were no longer connected to anything. The engineers believe it had to have been done very recently. In short, it had been intentionally sabotaged, apparently, with the intent to harm Elsie." Mark stopped for the information to sink in.

Elsie laid her head on her arms on the table and sobbed loudly. Polly on one side of her and Siobhan the other both patted her back. Polly handed her a tissue. She straightened up. Tears streaked down her cheeks.

"This means it was always me they were after," she said. "It was never Hubert. My home burned to the ground because someone was trying to kill me, not him." She blew her nose. "I was certain it was someone from Hubert's past since the fire started in his room. It's crystal clear that someone wants me dead. I don't think they're going to stop until I am lying in the grave next to Hubert." She wiped her cheeks with the wadded-up tissue.

Mark reached across the table and grasped both Elsie's icy cold hands in his own much larger, warmer ones. "Has anyone harassed or threatened you that you didn't report?"

She shook her head vigorously.

"Any financial or business misunderstandings at the store? Someone threatening to sue you? Or take other legal action?"

Again. A head shake.

"Do you have any idea who is behind all of these attacks?"

Elsie stared into Mark's eyes unblinking. She squeezed his hands hard. She moved her lips. No sound. No words. Tears began anew.

Mark walked around the table and hugged her. "C'mon, it's late. I'll walk you home. We can discuss this in morning. After a good night's rest everything will become clearer. You look dead on your feet."

Mark walked the trio back to Polly's house. He asked Polly to keep a special eye on Elsie who, he was sure, was in shock from this most recent news. As a police officer he'd faced people who tried to kill him, but it even unnerved him when Elmer Claridge was stalking him. Why would anyone want to harm the proprietor of a small yarn and fiber shop in Lansdale, Wisconsin? This wasn't making any sense. He had to be missing some important pieces.

****

Mark jogged over to Polly's the next morning. Polly answered the door shaking her head. Elsie was at the kitchen table still in her nightgown. Her bloodshot eyes told him he hadn't seen all of the tears Elsie shed last night. He had never seen her so pale. He slapped on a broad grin and went over to her, leaned down, and kissed her cheek.

"Good morning. It is a glorious, sunny day out with a bit of a breeze. Domino slept in this morning. Would you like to go on a short run with me?"

Elsie peered over her coffee mug at him. "Your dog can't go running with you so I'm second choice?" The words dripped with sarcasm.

"You know that is not what I meant. I can see you are neither dressed for nor in the mood for a run. I'll be back about eight-thirty to take you to work. We can stop at Siobhan's for a latte, and I'll help you open the shop. Okay?"

She barely glanced at him. "Sure."

He kissed her again and left to run the rest of his route.

Polly refilled her own cup of coffee and offered

some to Elsie who shook her head. The older woman sat down across the table from her. "I know you've been through a more than rough patch, but Mark Trask is the last person you should give a hard time. It is very clear the man loves you and he's trying his level best to find out who is harassing you. Cut him a little slack."

Elsie smiled weakly. "Mikal said you were the queen of tough love. I guess I just got a little taste of it."

"Caleb's Mikal told you that? She's never gotten any of it, although my grandson certainly did in the beginning. Yes. You did get a little dose of it—whether you wanted it or not. You needed it."

Elsie pushed away from the table. She walked to Polly's side, bent, and kissed her cheek. "Thanks for caring enough to jerk me out of my pity party. If Mark is stopping back at eight-thirty for me, I'd better go get dressed."

****

Siobhan made Elsie and Mark their lattes herself. "Go through my shop to the alley. They're hard at work repairing the mess already."

They walked out to the alley. This time the balcony was held in place by multiple metal I-beam legs with a metal plate and frame spanning them to hold the concrete balcony solidly in place. The railing would be bolted to the balcony at the point where it was firmly supported by the legs extending to the ground. They had taken down the Stalatti side and were reconstructing it the same way. The construction engineer came over to talk with them and declared this balcony could withstand hurricane force winds. Surprisingly, they expected to finish it all in one day. If they met their target and passed inspection in the morning, Elsie and Siobhan would be able to move back in tomorrow afternoon.

They went back into the coffee shop to finish their drinks. "It looks really solid. I'm glad we won't have to worry about any further balcony falls," Siobhan said.

"Me, too. Now all we need to know is who sabotaged it to begin with," Elsie said.

"You're right. I'll go and buy some wireless security cameras today. They should be simple to install and can record activity to your computer or phone or both. Siobhan, do you want me to get enough cameras to cover your side of things, too?"

"Yes, please. I'm sure Sully would approve it, if he were here. It will make me feel safer knowing who is frequenting our alley."

"I don't know why I didn't think of it sooner. I can install the cameras tomorrow after we get access to the alley again and before I go to work. Well, Ms. Dennis, we'd better get *Knitting Pretty* open before someone has an emergency and the Yarn Doctor isn't in."

After seeing Elsie into the shop, Mark headed to a local security service where a buddy of his gave him the best options for the cameras. Of course, he also offered to set the building up with a state-of-the-art security system. Mark said he'd relay the offer. For now he needed the cheaper cameras they could quickly put in place.

Mark dropped the cameras off at Elsie's. She was with a customer. He ran next door and bought a salad and sandwich for each of them. Siobhan knew what Elsie liked best on the limited menu. When he returned the customer was gone. He carried the sack of lunch to the back counter. "Soup's on. C'mon and eat."

"I'm not hungry, Mark. Really."

"I happen to know you ate no breakfast and it has been a long time since last night's dinner. Sit. Eat. No arguments."

"I think you've been around Polly too much. She's rubbing off on you."

"Thanks. I'll take that as a compliment. Now, no talking. Just eating."

After they both finished, two customers came in. Mark cleaned up the counter while Elsie waited on them. She walked to the back to check them out. Mark gave her a quick kiss on the cheek and went home to get ready for work.

****

Chief Miller had also come to the conclusion Elsie Dennis, not Hubert Dennis, was being targeted. He'd started doing some research into her life before Lansdale. He couldn't find any Elsie Dennis fitting her age and general description anywhere in any law enforcement data base.

"Mark, are you sure she said they lived in Pennsylvania before coming here?"

"Yes. Hubert might not have since they weren't in the same place, but she definitely said Philadelphia."

"Something isn't jiving," the chief said. "The Elsie Dennis we know can't be found prior to a little over ten years ago. If we're going to get this mess resolved, I'll need to personally interview her."

"I understand, Chief. Can we wait a couple of days? She's still pretty shell shocked. I'll keep a close eye on her."

The chief winked. "I'm sure you will, Officer Trask."

Chapter Thirty-Two

On Thursday morning, Elsie joined Mark and Domino when they jogged past Polly's. "I figured I better take this last opportunity to run with you before I move back into the apartment."

"Looks like maybe you got a little sleep last night."

"I did."

"Everything is going to be all right."

"Polly would say 'from your mouth to God's ear'."

"Amen," Mark said with a smile, then accelerated to see if he could outrun Elsie.

They were almost to the picnic table in the park marking the end of the route when Elsie made a beeping roadrunner sound and tore around him. She was standing by the table with her hands on her knees panting when he arrived a few minutes later. "Show off," he chided her.

"No. Just proving to myself I still had it in me."

Mark grinned and took off back the way they'd come. At Polly's he waited for her. "Call me when you know for certain if you're approved to move in today. If there's enough time, I'll install the security cameras before I go to work." He kissed her cheek and coaxed Domino back to his feet to run the last two blocks.

Arianna and Phil were in the kitchen when Mark arrived home.

"What about some French toast?" Arianna offered.

"I'd love some. Phil, why didn't you get married a long time ago. I could get used to someone else making the coffee and the occasional breakfast."

"Don't get too accustomed to this service. I'm not sure how much longer we're going to be staying," Phil said.

"I thought you both liked it here."

"We do," Arianna said. "We're thinking ahead to the cold Wisconsin winter. Moving south looks very attractive since Phil can work from anywhere."

Arianna was a good cook. She made French toast exactly the same way Mark's mom did. Maybe it's something about learning to cook in Philadelphia. "Thanks. It was delicious. I need to hit the shower."

Elsie called at ten o'clock to say the new balcony work passed inspection with flying colors. She asked Mark if he could go by to get her things and Siobhan's at Polly's. He was happy to do it.

The new balcony and railing looked very sturdy. Mark installed ten cameras at various angles so that he was assured full coverage of the area. He added a monitoring app to Elsie and Siobhan's cell phones and both their home computers for permanent video storage. He also added the app to his cell phone. He wasn't being a crazy stalker. He'd tell Elsie about it— eventually when she was less on edge.

"Thank you for the security system. Tell me how much it cost," Elsie said. "I'll write you a check."

"I expect to be paid...not in dollars."

She raised an eyebrow. "What did you have in mind, Officer Trask?"

"A home cooked meal...no...three home cooked meals and one long over-due formal dinner date."

"Seems a little pricy, but I'm willing to be overcharged considering the workman came on short notice and stayed until the job was done."

"Boy, you're easy."

"How much does Siobhan owe you?"

"She has enough to deal with right now," he said. "I'll settle accounts with Sully when he returns."

"That's kind of you. No one has heard a peep from Sully or Poppy. The good news is they haven't appeared in a hospital or morgue either."

"If you're awake when I get off work, I'll check in on you."

"Actually, I was hoping you'd be the first person to stay in my guest room/office. I know it's silly, but I'm not comfortable being alone tonight."

"You've stayed in the apartment alone before."

"Yes, before I knew for certain someone was trying to kill me. Could you please stay?" Elsie's eyes threatened to spill the tears welling up in them. "I'll even take the futon and give you the real bed."

Mark wrapped her in an embrace. "You sleep in your own bed. I'd be happy to be your on-site security guard. I'll pack a bag. With Phil home for the moment, Domino will be taken care of. I'll see you before midnight." He tilted her chin up and kissed her softly.

"Have a good shift. Thanks for humoring me."

"My pleasure, Ms. Dennis."

He gave her a mock salute and left.

****

Since Chief Miller had not unearthed any additional information about Elsie Dennis of Lansdale, Wisconsin, he told Mark to tell her she needed to come in Monday afternoon to meet with him. The chief was certain whoever was threatening her was from her past, not Lansdale, and wanted to resolve the gaping holes in her personal history.

Mark took the call from Miss Clover. The older woman had heard about Elsie's apartment accident and was concerned about how Mark's young lady was doing.

Mark parked his truck in the alley behind Elsie's store at eleven forty-five and the security app pinged his phone to alert him there was activity. Good. Everything seemed to be working properly. It also told him someone was on the stairs and at Elsie's door. He knocked. No response. He tried the knob. Locked. Good. He knocked harder. He peeked through the gap in the blinds on the door. Elsie came racing across the kitchen in a bathrobe with her hair wrapped in a towel. She took the key off the magnetic hook on the refrigerator and unlocked the deadbolt and then the knob. She pulled the door open.

"I'm sorry. I got started with my shower later than I planned to."

"I didn't mind waiting. I was glad to see the door was locked."

Elsie blushed. "I have to confess, I didn't lock it until I was ready to take my shower."

"Given what's been going on, you need to automatically lock the door as soon as you come in and you need to keep the back door of the shop locked. Please do it, if for no other reason than to make me happy."

"Yes, sir."

Elsie turned away from him.

Mark reached out and bear hugged her from behind

resting his chin on her shoulder. "I care about what happens to you...and not just because I'm a police officer."

She turned to face him and snuggled against him resting her head on his chest. "I know you do. Thanks."

She led him to the guest room and adjoining bath. "Here's your bunk. Are you going to bed right away?"

"Not usually. I stay up a little while after I get home. I need some time to unwind. Do you want to talk?"

"I wouldn't mind. There is a lot I need to discuss with you."

"I'll grab a quick shower. Then we can sit down together."

Fifteen minutes later, Mark strolled into the living room in a white T-shirt with a football team logo on the chest and dark green P.E. trunks. He plopped down on the sofa next to Elsie who was dressed for bed in a blue flowered nightgown, matching robe, and pale blue fluffy mule slippers.

"Now we can relax and visit," Mark began. "Have you thought anymore about who could be behind this havoc in your life?"

"I have. I can't think of a single thing that has happened in the past ten years that would trigger Hubert's murder. Nothing."

"What about from before you moved to Wisconsin?" If he was going to be able to help her now, he had to understand her past.

"There was a dangerous situation I fled from in Philadelphia, but recently it was fully resolved. I can't imagine that episode could follow me here." She didn't look at Mark. "I took extraordinary efforts to make certain it didn't."

"I don't want to pry." He took her hand in his. "Can you tell me what the problem was in Philadelphia?"

"I don't see the point in dredging all of it up again." She pulled her hand out of his grasp. "Everyone involved is dead now."

"Except you?"

A tear escaped and ran down her cheek. "Yes, everyone except me."

"It has to be related. Don't you see? Please, let me help," Mark begged.

"I can't. They'll come for you, too." Elsie stared at him. "I can't risk you. I won't."

"I need to tell you something, but I don't want to upset you." He sandwiched her hand between his again. "Chief Miller has been doing some research as part of the investigation into Hubert's murder. He can't find any Elsie Dennis matching your age and description prior to you coming to Lansdale. He wants you to come into the station on Monday afternoon to discuss the gaps in your history with him."

She shook her head. "I won't."

"Elsie, it's a criminal investigation. You will appear as requested or you'll be a guest in the jail."

She took a deep breath and looked at him with teary eyes. "Will you come with me?"

"Of course." He leaned toward her and hugged her tightly.

The discussion was over. Elsie went to bed. After sitting in the dark for what seemed like hours, Mark did, too.

Chapter Thirty-Three

Mark woke at seven and rapped lightly on Elsie's bedroom door.

"I'm awake," she answered immediately.

"Do you want to go for a run?" He hoped he sounded enthusiastic.

"Not really."

"Do you mind if I go? It'll be a different route. A little variety."

"Have a ball," she said flatly.

He unlocked the door and hung the key back in place. He relocked the knob and pulled it closed behind him.

****

Forty-five minutes later, he took the stairs up to Elsie's apartment. He knocked. No response. He knocked harder. And again. Finally, Elsie came down the hall in her nightgown rubbing her eyes. She unlocked the door and let him in. "Sorry." She yawned. "I finally fell asleep after you left."

"You mean you hadn't slept all night?"

"Very little. I had too much on my mind."

"I'm sorry. I shouldn't have told you about Chief Miller's request yet. I didn't think it would keep you from sleeping."

"It wasn't only the chief's request. It's this whole situation. I can't believe something that happened so

247

long ago is continuing to haunt me, menace me. I sacrificed so much to try and avoid this happening. Everything." Her voice quivered. "My whole life."

"Are you ready to talk about it? I'm a good listener."

"I know you are, but I'm not ready yet. Go take your shower. How do you want your eggs? Bacon, ham, or sausage links?"

"Scrambled and links." He kissed the top of her head. "Thanks."

Mark quickly showered and dressed. Elsie was at the stove when he walked into the kitchen. She put his breakfast in front of him then retreated to her room. Thirty minutes later, she reappeared dressed for work. Judging by the dishes in the sink, she'd never eaten a bite herself. He started to fuss at her but thought the better of it. He needed her to talk to him, not clam up to avoid being scolded.

"Your futon is pretty comfortable. The only thing missing was Domino snoring. Do I need to plan to bunk here tonight again?"

"I'll be fine."

He walked out of the apartment and down the stairs with her. He got in his truck and watched her unlock the back door to the shop. "Oh, thanks for the security app." She turned to him and said, "I'm getting pinged when people are around. Guess it's working."

"Yep. Be sure to lock the back door when you're inside." He wasn't certain she was emotionally ready to know he was monitoring the activity, too. At least, that's how he justified staying quiet. He smiled when he heard the deadbolt snap into place on the back door.

****

At five o'clock, Elsie flipped the sign on the front door from *Open* to *Closed* and locked the deadbolt. She reached overhead to scratch Cocoa's ears and was rewarded with a low purr.

She walked to the back of the store to balance the day's receipts. She took the cash out and carefully counted one hundred dollars—her starting amount for giving change—although fewer and fewer people used cash anymore. She put the starter cash in a manila envelope and slid it through the slot in the safe. Then she counted the rest of the cash for the bank deposit and wrote it on the slip. She slid it into the safe, too. She'd walk over to the bank and make the deposit in the morning before she opened.

She pulled the divider out of the drawer to double check that nothing was in the bottom of the register. She didn't usually take checks unless it was a long-time, reliable customer. If she did, they'd be stashed under the divider. There was a long, white envelope. She didn't remember putting it in there. She carefully pulled it out.

Her name—her real name—was carefully printed on the front in large, bold, block letters. Reading the name from her past made her hands tremble. The flap was tucked into the back of the envelope—not sealed. She opened it. Two pages drifted to the floor.

She picked up the paper that landed on the top. Another note from capital letters cut out of magazines:
REMEMBER
NO ONE IS GUARANTEED TOMORROW
NO ONE
She braced herself against the counter to remain standing and shook violently. She took a deep breath

through her nose and slowly let it out through her mouth. Then she took another. She forced herself to bend down and retrieve the other page that had fallen from the envelope. She gasped and closed her eyes tightly willing the picture in her hand to go away.

"No. No. No."

She stared at the page she'd laid on the counter. It was a picture of a dark gray granite headstone with two names engraved on it:

Kevin J. Tucker, Beloved Husband And Father
Delores M. Tucker, Beloved Wife And Mother

She began sobbing; her legs slowly crumpled, leaving her sitting on the floor. She lay down, crying uncontrollably. She was paralyzed. She wanted to die herself.

Exhausted, she passed out. Two hours later, she woke and stretched out of the fetal position she had curled into and slowly pulled herself to her feet. It hadn't been a nightmare. The picture remained on the counter.

She had seen her father's tombstone when they buried what was left of him after the horrible fire—the one she'd witnessed.

She always assumed her mother had been buried next to her father. It was intended for them to be together in eternity. But she'd never seen their resting place after her mother joined her father there. She had been living here. In Lansdale. In the witness protection program unable to go home—even when her mother was dying. She couldn't be there to care for her and comfort her and now, all those precautions appeared to be for naught.

Someone had found her. There wasn't room on the

headstone for a third name. Morgan Tucker, beloved daughter. Who was carrying out this delayed vendetta? She gathered the papers and put them back in the envelope, then put the envelope in her pocket. She needed Mark's help and much more.

Lord, please don't let it be too late to pull me back to the daylight, to safety.

****

Mark's shift began uneventfully. A shoplifter at the Five and Dime store turned out to be an elderly lady with dementia who had drifted away from her caregiver while they were shopping. The handkerchiefs she'd taken were paid for and no charges were filed.

At about six o'clock, Chief Miller called him into his office. "We finally got the report back from the National Ballistics database on the bullets that killed Hubert Dennis. It took so long because they were from a case over ten years ago in Philadelphia with a similar MO—arson to cover up a murder. A mobster and one of his henchmen went to prison for the crime, but the actual murder weapon and the shooter were never found." He passed the report across his desk. "It's more important than ever that we officially talk to Ms. Dennis to discover what her connection to this Philadelphia case is, if anything."

"I told her she needed to come in on Monday afternoon. She was upset about it. I know she's keeping a secret. She's afraid other people will be hurt, if they know what it is."

"It's our business to know all her secrets and to protect whoever needs it. We should try to see her before Monday, maybe tomorrow," Chief Miller said.

"Monday was good because her shop is closed on

Mondays. She'd have to close early or something tomorrow."

"Okay. As long as there are no other incidents. Do you want to share this report with her before the meeting?"

"It might help her be more prepared, if you would make me a copy."

The chief handed a copy of the report to Mark. "I thought you would want it."

Mark's cell phone text alert pinged.

—*Pls come home now. Urgent*—

It was from Elsie.

"That's her now. She said urgent. I don't see any alerts from the cameras I installed, but she would never call for me to come from work without a compelling reason."

"Go. Call if you need backup."

Mark struggled to stay below the legal speed limit all the way to Elsie's. He parked in the alley behind the building. There were no lights on in her apartment. He knocked on the back door of the shop. She immediately unlocked it as if she had been waiting just inside the door. She fell into his arms.

"Are you okay?" he asked, gently shaking her. "What happened?"

She stared at him with unblinking red eyes.

"Was someone here? Why are you still in the shop?"

"I need to tell you something. No—I need to tell you everything, if it's not too late."

He pulled out a folding chair. "Sit down." He gently lowered her on to it and knelt next to her. "What has happened?"

"You were right. Someone from my past is trying to kill me."

"Who?"

"I don't know, but I'm certain they're from my past. They have to be. It can't be anyone else."

"Someone from Philadelphia?"

She nodded.

"Maybe this is related. We got the ballistics back on the bullets that killed Hubert. Do you know anything about a decade old case in Pennsylvania?"

Her eyes got wider. She visibly paled.

"Over ten years ago a man was murdered and his business set on fire to cover the crime. The arsonist and the man who ordered the fire went to prison, but the murder weapon and murderer were never found. It was in Philadelphia. Does it sound familiar?"

She nodded again. A tear escaped and ran down her cheek.

"The weapon used to kill your brother is the same gun that was used to kill a man named Kevin Tucker ten years ago."

Elsie screamed as she fainted. Mark kept her from falling out of the chair. He gently lowered her to the floor and called for an ambulance. Then he called Chief Miller.

The ambulance crew revived Elsie. She refused to go to the hospital. Mark confirmed she had not hit her head when he assisted her to the floor. They helped her up to the apartment and agreed she could stay home, if she was not left alone. Mark said he would stay. After receiving an order from Dr. Lovelady in the Emergency Room, the medics gave her a sedative, saying sleep was the best thing for her.

Chapter Thirty-Four

Mark didn't go for a run when he woke. He didn't want Elsie to wake with no one in the apartment. He'd gone in her room several times during the night to check on her. The sedative did its job. She never moved out of the fetal position she'd curled into after getting in bed. One time he found her sobbing in her sleep. When he bent down and rubbed her back gently telling her she would be okay, the sound stopped.

He heard stirring in the bathroom. A few minutes later the shower came on. About half an hour later Elsie came into the kitchen where Mark was pulling a pan of bacon out of the oven. "Good morning, sleepy head. How do you want your eggs?"

"My eggs? Oh, scrambled with a little of the shredded cheese out of the refrigerator drawer, please."

"It's going to be a beautiful day. How would you like to go over to the river this afternoon and pretend we're fishing?" He tried to be upbeat and positive.

She sat down at the table. "I guess fishing would be a good way to relax."

Mark put a plate in front of her with the cheesy scrambled eggs, rye toast, and bacon. "Cup of coffee? Juice? Milk?"

"Yes."

"To which one?"

"All three, please."

He lined the drinks up in front of her. Mark sat at the small table on the opposite side. Elsie concentrated on the food in front of her.

"I'm glad to see you eating. I checked on you last night and it looked like you finally got some sleep."

She smiled weakly. "More like crashed and burned. Thanks for staying to babysit me."

"You were exhausted. I was glad I could be here, although I feel partially responsible for your distress. I didn't have to dump the ballistics findings on top of you just then."

She shrugged.

"Elsie, I think it would go more smoothly on Monday with Chief Miller if you and I talk about all this before we get there."

She wiped her lips with a napkin, pushed away from the table, and put her dishes in the sink. "You finish your breakfast. I'll be right back."

She disappeared into her bedroom. He heard drawers open and close, and a closet door slam shut. When Elsie returned, she walked over to the sofa. "Let's sit on softer seats. This may take a while." She patted the cushion next to her. Mark sat beside her.

"Could I say one thing before you start?" he asked.

"Sure."

"Elsie Dennis, I love you and there is nothing you can tell me about your past that will change my feelings in any way. Okay, you have the floor."

"Thank you, Mark. You keep running to my rescue. I think you need to know my whole story before you make any life-changing declarations."

"Duly noted." He settled back farther into the sofa cushions. "I'm listening."

"First, my name is not Elsie Dennis. It is Morgan Tucker."

Mark's mouth gaped. "Related to the Kevin Tucker of the ballistics match?"

"Yes." She took a deep breath. "He was my father."

"No wonder you fainted." Mark shook his head. "What are the odds of having your father and brother killed by the same weapon hundreds of miles and more than ten years apart?"

Elsie took a deep breath and slowly exhaled. "Hubert was not my brother. I was an only child. Hubert was the special marshal assigned to protect me while I was in the witness protection program. For his safety, and mine, I never knew his real name. When the men my testimony sent to prison died while still incarcerated, my official witness protection life did, too." She stopped and peered at Mark trying to read his face. "I didn't know until recently Hubert retired from the U.S. Marshal's office then also. He decided he liked living here and we continued the charade of being siblings."

"I'm a little confused." Mark cocked his head to one side. "Maybe you should start at the beginning."

She looked down at her hands, took a deep breath, then raised her gaze to his. "About eleven years ago, our family's business burned to the ground. Dad, Mom and I were all working in the store that day. Three of Dad's business associates came to meet with him. None of them saw me in the back storeroom, but I saw them. Mom was in the front of the store, helping a customer." She stopped and closed her eyes a moment. "Two of the men followed Dad to his office. After the customer left, the other man went to their car parked in the alley and returned carrying two large cans. The smell told me it was gasoline. He poured a trail through the store and directly to my father's office. The door opened and the two men came out of the office, but my father did not. When they reached the back door, a man I whose face I never saw left, then the older man said 'Finish' and went out the back door."

Her voice became markedly weaker. "The man who had poured the gasoline tossed a flaming rolled paper toward the office and the fire spread quickly. Then he went out the back door and I heard the car leave the alley." Tears ran down her face. "I found mom injured on a chair near the front of the store. She was badly burned before I was able to drag her into the alley behind the store. I went back inside and tried to get to my father. The heat drove me back outside. I couldn't try again because of all the billowing smoke."

"Then you know exactly how I felt when I couldn't rescue Hubert." He hugged her. "I'm so sorry. What did you do?"

"The business next door had called the fire department as soon as they saw the smoke. I called the police. I told them what I'd seen. The next several weeks were a blur. Dad's funeral. Mom's burn treatment, and her hysteria. They caught one of the men. I identified him as the one who poured the gasoline and lit the fire. I also identified the man who had ordered it done. The third man who pulled the trigger was never identified."

"I can't imagine. Weren't you frightened?"

"Yes." She nodded. "Especially after the man who ordered the hit and one of his henchmen appeared at our house one afternoon a week before the trial. Turns out the older man was a second cousin of my mother. I'd never met him because we didn't socialize with her side of the family. They'd come to the house to persuade me to not testify."

"Does *persuade* mean hurt you, if you didn't cooperate?"

"More. If I insisted on testifying, their intention was to kill me. Mom helped me escape. I did testify, but I never saw her after the trial. I was whisked away into witness protection only hours after the trial ended. An agent was assigned to play my older brother housemate, and I received the funds to start my own business. I sacrificed every bit of my former life to ensure justice for my father. Witnesses against The Family had a way of forgetting what they'd seen by the time the trial came around. I didn't. I couldn't let my Dad's death mean nothing."

"I know how hard it is to walk away from your past. I've done it. The difference is I could always decide to go back. I just haven't yet."

"What happened?"

"It's a long tale." He took a deep breath. "We're in the middle of yours. Let's finish one saga at a time."

"You and I moved to Lansdale about the same time. I've made a new life here with no contact from my past until about six weeks ago when these started coming." Elsie opened a large manila envelope and emptied its contents on the coffee table in front of them. She handed a newspaper clipping to Mark.

"This was the first one. It was delivered through the U.S. Mail to Elsie Dennis at my address here in Lansdale. Scachhi is the mobster I testified against—the

Don of The Family. I was notified by the authorities the guy who set the fire was killed by another inmate about five years ago while he was serving time for the arson charge. I had nightmares the night I received the newspaper clipping. I didn't sleep well for weeks."

"Did you go to anyone? Report it?"

"Hubert and I discussed it. There was no clue who had sent it. You can't even read the postmark. We decided to be extra vigilant. He believed it was someone who found out where I was but was never going to come here. They only wanted to scare me. They certainly accomplished that."

"How soon after you received the clipping did we find Hubert unconscious?"

"Less than a week. Honestly, neither of us connected it with the newspaper clipping. If it had been me instead of him, I think we might have. Then about a week after Hubert's hospitalization, this message was pushed through the mail slot and was on the foyer floor when I went to leave for work."

WE R WATCHING U

"Hubert and I had no idea who 'we' was. In hindsight, I should have had it dusted for fingerprints by the authorities, but I didn't. I put it in the envelope with the clipping and put them both in my safe at work."

"Smart thinking. When did the Stalattis move to town? Hey, have you got paper and pencil? I'll make some notes for our meeting on Monday."

Elsie grabbed a pad and ink pen off the desk and handed it to Mark. "Here you go. They arrived a couple of days after the first cut out letters message. Why?"

"Just curious. They're from Philly. They're Italian.

Maybe a connection?"

"Not every Italian living in Philadelphia is part of a mobster's family. Whomever is doing this is going to an awful lot of expense and wasting a lot of time, if they just want to take cold revenge on me." She sounded disgusted.

"Sorry, I interrupted. Continue." Mark made notes.

"Then there was the fire and Hubert's death about a week after receiving the first mail slot note."

He reviewed his mental calendar. "Right. And it happened only two days after you'd invited me and the Stalattis over for dinner after the rodeo."

"Right. Then I stayed with Polly until my apartment was ready. A day or two after I moved in here this note was slid through the mail slot in the shop door."

IT ISN'T OVER
NOT EVEN CLOSE
I'D SLEEP WITH ONE EYE OPEN
IF I WERE YOU

"The next terror was the rattler in the yarn shipment. And shortly later, the balcony collapsed. The final message was last night. I opened the cash register and in the bottom of the drawer were these."

Elsie unfolded the note and the picture of her parents' tombstone on the table. "I found it and apparently fainted. I was out for a while. As soon as I came to, I called you. How did someone put these in my cash register? I'm positive the back door was locked all day yesterday. And the register key has to be inserted to open the drawer."

"Where do you keep the register key?"

"In the little drawer under it."

"Was Sullivan Stalatti upset when you rebuffed his advances after the dinner out?"

"Obviously not. He has apparently run off with Poppy Caldwell. Why do you keep harping on him?" She was clearly annoyed.

"Because there are too many coincidences about him intersecting with you at critical periods in the last six weeks." He shrugged. "I could be wishful thinking."

"Because you're jealous?"

"Yep. I'll be the first to admit it. Chief Miller can objectively help us sort this out. I think this link to your past establishes the *why* your life is in danger. Now we have to determine the *who*—a much more difficult nut to crack."

She laid her head against his chest. "Thank you for being here for me."

He squeezed her shoulder. "Why didn't you tell me all this earlier?"

"You were dealing with a crazed black pickup-driving stalker and a mysteriously missing roommate. I didn't think I'd have your full attention." She looked up at him with teary eyes. "And after Hubert's death, I was afraid to involve anyone else for fear of their life being sucked into this chaotic vortex of evil swirling around me."

"Well, my mysteries are solved. Do you want me to call Chief Miller, and we can meet him now—today—while this is all fresh in your mind?"

Elsie shook her head. "I'm not sure I can be calm enough and I'm totally mentally exhausted. I'd rather wait until Monday."

"All right. Should I start calling you Morgan or are you going to stay Elsie?"

"I don't really like Elsie any better than Phil's wife liked Hazel, but until this is resolved, I think we need to stick with it. If someone hears you call me Morgan, they'll know you are aware of my past. It's knowledge that could be dangerous for both of us."

"Agreed. Thank you for telling me the truth. I think we need to relax the rest of the day. Do you feel up to a picnic lunch on the river?"

"Great plan. I'll be ready in a few minutes."

Chapter Thirty-Five

Mark had been right. Fishing—when you didn't care if you caught anything—was quite relaxing. They sat in the shade on the riverbank, absent mindedly bobbing their cane poles up and down periodically. All the talking had been done before they left Elsie's, so they sat in blissful silence. They managed to catch enough *keepers* to have dinner at Mark's and invited the Hugheses to join them.

Phil and Arianna announced they were moving to Alabama to get out of the cold Wisconsin winters and be in a more peaceful setting where they could start living again.

****

Sunday morning most of the congregation was seated when a couple walked down the aisle hand-in-hand to occupy the front pew. Poppy and Sully. Siobhan followed them. There were a few gasps and smiles, but no time to ask any questions. Reverend Knox started the service exactly on time.

Today's sermon was on the prodigal son. When Reverend Knox asked for prayer requests and announcements at the end of the service, Sullivan Stalatti stood and helped Poppy to her feet. "I'm sorry, if we caused any anxiety by our absence. I wanted to let you know Poppy Caldwell is now Poppy Stalatti, my bride. We've been in Hawaii on our honeymoon."

The congregation applauded.

Siobhan stood. "I'd like to invite everyone to *Sips To You* beginning at one o'clock today for a wedding reception for the happy couple. They'll be lots of food and drink. Hope to see you all there."

****

His sister must have had some advance notification the happy couple was coming home. A three-tiered wedding cake rested on the main table next to a large crystal punch bowl and matching glasses. Balloons and streamers decorated the main seating area. By the size of the crowd pushing through the door, it looked like most of the congregation had taken advantage of Siobhan's invitation.

Mark and Elsie went through the reception line together. Poppy hugged them both. Sully hugged Elsie and shook hands with Mark. "I hope there are no hard feelings from either of you."

"Thank you for introducing me to Sully, Mark," Poppy gushed. "If it hadn't been for the disaster dinner date we probably would never have met."

"We're very happy for you both," Elsie said.

"Good luck," Mark added.

Walt and Muriel Whistler were next in line. Muriel hugged Poppy. "Congratulations. I guess I'll be looking for a new waitress."

"I hope so," Poppy said glancing over at her new husband.

"Poppy may work wherever she desires, but I would love to have her at my side, helping with our store and Siobhan's shop," Sully said.

Poppy glowed at the stated idea. "Then yes, Muriel. You need a new waitress."

"That's what I thought," Muriel said.

"Good luck to you both," Walt added.

Elsie and Mark stayed long enough to see the cake cut and enjoy a piece before walking upstairs to her apartment. "You still think Sully is behind my terrors?" Elsie asked.

"I'm not sure."

"He was in Hawaii when the balcony collapsed, and the note was put in the cash register. It couldn't possibly be him. He and Poppy look very happy."

"Poppy looks euphoric. I thought he seemed to be tolerating all the hoopla but was not especially glad to be married. Maybe I'm reading too much into his demeanor. It didn't seem beaming enough or head-over-heels-in-love enough to be a man who was so smitten he had to elope on the first date."

"You are such a cynic, Officer Trask."

"I'll wear the label proudly. Did you hear any details about how they decided to elope?"

"Yes. He took her to dinner at a swanky place in Madison. When they had a little too much wine to drink, Sully suggested it wasn't safe to drive back to Lansdale and they should stay the night. Before Poppy could get upset at the proposition, he clarified they would stay in separate rooms. Then he said, 'Unless you want to put the money for the second room to better use'. She laughed it off, but the next thing she knew they were on a plane out of Madison bound for Honolulu. They went on a shopping spree when they landed to buy everything they would need. Then Poppy and Sully checked into a hotel bridal suite, cleaned up, and changed into their wedding clothes. They got married by a Justice of the Peace there."

Mark didn't believe it. "Who does that? Talk about a ridiculous way to kick off the rest of your life."

"Sounds romantic to me. I'd run away to Hawaii with you to get married in a heartbeat."

"Elsie, you wouldn't."

She gave him an exaggerated smile. "I would, if *you* ever asked."

"It's not the same. We've been dating for six weeks. Not one dinner date and poof you're flying on the wings of love. He's not off the hook with me."

She kissed his cheek. "We'll see what Chief Miller has to say tomorrow. Okay, Officer Trask?"

"I'll be by to get you about one forty-five for our appointment with Chief Miller."

"Thanks. Remember, I said I'd run away to Hawaii to marry *you*, not Sullivan Stalatti. Going anywhere to marry you would be romantic."

"Thanks for the ego stroke. I was getting worried you were regretting which guy you were stuck with."

"You are a goof." She cuffed him. "Goodnight!"

****

Sleep eluded Elsie most of the night. Any rest she got was marred by nightmares of stalkers, Hawaiian weddings, memories of the last day fleeing her mother's house, and flames engulfing everything—at her father's store and her house in Lansdale. When she finally drifted off, she slept hard. She didn't wake up until almost eleven in the morning. She would have kept sleeping, except someone was pounding on her door. She struggled out of the bed, grabbed her robe, and wandered to the front door to see who the unexpected, impatient visitor was. She peeked out the window in the door.

Sully.

And Poppy.

She opened the door.

"Oh, Sully, we woke her," Poppy said.

"Don't worry. It's about time I was getting around. I didn't have a real restful night," Elsie said.

"We just stopped to thank you and Mark again for putting us together," Sully said looking over her shoulder. "Is he here?"

"Of course not," Elsie said testily, glaring at him. "We aren't the newlyweds. You are."

"Don't get your feathers ruffled," Sully said. "I thought someone said Mark had been staying here. I must have misunderstood."

"If it is anyone's business, he stayed the first night I came back after the accident, and he slept in the guest room."

"Accident?" Poppy asked. "Elsie, what happened?"

"I'm sorry. I don't want to talk about it. Siobhan knows what happened. She was involved, too. If you'll excuse me, I'll say goodbye. Congratulations." Elsie shut the door. Almost in their faces.

****

When Mark came by to take Elsie to the meeting with Chief Miller, she told him about her morning visitors. He raised his eyebrows. "He's married and he still can't stay away from you."

"Not that at all. He thought you would be with me."

"Why would he think that?"

"Someone told him you'd stayed with me."

"You gotta love living in a small town." He laughed. "Now I have to marry you. I've compromised you in the eyes of the town gossips."

Mark brought along the timeline they'd worked out the other night. Chief Miller made a couple of copies to make it easier to follow along with Elsie's narrative. Elsie calmly told him everything she'd told Mark.

"It's getting a little easier to talk about it without getting emotional," she said. "But it's also frightening to see how it's all been building up to this point. I guess I was ignoring the obvious signs I was the target because I didn't want it to be true. And I felt guilty about Hubert's death being my fault."

"I think your reaction is natural. Please don't waste any energy on feeling guilty about Hubert's death. Putting himself in harm's way to protect you was his job. I know he had retired, but it had been his job for over a decade," Chief Miller said.

"Do you have any gut feeling about who is doing this?" Mark asked.

"Kind of. I need to see if we can get any fingerprints from the notes. I seriously doubt we will, but it's part of the process to home in on the suspects. The fact your father was killed by a professional and the ballistics matched with Hubert's death means we are probably dealing with someone who would not be sloppy enough to leave fingerprints."

"What do I need to do?" Elsie asked.

The chief carefully put each note in its own plastic bag to send for fingerprint dusting. "Be vigilant. Keep your doors locked. Report any strangers in the vicinity immediately to 911. If it's a false alarm, I'd rather have a couple of call outs over nothing than not know who is in the area."

"Are you going to share who you think is behind

it?" Mark asked.

"Sometimes if you zero in on a suspect too early it makes you miss clues to the real perpetrator," the chief said. "Mark, I need you to continue to be visible around Ms. Dennis. I think it's a good deterrent to anyone planning harm to her. Being around in uniform is even better."

"I can easily handle the assignment, sir." Mark grinned. "Speaking of which, if we're done, I need to take Elsie home since I brought her to the station. Then I'll report back to work."

"Sounds good. Don't worry, we'll find who is behind all this," the chief assured Elsie.

Mark led her to his truck and helped her up into the cab. She was very quiet. He was proud of her. She'd been calm and composed relating the story to the chief.

When they were almost back to Elsie's, she said, "Would you drop me at the front door of the shop? I was in the middle of preparing an order when we had to leave. I'd like to finish it and get it entered online this afternoon so that I'll have the supplies later in the week."

"Sure. I'd be happy to."

Chapter Thirty-Six

Mark pulled to the curb in front of *Knitting Pretty*. "Thanks for being there with me and for making all the notes the first time I told you everything," Elsie said. "Seeing everything written down made it easier to make certain I didn't leave anything out and helped take the emotion out of the situation."

"I was glad I could be with you. Please lock the door behind you after you get in."

"I will. Thanks again. Have a good shift. Hope it's a quiet one."

He kissed her goodbye. "Don't work too late. Get some rest."

Elsie got out of the truck. She unlocked the front door and slipped inside. Cocoa jumped down from her perch. Every time she took a step, the cat darted in front of her.

Elsie stepped on her tail. "See what happens when you act like a silly spoiled cat? If you're not careful, you'll trip me. Then we'd both get hurt." Cocoa yowled her unhappy sound.

Elsie walked to the back of the store. Cocoa's feed and water dispensers had both been knocked over. There was a morass of water and cat kibble pooled on the floor near the back door. "Did you do this? What a mess."

After cleaning up, Elsie righted the dispensers and

refilled them with food and water. "Those dispensers are heavy. How on earth did you get them down?" She walked to the back door. Everything was locked tight. She circled around the store. Nothing else seemed to be out of place. Cocoa followed her every step of the way periodically yowling.

"I'm making myself crazy. Seeing bogey men everywhere. You had to have made the mess." She picked the cat up and cradled her close to her chest. Cocoa began purring as Elsie stroked her furry back. "Okay. We can't do this all day. I need to finish that order. Down you go."

She set the feline on the floor and pushed a stool to the counter by the store computer to complete the order. Fifteen minutes later, the cat leaped onto the counter next to Elsie who let out a short scream.

"Don't do that. I'm already on my last nerve." She put the cat on the floor again. "Bad girl. Stay down." Cocoa curled in a ball under the stool.

An hour later, her supply order completed, Elsie logged off the computer. She was ready for a hot bubble bath and a good trashy novel. She walked to the back door with her purse over her shoulder, unlocked the door and opened it, then grabbed the trash bag to put in the can. She heard her phone ping. She stopped to check it. The security app said the back door was open. Duh. She threw the phone back in her purse. Cocoa darted out the door.

Elsie dropped her purse outside the door, threw the garbage in the can, and began calling for the escaped feline. She called several minutes. No Siamese appeared. Then she heard a yowl overhead.

Elsie locked the back door, grabbed her purse, and

tromped upstairs. "When did you become so pig-headed? You might as well come in the apartment. I'm not in the mood to try and wrangle you into the shop tonight."

Elsie unlocked the door, and the cat scooted inside the apartment eager to explore new territory. Her phone pinged. She didn't check. She was certain it was the app telling her she was home. She needed to remember to ask Mark if there was a way to reduce the number of things that made it ping. It didn't make her feel safer. It annoyed her. She dumped her purse on the desk near the door. Cocoa returned from her initial foray through the apartment. Elsie put a bowl of water down for her and fixed an impromptu litter box from a discarded cardboard container.

"You, my fine feline, may do as you like, but I am going for a soak in a hot bath with a British lord who finds me absolutely fascinating."

Elsie started her bubble bath, deposited her clothes in the hamper, grabbed her romance novel, and settled into the lavender-scented haze coming off the bathtub. Not to be left out, Cocoa made herself comfortable perched on the edge of the tub periodically batting at a passing bubble with her paw. Then the cat appeared to fall asleep.

****

"I wasn't sure about the guy at first. He seemed way too smooth," Mel Caldwell said. "Almost smarmy, but he certainly has made my little sister happy. I've decided he's a good egg."

"I'm not sure about him yet," Mark said.

"Are you still jealous over him asking Elsie out? He's married now. He's no threat to you and your relationship with her."

"It's not jealousy. It's a gut feeling there is something not quite right about him. I won't say anything else. I'm glad he's made Poppy so happy. She's a sweet kid."

The dispatcher told Mark the chief wanted to see him in his office. Mark knocked on the closed door.

"Come in...Good it's you," the chief said. "We got the national database ballistics report back on the second bullet."

Mark's phone pinged.

The security app.

Elsie was already in the apartment.

"Just a second." He tapped the app. And felt his blood run cold as the video from the past thirty seconds ran.

"I know what you're going to tell me, Chief. I've gotta go. Send silent backup to Elsie's apartment now!"

Chapter Thirty-Seven

Elsie woke up to icy cold bath water and no bubbles anywhere. She'd apparently had a nap. Thankfully—the dashing British lord was saved from drowning—she had dropped her book outside of the tub.

Cocoa was still asleep resting precariously on the edge of the tub. The cat didn't move even after Elsie had dried off and changed into sweatpants and a T-shirt. She laughed. "You must have worn yourself out with all your silly hi-jinks in the shop."

She turned on the overhead light and padded down the hall in her sock feet with her book in hand into the dark living room. She didn't remember closing the curtains. It had still been light when she went in for her bath.

What did she smell? She stopped when the odor of pipe tobacco scented with cherry and vanilla stirred something deep inside.

A wisp of smoke floated above the back of the paisley print covered chair directly in front of her. Another puff floated above the chair. She dropped the book and opened her mouth to scream but no sound came out.

He rose swiftly from the chair leaving his pipe on the coffee table. In less than a moment he had clamped his hand across her mouth. "Come now, Morgan. There is no need to be so dramatic. You knew it was me. No need to waste your breath. No one is nearby to hear you."

He made sure I'd be alone.

"Come with me."

He shoved her toward the dinette table where an open bottle of red wine and a single glass sat. He pushed her down into a chair and stayed standing over her with his hand still tight against her mouth. "I won't bother you much longer. It's practically over. I'm going to remove my hand. If you persist in screaming, I'm afraid it won't be pleasant—for either of us." He lowered his hand and sat down across from her.

Elsie stared into the face she'd once thought was handsome. "You're not a Stalatti."

"Bravo." He clapped his hands together. "You're figuring things out. Finally."

"You're Salvatore Scachhi's son."

"What gave me away? The pipe tobacco? Nasty habit—one I learned at my sainted father's side before you sent him to die in prison. The Feds could never trap him in anything. He was legendary in the rackets. It took the daughter of a furniture maker bent on justice to undermine the entire organization with her testimony."

Her eyes darted to the door over his shoulder. "What good does my death do? Why now?"

"We had to find you first. It took much longer than we ever thought it would. Even our people inside the marshal's office couldn't locate you. Not until your protector filed for retirement and stayed in place."

He glared at her with inky black eyes. "It will give me peace to know I avenged my father's death just as you did yours. I don't want my future hanging on whether one day you remember seeing the third person from your father's shop clearly enough to identify me."

"But I didn't see you except in the shadows. If I had, you would be in prison now or already dead." Her voice was stronger than she expected and much braver sounding than she was.

"It's funny how things become clearer over time. I am not a patient man. I couldn't chance it."

"The only reason you came here was to kill me? What about Siobhan? Was she part of the scheme? And Poppy?" Maybe if he kept talking...

"My darling sister is clueless. She thinks we changed our names because of the stigma attached to Scachhi and she really believes we will stay here. My dear naïve Poppy stumbled into her role in this vignette. Originally, I wasn't sure what was going to be your motive."

"My motive for what?"

"Your demise at your own hand brought on by a broken heart when the man you loved with all your being—that would be me—ran away and married another—my dear sweet Poppy. It was too much for you to bear seeing us together day in and day out. Right next door. A little cyanide in your wine and we'll both be out of our misery." His eyes showed the pure evil within him.

Elsie pursed her lips together. "It won't work. I won't drink it."

He poured a full glass of wine from the open bottle. She tried to get out of the chair and kicked at her captor landing a sharp jab to his shins. He abruptly stood up from the table and jerked her hair down, forcing her back into the chair. She screamed. He tried to pour the wine into her open mouth. It splashed on her cheeks and chest. Very little got in her mouth and that she spit back in his face. She bobbed her head around and quickly closed her mouth tightly. He pulled harder on her hair, then tried pinching her cheeks together to force her mouth open.

A noise sounded from near the door, followed by a deafening feline yowl. The wine glass crashed to the floor.

Just as Elsie screamed, Mark broke through the door and pushed Elsie away from her would-be killer. Cocoa had leaped from the floor to the table and onto the attacker's back, impaling him with her rear claws while draping over his head batting him with her paws and biting his ears. Sully couldn't shake the animal off. Blood ran down his back soaking his shirt where the feline strafed him with her rear claws.

Less than a minute later, two uniformed policemen, revolvers drawn, rushed into the apartment. Elsie held her arms out and the feline jumped into them after shaking her claws loose from Sully's shirt. The officers pulled his arms behind his back and handcuffed the assailant.

Mark embraced Elsie with the cat between them. "Did he hurt you?"

"Not really." She shook her head. "Wait. How did you know he was here?"

"The security app. I set it to ping me. I saw him on the video. He had a key to your apartment." She raised her eyebrows. "I'm sorry. I was going to tell you when things calmed down that I was monitoring the apartment and your shop."

"No need to apologize. You were right all along.

Thank heavens you thought to keep an extra watch on me. I couldn't see it." She shook her head. "I didn't believe it was him."

"It wasn't only the ping. The ballistics report came in from the night Stalatti shot the snake in your shop. The bullet was fired from the same weapon as your dad's shooting and Hubert's."

"Not Stalatti. Scachhi. He's the son of the man I testified against. He's the unidentified third man. He is the one who murdered my father."

"I guess Cocoa's a good judge of character. What was she doing in the apartment?"

She hugged the cat closer. "She ran out the back door of the shop and up the steps while I was locking up. I was too tired to mess with her so I let her go in the apartment. I'm glad I did."

"She must have sensed something was amiss."

"I think she had proof." Elsie led him to the door. "Will you come downstairs with me?"

"Sure, they need to finish processing the scene and we're kind of in the way."

Elsie, still carrying Cocoa, led Mark down the stairs and to the cash register in the shop. She opened the small drawer under the counter to get the key. She turned the register on and rang *no sale*, the drawer popped open. She lifted out the divider. "They're gone."

"What's missing?"

"My spare keys for the house and the shop. This afternoon when you dropped me off, I found a mess. Cocoa's food and drink dispensers had been knocked over and everything was spilled on the floor. I couldn't figure out how she was strong enough to push them down. She didn't."

"Then who did?"

"Siobhan and I had exchanged back door shop keys in case of an emergency. I'm guessing Sully took them without her knowledge, had seen where I kept my spare keys, and came in to get them while I was out. He probably had to leave in a hurry once Cocoa realized he was in the shop. He must have knocked the dispensers over while he was trying to flee the attack cat. Then he had my apartment key to use."

Cocoa purred loudly.

"I'm thankful you weren't hurt. I never thought I could be a cat person, but this Siamese may change my mind. She hasn't liked Sully from the beginning—any more than I have." Mark laughed.

Mark's radio squawked. The team at the crime scene had finished. Mark and Elsie left the shop, locked the back door, then stood at the bottom of the stairs while Sullivan Scachhi was perp-walked to the police cruiser with his hands cuffed behind his back. His sister and his new bride watched from the doorway of their apartment, clinging to one another, in tears.

The criminal stopped in front of his victim. "I'd set everything up perfectly. I should have taken care of the cat immediately. What was Trask doing here in the middle of his shift? How did he know?"

"Guess my guardian angels were working overtime," Elsie said with a smile.

The officer tugged Scachhi's arm and led him to the car. As soon as he was inside, they drove out of the alley to the station to book their murderer.

Mark wrapped Elsie in a long embrace. "Once again you ran to my rescue. How can I ever thank you?"

He kissed her gently lingering over her lips. "Marry me."

"How could I say no?"

"So the answer is yes?"

"Of course it is." Elsie kissed him. "Yes. Yes. Yes."

"Oh, one more thing. Am I marrying Elsie Dennis or Morgan Tucker?"

"I think Morgan needs to return to the past where she belongs. The name Elsie is growing on me, if it's okay with you."

"I've always liked the name, but I would love the woman in my arms with any name."

Epilogue

Three years later

"Hey Elsie, Phil and Arianna will be here any minute," Mark hollered from the entryway.

I carefully made my way down the stairs. Not an easy task with my arms full of a wiggling bundle. "I'm coming. Is everything ready?"

Mark met me at the bottom of the stairs and kissed my cheek. "I think I've moved all the toddler-attractive dangers to a place where little hands cannot reach. We'll see. What are the kids' names? I keep forgetting."

"The two-year old is Jonathon Mark, after you, and the one-year-old is Ariel Teresa, after Arianna's mom. I can't wait to see the kids and Phil and Arianna."

He nodded. "It will be good to be together again after so long. I can't wait to introduce them to this little guy." Mark took the chubby cooing baby from my arms, raised his tee shirt, and blew raspberries on his tummy until both father and son giggled with glee.

"This little one is drawing lots of visitors." I kissed the top of my son's head and breathed in the unique baby scent of him. "It was so nice to see your Mom again last month and to meet your brother and his family. I'm glad you've all made your peace. Nothing is more important than family." I kissed the baby again and his daddy.

"Well, you are responsible for the reconciliation, my sweet wife." Mark kissed my cheek. "I'm glad they're back in my life…in our lives."

The doorbell chimed.

I opened the door and found the Hughes family standing on the front stoop. "Come in. Come in."

"It's been an interesting ride from Alabama. I may have been wrong about driving being easier than flying with little ones. At least we had plenty of room for all the paraphernalia," Phil said as he embraced me.

Arianna introduced their children who both stayed behind their mother—clinging to her legs. "They'll warm to you once they've been around you for a little bit."

A black and white blur raced to the door. Domino wiggled around at Phil's feet obviously happy to see his old friend. Jonathon made happy little yelps when the dog greeted him with a tongue across the boy's cheeks. He threw his arms around the animal's neck, buried his face in the fur, and giggled. Ariel cautiously stuck her hand out for Domino to sniff and lick. When Domino's cold nose snuffled her neck, she squealed with delight and stuck her nose against his.

Arianna reached for my son. "May I?" Mark handed him over. "Who do we have here?"

Mark grinned, beaming with fatherly pride and said, "Meet our five-month-old son, Kevin Philip Trask."

"Is Kevin a family name?" Phil asked.

"Yes, my father," I said.

"I'm honored he has my name, too," Phil said.

Arianna sat down in the nearby rocking chair

cradling Kevin to her chest and cooing at him. The men went out to bring in the luggage. Phil brought two portable cribs in to set up in the guest room.

Arianna and I visited while the moving in was underway. Jonathon and Domino played in one corner of the room. Ariel stood by her mother and patted Kevin gently. Then she toddled over to me and crawled into my lap.

"Me baby," she said nuzzling against me.

Arianna laughed. "Looks like she's a little jealous. She's not used to seeing her mama holding other babies."

"Kevin's at the age where he doesn't care who holds him—as long as someone does."

"She'll need to adjust to being a big girl by February."

"You're not." Arianna nodded with a smile. "How wonderful! Life in Alabama must agree with you."

"It's better than I ever could have imagined." Kevin snuggled closer to her. "Sometimes I have to pinch myself—I'm living a beautiful dream," Arianna said.

"Funny the twists and turns life takes." Ariel watched her mother. Every time Arianna hugged Kevin, Ariel whimpered to be hugged. "Kevin comes to the shop with me. Mark moved to the day shift. We have dinner together every night. It's a life I never thought I would have."

After getting the car unloaded, Mark and Phil came in and sat down.

"When we drove through town, I noticed the coffee shop is a pita place now and the bookstore is a children's shoe store. Did the Scachhi sister leave

Lansdale after her brother's arrest?" Phil asked.

"Not immediately," Mark said. "People tried to be supportive of her and of his wife, Poppy, but I think they were both too embarrassed to stay here. Sullivan Scachhi went to prison for two murders and an attempted murder. Ninety-nine years for each without parole. He will die incarcerated just like his father did."

"Where did the wife and sister go?" Phil asked.

"I don't know. I work with Poppy's brother. All he would say is they left together and were all right," Mark said.

"I miss Siobhan, but it is much easier to put the past behind me without them here as reminders," I said.

"Why don't we take this party outside?" Mark stood. "I plan to fire up the grill and we'll have a picnic."

After going out and closing the gate across the stairs, Phil herded Ariel, Jonathon, and Domino onto the deck. Arianna carried Kevin outside and sat down in a rocking chair. Mark got the meat out of the refrigerator where it had been marinating.

I stood at the sliding door looking out on the deck. The sun came from behind a lone cloud, illuminating the people and the place I adore. All the darkness had vanished—only love and daylight remained.

Thank you, Lord.

A tear ran down my cheek.

My sweet husband noticed. "Hey, what's wrong?"

"Nothing at all." I smiled at the man who completely changed my life.

"Are they happy tears?" He swiped his thumb across my cheek to remove the offenders.

I nodded. "All of this is because you kept running

to rescue me from evil. You led me out of the darkness and into your arms—forever."

He kissed the tip of my nose.

Life was nothing, but good.

A word about the author...

I grew up the oldest child of a veterinarian in a small town in Wisconsin. I retired after a career in Healthcare Information Technology and live in Alabama where I am focused on creative endeavors:writing, spinning, weaving, knitting, crocheting, and creating buildings for my husband's model railroad. I have been married to my own romance hero for almost forever.

Follow my adventures at www.spinningromance.com.

E-mail me at kimjanine@spinningromance.com. I love to hear from my readers!

Thank you for purchasing
this publication of The Wild Rose Press, Inc.

For questions or more information
contact us at
info@thewildrosepress.com.

The Wild Rose Press, Inc.
www.thewildrosepress.com